HELL GATE

DAVID STOUT
& RUTH FURIE

THE MYSTERIOUS PRESS

New York • London
Tokyo • Sweden • Milan

The Mysterious Press, 129 West 56th Street, New York, N.Y. 10019

Printed in the United States of America
First Printing: July 1990

10 9 8 7 6 5 4 3 2 1

Library of Congress Cataloging-in-Publication Data

Stout, David.
    Hell gate / by David Stout and Ruth Furie.
        p.   cm.
    ISBN 0-89296-414-6
    I. Furie, Ruth.   II. Title.
PS3569.T658H4   1990
813'.54—dc20   89-40521
                                        CIP

For Shelley, Cheryl, Clay, and Craig

We apologize to mapmakers for our geographical revisions of Long Island, New Jersey, and Westchester and Rockland counties, and to the New York Jets football team for giving them yet another new home. This is a work of fiction, and the events herein happened entirely in our imaginations.

We wish to thank Judith Weber, Nat Sobel, and Sara Ann Freed for their careful editing and helpful suggestions.

Prologue

Man and boat blended noiselessly into the gentle darkness of the waves, the oars moving with the silence of an owl in flight. The small rubber dinghy was almost invisible as it moved between the sailboats bobbing on their moorings. Black water, black boat, and black clothing. Although he had done this before, he was sure that the pounding of his heart could be heard over the easy lapping of the tide.

Across the bay the also-rans of the sailboat race were fastening the sail covers, coiling the lines, and closing the hatches. Occasionally a boat horn would sound, signaling that the captain was ready to come ashore. Many of the racers were headed for drinks and backslapping at Chowder's. The man would go there, too, after . . .

He rowed to a sloop at one of the farthest moorings and tied the dinghy to the side facing the bay. As he climbed over the gunwales of the bigger boat, he kept low, almost slithering as he shifted his weight onto the cockpit seat. Squeak! The rubber dinghy rubbed against the hull. He stopped, waiting to see if the noise would repeat, to see if he should retie the small boat to keep it silent. Nothing. Just a soft bump. Good.

He told himself not to hurry, to be careful, but above all to be silent. He tried to ignore the thumping in his chest that echoed in his head. He told himself that no one else could hear it. He had been on boats for most of his life, felt easy on the water. But tonight his confidence had fled. Terror floated next to him.

It wasn't until he was safely away from the sloop that he felt the evening breeze on his face, that he began to enjoy the summer evening. As he neared the dock, he pulled freely on the oars. Out of danger now. A beer. Maybe a shot, too. At Chowder's.

1

A freshening breeze blew off Long Island Sound, bearing the smells of salt water and fish and the hint of coolness. It was a beautiful August evening, just after dusk, and the running lights of sailboats were visible in the distance through the window behind the bar at Chowder's, where Kevin McNulty was hunched on a stool. He could see the pinpoints of greens and reds as the sloops, ketches, and yawls maneuvered in the dark.

The sea smells came through the open window near the end of the long, curving oak bar where Kevin hunkered over his beer. The smells blended, not unpleasantly, with aromas of gin and beer and fried sole and the spiced fish soup for which Chowder's was famous.

The sounds that skipped across the water were of engines, winches, dinghies bumping against hulls; there were also wisps of voices and laughter. And occasionally, over the bar babble and clinking ice, Kevin could hear the music of halyards jangling against masts.

Kevin McNulty loved that boat music. He thought there must be no better music in the world for a child to go to sleep by, or a man and woman to make love by.

Now the music made him almost want to cry—or, since he couldn't very well do that in public, made him want another beer, his fifth or sixth, whether he needed it or not. The beer would dull his consciousness, or wash out the wound in his soul, or—whatever.

He and Yvonne were selling their boat. Sometimes Kevin wondered if they should have put their own name on it, instead of keeping the name the former owner had christened it with: *Lark IV*. No, it made no difference.

They had already started talking about selling the house as part of the split-up, so it made no sense even to think of the boat as something that was part of what they had been, though it surely was.

Thinking about the boat made Kevin look around the bar for Harvey Green. There he was, thirty feet or so away, talking with a bunch of hard-drinking powerboat types. Harvey was a good mechanic, and he ran a tiny marina that was little more than a garage with a couple of long piers sticking out into the water at the back. His father had started the business, and Harvey had taken it over after the Second World War. Harvey was well off, if you figured the value of his property, though you would never know it to look at him. Word was he had gambled away a lot of money over the years. He was a weird duck, Harvey. But he was a good mechanic.

Kevin and Yvonne had kept their boat at Harvey's. Harvey didn't charge them that much for a mooring, and he was good with the engine. Keeping the boat at Harvey's wasn't quite like belonging to the Port Guinness Yacht Club, but Kevin and Yvonne couldn't have afforded a yacht-club membership even if they had been invited. The closest they had ever got to the club was the weekly sailboat races; they started at the yacht club, even though anybody could race in them. That way, Kevin and Yvonne had had a champagne social life on a beer budget, but that was all over, too.

"Harvey!" Kevin shouted, surprised that his voice sounded a little slurred.

Harvey didn't look his way. Hard-of-hearing, and too dumb to get a hearing aid. Christ, he was past sixty. How much pride does a guy need?

"Harvey!" Kevin tried again. He did not want to go over to him and risk losing his barstool.

Quince, the owner of a forty-foot yacht, was glowering at Harvey, obviously engaging him in some deep conversation. Kevin wondered if Quince was pissed at Harvey for keeping him waiting on some engine job. Quince, tall and dark, with neatly scissored hair, had large eyes that seemed to have no irises because they were so black. His boat had a flying bridge and an enormous array of electronic equipment, evidenced by a battalion of aerials deployed at the top and sides of the boat. Quince was a regular at Chowder's and on race nights bought drinks for the winners, who often had lost their sea legs by the time they went home.

Kevin decided to look for an opening before trying to get Harvey's attention. He watched, sipped his beer, listened with one ear to the talk around him, with another to the exhibition football game on television.

Kevin didn't know what to make of Quince—that was what everyone called him, just Quince. He had an inconspicuous office over on Guinness Boulevard. Trucks, something to do with trucks, Kevin thought. Sometimes Quince drove a van, sometimes a pickup. Sometimes he drove a car. Whatever he drove, it had a phone. Quince usually had a serious, busy expression, especially when he was driving with one hand and holding the phone in the other.

Kevin had heard, variously, that Quince was from Argentina, or Cuba, or Bolivia, or Ecuador, or Colombia. Kevin thought Quince looked like a younger Omar Sharif. Quince definitely had a no-nonsense way about him, and Kevin could imagine him making a lot of money at . . . something.

Sometimes Kevin wished he had more money. But newspapermen didn't make that much. As a sportswriter, Kevin got to travel now and then, but that was getting to be a drag.

Kevin looked over again at Harvey, whose head was bobbing up and down. Quince was smiling now, maybe Harvey had a satisfied customer.

At least three times in as many weeks, Kevin had asked Harvey to make certain the boat's engine was working right, because he and Yvonne wanted to sell the boat. Harvey had said he would look around for a buyer. He had promised to check the engine every so often and look into the bilge whenever he was on board.

It had felt strange and sad to Kevin not being on the boat all season, not since he had moved out of the house. He supposed Vonnie felt the same way. Well, a lot of things went by the wayside with a marriage.

Now Kevin had his own buyer, a sportswriter friend from *The Bugler,* up in Rockland County. But had Harvey tuned the engine?

"Harvey," Kevin said again, waving. This time, he caught Harvey's attention, so he slid off the stool, hoping the glass of beer in front of it would save his place at the bar.

"Listen, Harv, have you gotten to the engine on the Pearson? We want it right for when we sell it."

"You kidding? Anyhow, the engine's fine. I tuned it up two weeks ago. Running like a top. You don't put no strain on it, the kind of little trips you two take. You ain't been on it all season anyhow."

"Great, Harv. I know you're busy as hell." Kevin had been deliberately vague with Harvey; he hadn't told him, in fact, that he already had a buyer and that they were taking the boat the next morning and never bringing it back.

Kevin wasn't sure just why he had played it so close with Harvey. Yvonne trusted his intuition up to a point, and if she ever asked him he would say that he didn't trust Harvey a hundred percent, even though he liked him some of the time. If Harvey had known they intended to sell to a guy way up in Rockland he might have invented a mechanical problem to keep the boat, saving it as a bargain for some friend of his. Meanwhile, he'd tell Kevin and Yvonne they'd have to take a little less than they wanted, because the boat really had a problem.

Harvey was short and lean, with a leathery face that had been more handsome a lot of sunburns and beers ago and that was still not bad, considering. Although he was a two-fisted drinker, his face never bloated and turned scarlet like most of the Irish drinkers Kevin knew, including some in his family. His hair, what was left of it, probably had been blond once, but now it was the color of old lace curtains.

Kevin went back to his beer. He could drink as much as he wanted to, as long as he was willing to balance it off against a hangover. He wouldn't think about the boat anymore tonight. Getting rid of the boat wouldn't be half as bad as selling the house. . . .

Jesus, the house. He couldn't think about that, couldn't handle it at all.

Bruce the bartender slid the beer to him, and he took a gulp.

"On me, Kevin," Bruce said. Bruce was friendly, and he used his powerful, ham-thick forearm to nudge Kevin's. Or maybe Bruce, who collected Kevin's bets, was just feeling sorry for him.

"Thanks, my man," Kevin said. Kevin figured he must be doing a lot of drinking to get a free beer from Bruce. Or maybe Bruce knew, like everybody else, about his troubles.

"Hear about Tolly from the yacht club?" Bruce asked, leaning over the bar.

"No, what?" Kevin said. Tolly was the club's launch operator and sometime mechanic. He had towed Kevin and Yvonne back to

Harvey's once when their engine had conked out on a choppy day, which made Tolly fine forevermore in Kevin's book.

"He bought the locker," Bruce the bartender said. "Found dead this morning, lying on his back in a boat. A big inboard. Monoxide, they think."

"Jesus," Kevin said. Tolly was a nickname; nobody knew his real name, except perhaps Harvey, who had been a drinking buddy of Tolly's. Maybe that's why Harvey was such a jerk just now, Kevin thought.

"Yeah," Bruce went on. "Owner of the boat came on board, and there Tolly was, lying there. Face all bloated. Could be he had some leftover booze in him, too. Could have made him pass out quicker, you know?"

"Damn. He used to come in here sometimes, no?"

"Yeah, sure. Truth is, they didn't want him hanging around the bar over at the club, so he had to come here to do his drinking. Damn shame."

"Yeah. Jesus." Though Kevin had not known Tolly well enough to feel remotely close to him, he did remember the favor. That, plus the simple fact that someone he had known in the world had left it forever, made him feel all the gloomier. Maybe he would say something to Harvey. . . .

The voices and laughter of the racers only deepened Kevin's grief. He tried not to let the noises get to him. Just two and a half weeks to go until Labor Day, so the racers were getting in as much sailing as they could, knowing the summer was winding down. For some sailors, the races were cheerful tests of seamanship, for others they were as serious as the America's Cup.

Once, a couple of summers ago, he and Yvonne had come close to winning a race in their division. They had been having a great sail, even though Kevin had just had a couple of beers. Vonnie was pretty good at reading the ripples coming over the water and sensing how the wind would shift. They had caught the wind just right on a couple of tacks in a row, and suddenly they had the lead.

Then Kevin had screwed it up, failing to cleat the mainsheet properly, so that it came loose and the sail flogged and Yvonne almost went over trying to right things. She had been angry as hell over missing the chance to win the race. No, mostly at him. And Kevin had made the mistake of laughing, just laughing. Because mostly he didn't give a goddamn about the race, it was the sailing he liked, just being out on the water with her, having a few beers. But she hadn't quite understood that, and he couldn't blame her too much. She hadn't forgiven him all that summer, the way he hadn't given a damn.

Now another summer was almost over. The exhibition football game on television, the game Kevin was watching with interest, since he had bet on it, was another sign of that.

The sailboat racing was one of the more lovely things about Port Guinness, a North Shore village tucked between Port Washington, to the west, and Huntington, just to the east, and less crowded than either. Port Guinness was a little enclave, reachable by a two-lane road off the Long Island Expressway, and most everyone had a boat, or sailed with someone who did, or was about to buy one.

The races were organized more or less along lines of sailing experience and boat length and were almost always followed by beer or gin and tonics at Chowder's. Indeed, there were lithe, suntanned young men and women who had grown up hearing their parents talk about the races. Having heard so much boat talk, they thought everyone lived the way they did.

Kevin hadn't grown up like that, and although Yvonne was a Port Guinness native, her parents had never owned a boat. But Kevin and Yvonne had enjoyed the races, together, for a while. Now, the races and the merriment seemed to Kevin farther away than Montauk, way out at the tip of the Island, or Cape Cod, or Greenland, or anywhere.

Things are bad, he thought. I'm the only one here who cares about that football game and can't enjoy what's left of the summer.

He had always loved football, though he played it only well enough to sit on the bench in high school, and had been happy at first when his newspaper, *Long Island,* assigned him to cover the Jets. After they moved from New Jersey back to Long Island, the Jets were a choice beat for any reporter. But he had covered them for two years, and the novelty was wearing thin. Besides, Yvonne had been bothered by the trips he had to take, by his staying out too late after practices, drinking with some of the players. She had heard the stories of groupies following the pro jocks. Jesus, she flattered me, Kevin thought, taking a big gulp.

Now, as he watched the Jets going through the motions against the

Packers on an incongruously steamy evening in Wisconsin, he knew he would be out another twenty bucks.

Shit, betting on an exhibition game was stupid. The Jets had no cornerbacks, and their linebackers weren't putting the pressure on the quarterback, and so the Jets wouldn't cover—cover!—an exhibition game, and he was already thinking about covering spreads!

Yvonne was right; he bet too much. Drank too much, too. And she was a better sailor than he was, with a much better head for detail, more patience, more precision. Which was what you needed on a boat, big or small. Probably would have been a better parent, too.

No, not now for that subject. Not now . . .

Tomorrow might be the last day they would do anything together on the boat, and it probably wouldn't be a lot of fun. They would take it from Port Guinness all the way west on Long Island Sound, into the East River, down to the tip of Manhattan and up the Hudson, way up the Hudson to Haviland, in Rockland County. They were moving the boat themselves, because to have it trucked over to Haviland would cost five hundred bucks or more, and they needed the money. It was as simple as that.

It was a good boat, a damn good boat. A Pearson Ariel, a twenty-six-foot sloop. A classic, some boat people had told him, Pearson didn't make them anymore. Yvonne always called it a boaty boat. Well, they couldn't afford a classic, not now. More to the point, neither could afford it separately.

It would be a long, long trip. All day long. Kevin had told the buyer, Marty Diehl, a young sportswriter whom he sometimes saw at Jets games, that they would try to be there before dark, but that he couldn't promise that. Marty Diehl had agreed to give Kevin and Yvonne a ride down the Palisades Interstate Parkway and across the George Washington Bridge to the bus terminal, where they could get a subway to midtown Manhattan and catch a train back to Long Island.

The more Kevin thought about it, they would be really lucky to make it by dark. Getting there by dark depended not only on getting an early start, but on the engine's running right all the way and nothing else going wrong. And they damn well had to get to Hell Gate for the right tide or they could forget it.

Hell Gate was where the East River turned south and the Harlem River joined it. Long Island Sound's currents pushed at the river's eastern mouth and the Atlantic pushed at its south end. Hell Gate was where it all swirled together, and depending on the state of the tide the water could be going up to six miles an hour in addition to its cross-currents. A boat the size of their Pearson could only go with the tide.

Between sips, Kevin smiled smugly for a moment, remembering how surprised Yvonne had been (she being the better sailor, and all) to discover that he had been right: They couldn't cut their trip almost in half by going through the Harlem River into the Hudson. That's because there were bridges that were too low for the mast of their Pearson, so they had to go clear to the tip of Manhattan. And they weren't about to pay Harvey to unstep the mast. . . .

Maybe they would have to stay overnight somewhere. Kevin wondered how they would handle that.

He hoped they wouldn't fight too much on the boat.

2

From the deck off the living room, Yvonne watched the racing boats turn at the buoy. Sails puffed and flapped and puffed again as the craft rounded the marker.

The breeze is just right, she thought, an easy turn. Sometimes the best entertainment was watching the boats try to turn when the sailors had misjudged the wind or trimmed the sails wrong. When she wasn't racing herself, Yvonne liked nothing better than playing dockside captain. Kevin often laughed at her as she prompted from her deck chair: "Trim your main, fall off, you're turning too tight." A smile flitted briefly on her lips, replaced almost immediately by the pouting, worried expression that she more often wore these days.

Some of the racers had hailed her as they passed. Then Scotty Durer yelled, "Why don't you get your landlubbing ass out here? Afraid we'll beat you again?"

He had a cheerful voice and knew that it carried like a boat horn. She couldn't pretend she hadn't heard him. She went to the railing, leaned out and forced a smile she didn't feel.

"Didn't you hear? My crew mutinied."

Scotty Durer's white teeth flashed in his tan face. He kept looking at her, waiting for more. His wife, Melba, said something to him that Yvonne didn't and wasn't supposed to hear.

"Watch out," Yvonne shouted. "Your main is luffing."

Scotty lifted his drink from the holder near the helm and raised it, saying, "I luff you too."

At this, Melba brought a Top-Sider up to Scotty's backside and, turning toward Yvonne, she cupped her hands and shouted, "Meet us at Chowder's, we'll buy you a drink. At the rate we're going, we'll get beat by the dinghies."

Scotty, brought up by Melba's assessment, turned his attention to his captain duties and yelled, "Ready about." Melba moved to tend the jenny. Yvonne smiled as she watched Melba's short, plump frame scurry about the deck of the thirty-seven-foot Hunter. A beautiful boat, an expensive boat, and polished like a jewel. Yvonne wondered how much they spent on the boat every year.

If you have to ask, you can't afford it, she thought.

In Port Guinness there were plenty of people who spent more on their boats than on their houses. Scotty spent lavishly on everything. He had never learned to do anything else. His mother had always spoiled him. Always got him the latest toy, whatever clothes he wanted. And yet, Scotty was a nice guy, always had been. Maybe wanting things makes people mean, Yvonne thought.

"Should I go down to Chowder's and let Scotty spend some of his money on me? Or sit around feeling sorry for myself?" Yvonne said aloud. Tess, the Doberman lying on the deck catching the last warmth of the day, opened one eye and wagged her little stump of a tail a few times. "You wouldn't mind if I went, would you, old girl."

The dog's tail thumped on the deck. Ah, Tess was getting old. Gray in the muzzle and a little hard of hearing. Yvonne remembered when she and Kevin had bought her as a puppy, when they had moved into the house. Tess was supposed to protect Yvonne on all those nights when Kevin was out late or out of town covering a game. Well, she was protective. She'd growl when anybody came close to Yvonne, even Kevin sometimes.

Yvonne remembered the first time, when Tess was barely out of puppyhood, that the dog bared her teeth when Kevin hugged Yvonne. After that, it was a joke. "Don't touch me or I'll call Tess," Yvonne would say. But the dog grew out of growling at Kevin just as she had grown out of chewing Yvonne's shoes. And now, suddenly, she was an old dog, and Kevin and Yvonne would go their separate paths. Yvonne stifled a sob and rubbed a wrist across her eyes.

Cool it on the self-pity, she told herself. Melba's invitation is just what you need. Get up and get out. Chowder's was made for summer evenings. So what if Kevin is there inhaling suds at the bar. That doesn't have to keep you away.

Yvonne couldn't go to Chowder's by herself. Not yet. Not until everybody knew, until people didn't expect that she would be with Kevin, until she didn't have to explain.

The invitation, hollered casually across the water, was perfect. She had someone to be with. But the more she thought about Kevin and Chowder's, the angrier she got. Chowder's was mostly a bar for Kevin, some place for him to curl a foot around the rail and lose himself in a beer glass. Well, she would let him stay draped over the bar. Tonight she would party.

Yvonne lingered on the deck until most of the sails had passed and made their turn to head back into the harbor. The watercolors that she had been dabbling with earlier had dried. She held up one and then another, eyeing them critically. She thought she had improved; she could do with just a few strokes what used to be a labored rendering. She wondered whether suffering really made a difference, somehow made her painting better.

A few other sailors who passed close to shore yelled and Yvonne waved, although the sinking sun behind the boats made it impossible for her to distinguish even the boats, let alone the sailors.

She would give Scotty and Melba plenty of time to get there before her. And she would put on some of that new eye makeup she'd just bought at Bloomie's. She admitted to herself that she wanted Kevin to think she looked great. But why? Spite? Or was there still a spark?

Damn him. She had loved him, but not the person he had become. The drinker, the gambler, the guy who always wanted to be right, who couldn't see his own faults. She tried, most of the time, not to lose the memory of the Kevin she had loved, the sensitive, good-natured, funny, even adventurous Kevin. The friend who could really hold up his end of a conversation, who was right there in the next paragraph.

He had messed it up. Too much drinking, too much betting on stupid games. Too much of God-only-knew-what on the road, and too many lies covering up when he got home. At least, she thought he had told some lies.

The drinking, that had done it. A person should put up with only so much. As though she hadn't felt bad about the baby.

Before she knew it, the tears were there again.

No! Don't go to Chowder's with red eyes. People will think you've been crying or drinking. That's not what you want them to think of you. You're self-sufficient, you're jolly, you're the former cheer-leader. You're also too damn proud and an asshole. So put that emotional baggage away for tonight.

Her hot-pink sundress was tied at the nape of her neck. Her shoulders and back were tanned. The soft cotton fabric flowed gently as she paraded in front of the full-length mirror in the bedroom, where the king-size bed looked too big now.

Dressing up lifted her spirits, made her feel like a teenager for a moment. (God, her fifteenth high school reunion was coming up next summer!) Now, looking at herself, liking the way she looked, she giggled and tossed her head.

Ah, what a salve vanity can be, she thought. But maybe it's just a case of arrested development; I'm still a seventeen-year-old cheer-leader.

She turned to one side, then the other, and then tried to leap as she used to at the end of a cheer. She muffed it and looked around, grateful then that she was alone.

These days, self-administered pep talks were common. "You have your health and food in the fridge. You have options. . . ."

Losing the baby had been like losing a piece of herself. The baby. She thought of it as that. Even though it hadn't been that far along. But far enough along for the tests to show that it would have had Down's syndrome.

Quite rare before thirty-five, the doctors had said. Not really a person, just a developing mass inside her. A mass that was developing wrong, the tests said. A mass that neither she nor Kevin could deal with. But it had been a baby, hers and Kevin's, planned for, wished for, eagerly awaited. Mongoloid, special care. It might have had other defects, too; they often did, the doctors said. What to do?

They had begun to have long discussions late into the nights. They had called on a couple of support groups. Kevin had even gone to see a priest. But the gods or fate or chance made the decision for them. (Blessing or punishment?) And so the baby—they never knew what sex it was, didn't want to know—had become a mass, a mass that was delivered after the most excruciating pain Yvonne had ever felt. Was childbirth that bad? Her mother had said that when the baby is okay, it's worth it. Yvonne had felt close to her mother during the days her mother had spent with her after she came home from the hospital. Her father had called, but he had stayed in Florida. The beloved chauvinist thought it was women's stuff.

Kevin and Yvonne were told to try again. But now that was unlikely. Their marriage hadn't stood the strain; maybe it was a test that they had somehow failed.

Oh, more than that. At least she was willing to admit that she had felt partly relieved when she miscarried. Kevin hadn't been willing to admit it (he had lied to himself again), and had blamed her. He couldn't admit that, either.

Enough. Stop wallowing. Tonight the lady's not for mourning.

Today, tonight, she was dressed to kill and she was going to have a good time without Kevin. Tomorrow she would have to spend the whole day with him, moving the boat, and for sure there would be more Kevin than she could stand. Probably a hung-over, hangdog Kevin, at that.

Yvonne left a few lights on, set the phone-answering machine, and turned on the radio before she went down the steps to the garage where the roof of the aging Chevy Caprice reflected the overhead light. Yvonne put Tess in the run that opened from the garage. She put down fresh water and gave her a biscuit, a ritual that told the dog she was to stay behind. "Here's your cookie, old girl, now stay and mind the house."

It was only a mile and a half to Chowder's, but in that distance the rocks and marsh grass and sand and sparse housing gave way to the rows of village Cape Cods and then the shops and marinas. Chowder's was one of the few restaurants in town that had their own parking lot. That lot too, in recent years, had become an expensive piece of real estate. Almost too expensive to leave as a parking lot. There had been rumors that the restaurant would be sold to a developer who wanted to put up condos, but no developer had shown up at the planning board yet.

Yvonne had been aware of real estate for as long as she could remember. Her father had owned the office where Yvonne now worked on weekends, the office that Scotty's mother, Rosalie, had purchased when Yvonne's dad decided to retire and go to live in Florida. Her dad had always made a good living, but Rosalie had doubled the business before she'd had it two years. Her dad had liked Rosalie, admired her capacity for work. Yvonne's mother would get kind of quiet when Rosalie was mentioned.

Once, when Rosalie was still working as a real estate salesperson, before she bought the office and became a broker, Yvonne's dad had come into the kitchen to talk to Yvonne and her mother and he started praising Rosalie. A deal she had been working on was turning out to be really big, largely through Rosalie's efforts. Yvonne's mother had slammed down whatever it was she had in her hand and said, "She never does anything the way everybody else does it." Her mother had stormed out of the room, and her father had said, "Your mother thinks women ought to be less aggressive than Rosalie is."

Yvonne parked the car and turned off the engine and the lights, but before she got out she checked her makeup in the rearview mirror and took a few deep breaths because her heart was racing and her stomach felt as if it were turned upside down. "Shit, Kevin, why can't I stop this?" She waited in the darkness for a few minutes, rehearsing what she might say if she saw him, or if he came over to the table, or if she met him on the way in.

When she finally walked into Chowder's, despite all of her resolve, she immediately looked toward the bar, her pulse pounding in her head, and saw Kevin, who looked at her as if he had been waiting for her to arrive.

"Vonnie," he called across the bar.

Yvonne walked toward him, resenting his presumption, wishing she had the nerve to snub him and at the same time longing for the days of the old Kevin and Yvonne perched at Chowder's bar, exchanging jokes with the other regulars.

On the other side of the room, at one of the tables, Melba had been watching for Yvonne. When she saw her, Melba read the pain in her friend's face. Before Yvonne reached Kevin, Melba was at her heels, chattering a busy greeting full of words and empty of meaning. Yvonne and Kevin exchanged wide-eyed looks of hurt and recrimination, but he said only, "How's Tess?" and she answered, "She's fine. I took her for her rabies shot."

Melba stepped into the awkwardness. "Kevin, you old sot, Yvonne is joining us for a few drinks, and maybe we'll even persuade her to dine with us. When you're through here, why don't you stop by our table for a few minutes. Scotty would like to say hello, I'm sure."

She's a genius, Yvonne thought with some relief; she's friendly but she's obviously not including Kevin in the evening's festivities.

Kevin looked toward the table where Scotty, Rosalie, and a young guy who looked like a tennis star were in an animated, good-natured exchange. "Scotty seems to be all taken up in conversation right now, Melba, but thanks. I'll be leaving soon. I'll stop by before I go," he said.

His lips were drawn tight across his teeth in what passed for a smile with everyone but Yvonne. His glass was full, but Yvonne did not call attention to it; it was probably high time he went home. Yvonne recognized the signs: Kevin's eyes slightly out of focus, his lips pursed ever so slightly when he talked so that he wouldn't slur. She could also tell by the way his trousers were wrinkled at the crotch that he had been sitting at the bar for a couple of hours.

Kevin turned to Yvonne and said, "I'll meet you at Harvey's at eight, unless you want me to pick you up."

"Harvey's at eight is fine," Yvonne said, not wanting to continue the conversation in which a decision would have to be made. Let her make it now and be done with it.

"Is . . . is that a new dress?"

She had bought it the week after Kevin left, but this was only the second time she had worn it. "Not really," she said.

"It's smashing," Kevin said. "Isn't it smashing, Melba?"

"You're absolutely right," said Melba. "Now I think I will whisk her away and show off that smashing dress to the rest of the bar. Maybe you'll even be on one of the videos." Melba nodded toward a corner, where a captain and his crew, red-faced and beaming behind a trophy surrounded by empty beer cans, were being videotaped and photographed.

As Melba guided Yvonne away, Yvonne gave her arm a little squeeze and said, "Thanks for getting me through that."

"I didn't know he'd be here when I invited you. I know you two are having it tough. But what the hell are you doing with him tomorrow?"

"We're taking the boat to its new owner. We can't afford to keep it and it's too big for one person to sail alone, at least the way it's rigged. And whenever I miss sailing, I'll offer to crew."

"You can crew for us anytime, if you can put up with a sloppy captain. And I'll just sit back and watch."

"You've got yourself a deal. I love the way your Hunter sails. Hi, Scotty, thanks for the invitation. Hello, Rosalie, how's the Millridge deal going? Did they get their mortgage?"

"Yes," answered Rosalie. "Your commission should be rolling in about a month from now." Rosalie was a smaller, more compact version of her son. The same deeply tanned and lustrous skin, the same large sherry-brown eyes ringed with thick black lashes that matched the hair. Their clothing was always neat and well-tailored—excessively neat, Yvonne sometimes thought. Rosalie was flashier, though. She had flair and an eye for color.

Tonight she was wearing a powder-blue blouse with matching trousers. Yvonne thought the trousers were linen and the blouse silk. Over them she wore a lavender coat-length, sleeveless cashmere cardigan. Yvonne was certain that Rosalie had crocheted it herself; it had a little drama to it that store-bought things couldn't match. Yvonne noticed that Rosalie's eye makeup was the same as hers and wondered how many others had been sold that combination this week at Bloomie's.

"Good, I'll be able to use the money," Yvonne said.

"You ought to give up teaching and work with us full-time," Rosalie said. "It's in your blood, you know."

"So's teaching. I've never been able to choose." It was true. Yvonne's mother and several of her aunts had been elementary school teachers, and she had been raised with funny stories about the antics of little children. Her father's conversation was more often than not about what house sold for what, who was asking too much for a house, which neighborhood was appreciating. . . . So Yvonne had studied art at Bennington and worked in the real estate office during vacations.

"That's a great sweater," Yvonne said. "Another original?"

"Not exactly. I borrowed the idea from an old drawing."

"It's still great."

"Thank you."

"I bought that computer you recommended," Yvonne said as she slid in beside Rosalie. Rosalie shifted a bag of yarn to her other side.

"So soon," said Rosalie. "Well, the sooner, the better. Keeping the listings on the computer is so much easier. And being able to work from home will be even better. You'll see."

"I'm ready to go as soon as you can get me hooked up. I have a modem and I've copied the office programs. I may need some help getting my machine set up at home, though."

"You won't need all the office programs. I have one program I use to plug into a network where I get crochet lessons."

"You don't need lessons. You could be giving the lessons."

"There's always more to learn. Just the other day . . ."

Rosalie was interrupted by Scotty at this point, complaining, "You girls are always talking shop. Besides, Yvonne, I haven't introduced you to Erik Walters. He's working with me now."

Scotty's work, which didn't seem to occupy much of his time, was running a travel agency in a storefront office adjoining his mother's real estate agency. Yvonne suspected that Rosalie paid most of Scotty's bills.

"Hi, Erik," Yvonne said. "Don't let Scotty work you too hard."

"No danger," Erik said, grinning beautifully with his wide mouth and big, even teeth. "I'm your basic sloth."

"The only things busy in that office are the spiders," Melba said, "spinning webs between you and Scotty."

While this exchange was going on, Rosalie nudged Yvonne and said, "I'll come over some night soon and get you started on the office programs."

Kevin stopped by on his way out and said to Yvonne, "I'll meet you at Harvey's at eight. Unless you want me to pick you up."

"Eight is fine," Yvonne said. "That should get us through Hell Gate at the right time." She wondered if he was drinking so much that he blacked out. They had already settled the arrangements about meeting at Harvey's.

Rosalie got up to leave the group shortly after cocktails and hors d'oeuvres, enough hors d'oeuvres to make a meal. Yvonne felt sated after sampling the trays that Scotty had ordered: a platter of shrimp, a bucket of steamers, another platter of oysters a la Chowder's (oysters with bread crumbs and Dijon mustard, baked in the shell), and several servings of fried mozzarella.

"You young folks have a nice evening," Rosalie said. "I have to go back to the office and then I'm going home. I have to get my beauty sleep. If I told my nutritionist what I ate tonight, he'd be apoplectic."

"What's that guy supposed to be doing for you anyway?" Scotty, always the diplomat, asked.

"Haven't you noticed how much more energy I have lately? And I think my skin is better, too."

"So now you can work sixteen hours a day instead of fourteen. Terrific. And there was nothing wrong with your skin, Ma."

"I'll consider those remarks as compliments and quit while I'm ahead. When you get back, Yvonne, I'll show you which programs you need. And I'll stop by to check on Tess."

"Terrific," Yvonne said.

Scotty continued to order huge amounts of food and drink, and the conversation stayed pleasant and gossipy. Erik fawned over Yvonne all evening but wasn't so pushy as to ask to take her home. He was younger than Yvonne, intelligent, polite, and dressed in very expensive casual clothes. Yvonne thought she remembered seeing the same grayed mauve sweater in an ad for a very chichi Italian designer.

When, during a trip to the powder room, Yvonne accused Melba of matchmaking, Melba laughed.

"Just window dressing, my dear, and ego nourishment. Erik is as gay as a fruit fly, which he will tell you if you try to get fresh with him."

This sent Yvonne into a fit of giggling that infected Melba as well and delayed their return to the table and had them wiping tears from their eyes when they joined Scotty and Erik.

"Are you going to let us in on the joke?" Scotty asked.

"It's just women talk, I'm afraid," Melba answered.

"You had to be there," said Yvonne.

"You girls have all the fun," Erik said, igniting the hilarity once more.

"We don't tell you guys everything," Melba said, a remark that successfully unfurled Erik's brow.

That started a whole round of jokes. Erik told gay jokes. Scotty, whose maternal grandfather's last name was Bernardo until the officers on Ellis Island changed it to Bernard, told Italian jokes.

Yvonne and Melba told knock-knock jokes as the foursome dropped all pretense at adult behavior.

When the waiters started to yawn and count their tips, Melba suggested that they continue the festivities at Scotty and Melba's place.

"I'm tempted, Melba. This has been such fun. But tomorrow is another day. I've got to go up the river."

"It sounds like a sentence," Scotty slurred.

"It is," Yvonne said. "It's got a perfectly good subject and predicate."

"Smart ass," Scotty said, his pronunciation of the letter *s* not improving.

Scotty, Melba, and Erik saw Yvonne to her car and asked whether she was all right to drive. Yvonne told them that she was only tipsy with enjoyment and thanked them all for the wonderful evening. Yvonne hummed and smiled as she drove home, realizing that it was the first time since the miscarriage that so many hours had passed without thought of her grief. She promised herself that she would do something nice for Melba and Scotty.

Though he was still smarting from the encounter with Yvonne, Kevin was glad he had stopped drinking when he did. He was sure he would have stopped when he did anyhow, even without seeing her, but he was glad just the same. The Port Guinness cops knew him from his days on the police beat, and he could probably call in a favor if he had to, but he didn't want a DWI charge.

Melba frustrated him sometimes. Like tonight. Oh, hell, there was no getting away from the frustration. Not when all he wanted to do was punch her in the mouth, so hard that she'd fall backward over the booth in Chowder's, right through the window and into the street. . . .

She had cut him out of it, the bitch. . . .

Jesus, good thing he had stopped drinking when he had. Fucking Jets . . .

What he should do, he told himself, was drive straight by the turnoff to Duck Point Lane, without even looking, and go straight to his apartment and straight to bed. He should not even think about . . .

He slowed down as he neared Duck Point Lane. Suddenly, he was almost blinded by the high beams from a car behind him. The light shone off the dirt and film on his own rear window and windshield.

Cop, Kevin thought. Jesus, if the guy wanted to be a prick Kevin had no chance at all. Especially since his newspaper had recently run a series investigating how drunk-driving laws were enforced.

Dazzled by the reflected light, Kevin felt a panic both deep and childlike. Squinting into the rearview mirror as he slowed to a near-stop, he waited to see the whirling red gumball he knew would appear any second.

Self-disgust and fear washed over him. God, he was in deep shit. You couldn't fix up a DWI charge anymore by pleading down to reckless driving and paying a traffic fine. Drunk driving was a misdemeanor, a crime.

He flicked on his turning signal, saw in the mirror that the cop had done the same. He was almost to the Duck Point Lane turnoff.

Kevin didn't know what to do. He was afraid that if he pulled all the way over and stopped just before the turnoff, the cop car would rear-end him and blame him for it. Jesus, the cop would hang all the paper he could on him; it might even make a funny story for the TV reporters. But if he pulled over too slowly, in the cop's judgment, it would be just as bad. Cops were always sizing people up, checking out their attitudes.

He decided to turn onto Duck Point Lane, then pull over immediately. Tell him I wanted to get off the main road, Kevin thought. Act humble.

He turned, and the car followed close behind. The cop can wreck my life if he wants to, Kevin thought. Lose my license, get in trouble with the paper, pay hundreds of dollars, maybe a couple thousand, in fines and for the lawyer. . . .

Go to jail, go to jail . . . Vonnie would really be through with him for good.

He squinted in the mirror. Still no red gumball. Suddenly, the car pulled around him and sped by.

No cop.

Kevin sucked in the cleansing night air, essence of salt water and trees and grass. Better than mints. He offered a prayer of thanks. This time, *this* time, he really meant it. He would not lie to God by swearing he would never drink again, but he sure as hell would never *drive* like this again.

The car that had passed him slowed a few hundred feet ahead, the flash of its brake lights somehow conveying confusion and tentativeness. The vehicle turned slowly, hesitantly, onto a side road—a path, really—that Kevin knew was a short cul-de-sac. Lost, Kevin thought.

Easiest thing in the world, getting lost in Port Guinness, with all the side roads that followed the shoreline. Well, they could get directions without much trouble.

Port Guinness was a friendly place; he and Vonnie had always thought that. They hadn't known how lucky they were when they found the house. No, not lucky. Blessed. They hadn't known it, at least he hadn't. But that was when they were younger. . . .

You had to be rich to have a house on or near the water nowadays. They had stumbled onto the house almost by pure luck. Decades before, it had been the servants' shack for the Blair Estate, and it still sat incongruously, almost comically, amid the mansions of the wealthy on Duck Point Lane.

When they had first moved in, Kevin and Yvonne had been embarrassed when their far-from-new, middle-class cars had encountered the BMWs and Cadillacs along the lane. Then they had learned to laugh about it, and the people in the BMWs and Cadillacs smiled and waved more often than not.

Tonight, driving slowly down the lane, Kevin hoped he would meet nobody. He knew he had a while to spare before Yvonne came back, and he just wanted to be alone near the house.

He stopped the car and turned off the lights and the engine a couple hundred feet away. Maybe if he was real quiet and the wind was blowing right, Tess wouldn't start barking right away. She was a little hard of hearing. Good old dog. God, he loved her.

Kevin figured he wasn't too drunk, because he was able to walk pretty quietly on the gravel. Then he guessed he must have figured wrong because he was overcome by sadness. The sound and smell of the water, the soughing of the trees, the sound of frogs and crickets were too much for him.

Kevin heard the old Doberman stir in the run by the house. She growled and was about to bark.

"Tessie, girl. It's just me. Your daddy."

He knelt down unsteadily, feeling the wet grass soak through the knees of his trousers, and put his face near the fence. The dog's tongue came through the links, flicked off his ear, again and again. Kevin laughed, and the dog licked some more.

"You good old girl, I hope you live forever. How the hell you get so old so fast, huh?"

The dog licked harder still. That was one of the nice things about dogs: You could say almost anything to them, and if you said it in a pleasant tone, they were happy.

"Missed you, old girl. Had to come by and visit." He hoped Yvonne would remember to leave the dog plenty of water while they were moving the boat. Sure, she would. That was one thing they were together on; they both loved the dog.

Kevin stood up, not knowing whether he should savor the night all he could, trying to take some of it with him, or try to forget it entirely.

Fat chance.

"People like us . . . people like me, we get one chance at a house like this. . . ."

The grass and trees and water would belong to someone else.

"Bye, Tess. Take care. Tell her to water the plants."

He turned and walked quickly back to the car, looking straight ahead all the while.

As Yvonne's car entered the garage, Tess started her hello bark, and Yvonne hurried to let the dog out of the run to quiet her. Even though the neighbors were not close, they weren't far enough away not to hear Tess. The Doberman rubbed her head and then her side against Yvonne's legs, her short tail quivering and her nose stopping at Yvonne's skirt and then at her shoes, hands, and purse.

"Would I come home without a treat for you, old girl?" Yvonne patted the dog's head and started up the stairs from the garage to the kitchen. She expected the dog to follow her up the stairs, but Tess was standing by the closed garage door and growling a low, soft growl.

A chill ran through Yvonne, draining away all the warmth of the evening's camaraderie. Her breathing quickened and became shallow as she stood on the stairs listening. Usually the dog barked at strange noises or strangers, but this menacing growl was different, frightening.

Tess stood with her nose to the floor next to the overhead door. The hair on her back was up and her tail was still. Yvonne felt vulnerable standing on the stairs in the lighted garage. If there was someone outside, she was clearly visible through the panes of the garage door.

She turned and ran up the steps, calling to the dog in a loud whisper, "Tess, come." The dog, always obedient, followed. Yvonne wanted to see if she could catch whoever or whatever it was. She left the house lights as they were when she left, and, once the door was relocked, she hit the light switches that turned on the outdoor lights.

She ran to the window in the big bedroom, which was over the garage. Tess followed her and growled again. Yvonne sucked in her breath. The bushes had moved. Someone, something was there. She stood staring at the spot where the bushes had swayed and the wind moved among the leaves. Was it the wind?

"What was it, girl? I know you're trying to tell me," Yvonne said, rubbing Tess behind the ears. The dog growled again.

After searching the house, keeping the dog at her side, and scanning the yard several more times, Yvonne decided that some strange animal must have been nearby. Tess had stopped growling by the time Yvonne was making her second pass at the windows.

Yvonne had been planning to sit on the deck for a while before she went to bed. She had always felt so safe in the house, in the neighborhood. Maybe the dog was getting senile. But she didn't sit on the deck. Instead she locked up all the windows except for the high ones. And when she slipped into bed, the dog, wise as old dogs get, nonchalantly hopped up next to Yvonne.

"You're about as senile as a fox," she said, patting the dog. Tess grunted happily.

3

The gate on the chain-link fence was locked when Kevin got to Harvey's Boatyard the next morning. God, he hoped Harvey was in by now. Sometimes, early in the morning, Harvey would go inside, then relock the gate for an hour or so. Like he was doing something real mysterious. Kevin felt pretty sure he didn't have a woman in there. At least he had never seen one. . . .

"Yo, Harv," Kevin shouted. "Yo, Harv."

Kevin felt a little satisfaction having beaten Yvonne to the yard. He just hoped he didn't look too green around the gills. Good thing he'd stopped when he did; another glass and he might not have made it. As it was, the coffee and toast sloshed uneasily inside him.

The goddamn Jets. No cornerbacks. Couldn't cover against the Packers. He hoped Yvonne wouldn't ask him if he had bet.

Well, Kevin had kept his part of the deal: He had rolled out of bed early, even done a little weight lifting to sweat out some of the beer before showering and jumping into cutoffs and Top-Siders. Now, if Harvey would just open the gate and Vonnie would just get her ass here, they might make it to Hell Gate on time. . . .

"Yo, Harv."

Nothing yet.

Vonnie . . . He had thought of her just then as Vonnie, his affectionate name for her. Then he thought of Chowder's the night before and got pissed off again. Goddamn her, too. Goddamn it . . .

Kevin's head started to ache a little. Always did when he was hung over and mad both. . . .

A car door slammed. There, there was Vonnie. Cutoffs and a

noise with the sudden shift. "Enough is enough, Harvey. It has nothing to do with you or with the commission. And we thank you for the things you've done for us. . . ."

"Like towing us off the sandbar that time," Kevin said, trying for a laugh and missing. He owed Harvey that much.

"This has been a good place for us to keep our boat," Yvonne went on smoothly, not unkindly. "We're leaving and we're selling." Yvonne had already started walking again toward the end of the dock, where their dinghy was.

Harvey bumped Kevin as he trotted after Yvonne, who turned in alarm.

"Yvonne, talk sense to him, for Chrissake. Let me keep it and get a fair price."

Kevin was furious that Harvey would try to undercut him in front of Yvonne—no, *through* Yvonne—and about something Kevin was sensitive about just then: money.

"Not that it's any of your damn business, Harvey, but we got a good price. Seven thousand, which isn't bad at all. And I've known the guy for years. Marty Diehl. He covers the Jets for *The Bugler*. Now back off. All right?"

Kevin looked into Harvey's face, saw him move his lips silently. Sauce on the brain, Kevin thought.

"I need some time," Harvey stammered. "I mean, you might still owe me for the mooring, I can't keep everything straight all the time for you kids. Now you're up and leaving."

Harvey's eyes were dark—piglike, Kevin thought—and drops of spittle from the shouting had flown into Kevin's face.

"I don't owe you shit, Harvey," he said. "Don't owe you fucking shit!"

Kevin's voice had risen to a near-scream, enough to hurt his throat.

"Kevin!" Yvonne yelled, dismayed at Kevin's temper. When would he learn that he didn't have to counter stupidity with a tantrum? Nevertheless, she felt she ought to show she was on his side in this.

"Harvey, back off," she said. "You can't hold us back, whether we owe you or not. I want an itemized bill of all the charges you say we owe, and if I don't get an apology from you for this, I'll tell everyone in town how you treat the people who rent space from you."

Kevin brushed by Harvey and grabbed the front of their dinghy, which was lying upside down on the end of the pier. He flipped it over and slid it into the water.

Yvonne stowed her bags, stepped lightly into the dinghy, then held on to the pier to steady the small boat so that Kevin could step in.

"As for owing you," Kevin said, still in high dudgeon, "we always paid, and we know you let other people use our dinghy, which wasn't kosher. So we are damn well square."

"Kevin, let's go!" She hoped he wouldn't get into a fistfight.

Kevin hurled his bag into the dinghy and stepped in hard enough to rock the boat. He slammed the oars in the oarlocks and churned the water furiously, making more splashing than progress until he got control of his stroke. He felt sick, spent, disgusted by his anger. For the thousandth time?

"Harvey," Kevin called hoarsely.

"Just row, Kevin. Let it be."

"Harvey, if we owe you, we can talk at Chowder's some night. Buy you a gin."

But Harvey was out of earshot, walking away from them down the pier.

"Do we owe him anything?" Yvonne asked.

"No, goddammit!"

"Don't shout at me. It's not an unreasonable question. It wouldn't be the first time you forgot—"

"Oh, hey, spare me this crap—"

"Maybe I should have let you vent your spleen on Harvey. Then I wouldn't have to put up with it."

"Look, Harvey's a jerk. I don't owe him diddley-squat. He's just a drunk who sees a boat commission sailing out of his yard. You always run into morons in boatyards. Anyhow . . . I shouldn't have shouted."

When they reached their boat, Kevin tied the dinghy to the stern and Yvonne started the engine, which turned over like a top and purred as smoothly as a teakettle, making little bubbles and ripples in the water.

Engine couldn't be better, Kevin thought.

Yvonne had the drill down cold: God, she was a sailor, Kevin thought. She loosened the bowline and cast off from the mooring. Now she walked smoothly back along the gunwale, stepped into the cockpit, took the rudder (as if Kevin weren't even there, that always pissed him off).

Yes, she had the drill down, still had it down, and so did he. Yvonne let the boat drift back from the mooring ball a few feet, then said, "Okay."

And Kevin pushed the gearshift into forward, gunned the throttle slightly, and they were off. Just like old times.

The confrontation, especially his own outburst, had left him depressed—as though all the friendly exchanges with Harvey, the occasional favors he had done for them and their thanks, had been wiped out.

He would look Harvey up at Chowder's, soon, buy him a drink, smooth it all out.

Yvonne watched Kevin's face register remorse, then sadness, then the hopeful resolve of a child coming out of a confessional, or, more likely, she thought, the endless starting all over of the alcoholic, who expects an apology to erase an offense. She couldn't blame him for getting mad at the way Harvey acted, but Kevin should have had more control.

"Harvey was way out of line," she said. "He would have pissed off the Pope. But of course, when the Pope gets pissed, he prays. He doesn't say the f-word and all the other four-letter words he can think of."

Kevin sensed that Yvonne was trying to lighten the gloom, and appreciated it. "Yeah, well, I see your point. About the Pope, I mean. I guess it wasn't all my fault. I don't know. Maybe Harvey's mad because we're leaving him."

Enough, Kevin thought. They had many nautical miles to go, and promises to keep. Kevin fiddled with the throttle, finally getting it where he wanted it, about three-quarter speed.

"That's good," Yvonne said. "Just right."

Her voice was soft, not like before, and Kevin looked up and nodded. God, she looked good in cutoffs.

"Let me know when you want me to steer," Kevin said. He thought he saw her nod. He pulled his legs onto the bench and rested his back against the outside of the cabin so that he was looking toward the stern.

To his great relief, the water smell and the motion were perking him up, helping to dissolve his hangover. Sometimes he thought the water smelled like a big gin and tonic.

"We picked a good day for it," Yvonne said.

"Hmmm . . ."

Vonnie must still be jogging, Kevin thought. Her legs looked so firm and tan, even the tops, near the frayed edges of the cutoffs. He remembered when they had jogged together, usually in the morning and near the water. On the best days, the salt on their skin afterward had been part sweat, part sea spray. Showering together had been fun too. Sometimes a lot of fun.

Suddenly, without meaning to at all, Kevin remembered how she had looked when she got pregnant, her belly just starting to swell. That reminded him of all the rest, especially the tests, and the doctor seeming to say, without coming right out and saying, that it might be just as well if the pregnancy didn't go all the way.

Kevin swung his legs off the bench and stood up, facing the bow. He sucked in the air and the smell of the water. Then he clenched his teeth. Goddamn you, Vonnie, it's not just my fault we lost it. Goddamn me too. Goddamn everything.

After a while, he took the tiller and she sat near the throttle. She pulled a Thermos of iced tea out of her deep purse and gave a cup to Kevin. It tasted like it was from heaven, and he loved her again, not even minding very much when she gave little hand motions, wordlessly, to correct his course.

He wanted to tell her then that he still loved her, and hoped they could try again, boat or not, house or not. He really loved the way her hair licked around her face in the breeze. He remembered all the times on the boat, how her eyes had looked, intent on the tightness of the sails, the direction of the telltales, the surface of the water. Her pupils would shrink to tiny black flints in a field of cornflower blue. God, what a sailor . . .

All he could say was, "Really is a good day for it."

Near the Throgs Neck Bridge, they slowed down to let a freighter go by. And when the big steel hulk had slid off the horizon, Kevin saw a boat bobbing near one of the bridge towers. Funny place for a boat to be, he thought. When Kevin first spotted it, the boat was a few hundred yards away. As they drew closer to the bridge, Kevin thought it looked like one of Harvey's boats, a knockabout that Harvey used sometimes for fishing and sometimes for beer outings with his cronies. He would have sworn that the guy on the boat was looking at them through binoculars. Then the boat started up, spurted away from the bridge and headed back toward the open Sound.

Going under the bridge, Kevin heard the hum of the cars above.

"Did you see that boat?" Kevin asked. But Yvonne had her timetable on her mind. "Goddamn, freighter held us up," she said. "We don't want to fart around getting to Hell Gate." So she put the throttle on full, the stern dipped more into the water as the bow came up. When Kevin looked back for a moment, he would have sworn he saw the speedboat again, far in the distance and reversing course. But he wasn't sure.

Past the Throgs Neck, they were in a big calm basin that marked the start of the East River. The Bronx-Whitestone Bridge was at the other end of the basin and seemed very close. It took them twenty minutes to get to it. Another rumble-hum far overhead as they passed under the Bronx-Whitestone.

He's slacking off on the jogging, she thought. Probably drinking too much, not getting outdoors enough, eating a lot of hamburgers and heros and pizzas.

"Did you bring any sunscreen?" she asked.

"Nah. Real men don't wear sunscreen." It was one of their old routines about what real men and real woman do, and he had meant it to be light-hearted.

Yvonne didn't laugh. Health was an important item on her agenda. "Real men get skin cancer," she said. "I have some in my bag, but I'm not sure it will be enough for you."

"Thanks, Vonnie, really. It'll be better than nothing. I didn't think of it. But," he said, reaching into the cabin for his duffel bag, "I did remember to pack"—and he lifted each item with a flourish—"pickles, and apple juice, and turkey-and-cheese sandwiches."

Yvonne smiled in spite of herself, touched that he had remembered her favorites. She, too, had packed a lunch with things he liked, but she thought she would wait until later to tell him that she had packed roast-beef sandwiches with mustard, lettuce, and mayonnaise, and some V-8 for his hangover. She used to feel sorry for him when he woke in the morning with eyes cracked with red lines; she had even shared some bleary mornings with him early in their marriage, both of them bedbound till noon wearing cold washcloths across their foreheads and eyes. She had resented his drinking after she became more health-conscious, especially when she was pregnant. Then she hadn't drunk, had taken her vitamins, gone to bed early, had become a blooming incubator. And for what?

There were advantages to an aborted pregnancy: no stretch marks, and then there was the freedom. She had been willing, though, to give up the freedom, twenty years of it, for the next in line on earth. And stretched skin was a small price to pay to have a child that is part of you, that you made, that wouldn't be on earth except for you.

She was staring out across the wake, watching the churning greens and blues and grays darken as they receded. The colors claimed her attention and she found herself wishing she had brought along her watercolors. She had painted on the boat before, but usually at anchor or at the mooring. She felt the waves toss the boat slightly and thought that she would produce a sloppy watercolor while they were motoring. She would try to remember the colors and the way they changed.

"I think we'll hit Hell Gate in plenty of time," Kevin said.

His voice snapped the reverie. "Oh, let's see." Yvonne pulled out the charts and tables, which were marked with the arrival times on the route. She checked her watch and then the chart and then looked toward shore. "That's College Point. Yes, we have time to spare. Good."

An oil tanker with a Spanish or Portuguese name passed them on its way toward the ocean. Several suntanned crewmen waved to them from among the clusters of pipes and valves high above. Kevin and Yvonne waved back.

"Look at her," Yvonne said as the first waves from the tanker slapped at their boat. "A lot longer than a football field."

"Yep, easy. And she's nothing compared to the big supertankers. What do you say we let the engine slack off a bit?"

"Aye, aye," said Yvonne, with a little salute. That was another of their games. Whoever was at the tiller was the captain. She pushed back the throttle.

"Hey, that's better," said Kevin. "I can see over the bow sitting down now."

"Captains shouldn't be slothful," she said, looking back again over the wake, which now left small ridges in the surface.

Now they were crossing the landing path for LaGuardia Airport. One after another, it seemed like every minute, jetliners appeared as dots on the horizon, grew bigger, then roared overhead, drowning out the sound of the boat engine.

They were passing Rikers Island, the city prison, when it occurred to her that she had been seeing a small speedboat behind them for some distance. "Kevin," she said, "am I imagining that the boat back there is following us?"

"Where? I thought I saw a boat that looked like Harvey's back by the Throgs Neck."

"Harvey? What the hell is going on? I thought you said we don't owe him any money."

Kevin bit his lip; she still had the touch to piss him off. "No, we don't. The only bill we could have is the latest one for engine work, but he said it was okay. Remember?" Kevin paused to cool himself down. "To tell you the truth, I half-imagined I saw something myself."

"Okay, okay, I'm sorry. Why don't you kind of sneaky-like get the binoculars and peek out from the cabin. I'll take the tiller back."

Kevin climbed down the steps into the galley and pulled the binoculars from one of the cabin drawers. "We have to clean out these drawers, Vonnie, I don't think we need to leave all this stuff for Marty Diehl. Hey, there's some good stuff here. Cribbage board, that extra compass you got me last Christmas. . . ." Kevin stopped. There was a lump in his throat. He thought he saw sadness flash over Yvonne's face, too.

Yvonne indeed had felt a sharp pang when she thought how happy they had been at Christmastime, at least before the big fight about the Jets party. She recovered her composure, yelling, "Are you taking inventory or are you going to check on that speedboat?"

Kevin braced himself on the hatch and kept low as he focused the glasses. They were passing between the North Brother and South

Brother islands, and he scanned the river bank past Rikers toward the Bronx-Whitestone.

There. Yes, it looked like Harvey's boat, but he couldn't be sure. Lots of boats looked like that. Gray, or blue, or silver, or silver-gray, or silver-blue.

"Well?" she said.

"No way I can tell."

"You're sure?"

"I'm sure I can't be sure. How's that?" I'm not sure of anything anymore, he thought.

4

As the sound of the Pearson's engine faded, Harvey walked back along the pier toward the big garage and storage shed, a tiny corner of which served as his office. The pier bobbed only slightly with his steps, but Harvey felt that his world was turning upside down. He had to swallow to keep from losing the contents of his stomach from the nausea stirred by his hangover, self-disgust—and fear.

"Goddammit and Jesus Christ to hell and back!" How could he have been so goddamn stupid, not to have picked up on what those kids were pulling. Jesus. All summer they don't go out on the boat, then that snot nose Kevin nags him about the engine. Easiest thing in the world to see that they were going to take the boat away. Jesus Christ!

Harvey got to the end of the pier, gave one last hard swallow, and leaned his back against the garage, savoring the shade. All right, all right. If he could just think straight.

"Jesus Christ almighty."

Was he being punished somehow by God, or the gods of chance, for not being a hundred percent sorry his old friend Tolly had gone to the great big bilge? Well, shit, it had been Tolly's own fault and no one else's, doing what he did. Drinking so much he passed out the next day working on an engine. Plain common sense should have told him better. He, Harvey, had never done anything that stupid, not since he was a kid anyhow.

For a moment, Harvey felt naked in his guilty knowledge. Yes, after first feeling sorry about Tolly he had been glad that Tolly was out of the way. All right, sure, it was true. Harvey had been glad. Well, no wonder. Tolly had started to get careless, greedy, trying to take over what had been Harvey's idea in the first place. Wanting more of a split than he deserved, too.

Harvey left the shade of the building, went around the corner and into a side door. He sat in the old wooden chair that served as the main piece of furniture in his "office," actually an area bounded by shelves and boxes packed with various cans and bottles of boat paint, marine oil, varnish, grease, and God knew what else.

Again, for a moment, his mind wandered. This time, he thought way back, if not in time then certainly in circumstance, to how things had been before they came to him offering a business deal. The deal had changed everything, and there was no canceling it.

Sitting there, waiting for his heart to slow down, Harvey breathed deeply, taking small comfort in the smells of tar and rope, varnish and canvas that had been part of the garage since his father had run it. Good, warm, timeless boat smells. Comfortable and uncomplicated.

Damn, Harvey thought, I had the world by the ass *before* the deal.

Harvey picked up a work rag that wasn't too dirty, wiped his sweating face, tossed the rag in the corner.

He picked up the phone and dialed. "It's me," he said. "We got a problem. . . . Just listen. Them two kids with the boat. Well, they came here this morning and took the goddamn thing away. . . . Of course they don't know. You think I'm crazy, for Christ's sake? . . . Because I didn't have time, that's why. . . . Just calm down and listen to me. . . ."

After a few minutes, Harvey hung up. He felt better, having taken some action.

He really didn't have anything against Kevin and Yvonne, kind of liked them, in fact. Especially her, with them legs of hers.

Maybe it could be undone so no one got hurt. Then again, maybe not. Got nothing against those kids at all, Harvey thought, but first things first. Anything can happen, not my fault. They shouldn't have surprised me like that.

Harvey breathed deeply, wondering if he could retrace his steps.

The money had been so tempting, so easy, even before. . . .

He shook his head, swallowed hard, again and again. He had to keep his head, no matter what. If only things hadn't got so complicated.

He didn't know how long he sat there before he heard the phone.

Long enough to be startled by the ring. But not so long, he realized with alarm, for the call to be a response to his own.

He picked up on the third ring, concentrated on making his voice matter-of-face, bored.

"Harvey's Boatyard," he said. No, he had not quite pulled it off.

"Harvey," the familiar voice said. "It's that time again. Why don't you drop by for something cold."

Harvey pulled into the lot behind Quince's building and parked next to one of the rental vans. As he reached the door of the building, he was surprised that it was pulled open from the inside.

"Harvey," the door opener said as Harvey stepped in.

"Whaddya say," Harvey responded.

Harvey knew the man only casually. His name was Chuck, and he worked for Quince. He had a thick back and shoulders, heavy, with slabs of muscle that were perfect for heavy lifting or . . .

"He here?" Harvey asked hoarsely.

"Waitin' for you."

"Good. Hope he's got a cold one handy."

But Harvey's little stab at camaraderie was met with silence, leaving him embarrassed, edgy.

Harvey went down a dark corridor and knocked on a door at the end.

"Come," said the familiar voice inside.

Harvey entered and instantly was aware of globs on his face as the chill from the air conditioner bathed his skin.

"Say, Quince," Harvey said, trying his best friendly voice.

"Harvey. Sit down, please." Quince's voice was soft, businesslike, controlled.

Harvey sat in a Naugahyde chair facing Quince's barge-sized desk. Quince sat down at his desk, leaned back a little, crossed his legs.

"How are you anyhow?" he said. Then he smiled, but his eyes were flinty.

Harvey expected Quince to offer him a cold beer any moment. As a hint, he said, "I'm about the same as I was last night at Chowder's. Feel like I had maybe one too many. Getting too old to learn—"

"Tell me, do you have any problems at your yard? You know, with stealing? That kind of thing?"

"Well, no, I'm careful all the time." Harvey tried to sound casual, but his blood had gone to ice.

"How about with unauthorized use of equipment from your yard?"

"You mean . . ."

"I mean boats, say. Anyone ever use a boat from your yard without your say-so?"

"Well, no. Hell, no. Not that I know of." The chair arms were slippery now from perspiration.

"And it's just you at the yard, isn't it? You have no associates. . . ."

"No. Just me."

"Although at one time, I think I remember, you did do business with that fellow who breathed the wrong stuff. Tolly."

"Tolly? Oh, yeah, we go back a ways. Told you that. Shame what happened to him."

"A shame. But that's what comes from carelessness."

"Mmmm." The sweat was running down Harvey's face and arms. He thirsted for the cold beer he hoped to be offered any moment, and for the easy friendship Quince had shown toward him only the night before.

"I myself know about carelessness," Quince went on solemnly. "Back a while, when I was first getting started in trucking, I learned the hard way that I couldn't trust everyone. Petty thievery from the docks, employees filling their own gas tanks, that kind of thing."

"Right. Gotta be careful."

"But you've managed to prevent theft at your yard. Tell me," Quince went on, baring his teeth in a smile, "how do you do it?"

Harvey squirmed in the slippery chair. "Just me," he said, almost stammering. "Just me in the yard, so I know everything that goes on."

"Ah. Then you know why one of your boats is chasing those two who left a while ago with that Pearson sloop."

"Chasing . . . ?" Harvey's voice almost died in a croak.

"Chasing, following, whatever. You know, surely. You just told me—"

"No, not chasing. I mean, not really. I know where . . . See, I figure they might still owe me for . . . for engine work I did."

"Well, you could just bill them."

"Well, sure, but once the boat's gone—"

A flashing red light from above and off to his left had caught the corner of Harvey's eye. He looked at the ceiling corner closest to him and saw that a television security camera was trained directly on him. The red bulb light on top of the camera blinked regularly.

"You could just bill them. Unless there's something else."

"Something else? Well . . ." Harvey was dizzy with fear. The blinking red light . . .

"Tell me, confidentially and man-to-man. Do you think there's even a remote chance they found out about . . . you know. And that, having found out, they took advantage of your trust?"

"Well, I hope not. I mean . . ." Harvey was confused as well as afraid; he couldn't figure what Quince was driving at.

"He gambles, I hear at Chowder's. On football. And the lovebirds are flying their separate ways, so perhaps they have a money problem. Or perhaps *separate* money problems."

"Well, could be, I guess. About them and money."

"So you did have them followed so that . . . so that . . . well, *why* exactly?" Quince seemed both puzzled and annoyed.

"Well, like I said . . ." Harvey slipped and slid in the moist chair. "I mean . . ." The blinking red light atop the camera seemed like a laser beam drilling into his brain. "Say, that light is driving me nuts. Could you turn it off?" Harvey wanted more than anything in the world to have Quince break a gut-splitting laugh and hand him a cold one.

"It's just a camera," Quince said incredulously. "Like they have in banks. They have their money to look after, and we have ours."

"I was only . . ."

"I know this is a little unsettling for you. Please forgive me. But we all have our orders."

"Orders?"

"Mine are to check into what we think has been some, you know, pilferage."

Harvey's mind was racing in terror. He tried to remember how long the corridor was, whether he had any chance of running out of the office and . . . but where would he go?

"As I said, we have been concerned about pilferage."

"Mmm . . ." No use even thinking about trying to get away, Harvey knew. He would never get outside the building, and even if he did . . .

"You're bothered by that camera?" Quince had changed his tone. Suddenly he was friendly, smiling, jovial.

"Ain't that. I just take shitty pictures." Harvey managed a small laugh.

"Me too. I have some pictures of myself that you'll just have to see . . . I'm sorry. I forgot. Can I get you something?"

Harvey felt as if a stone had been lifted from his chest. "Just a beer, Quince."

"Please, let me join you in a gin and tonic. Please."

"Sure. Gin and tonic it is."

Quince walked to a near wall, opened a dark oak cupboard, took out glasses and gin. Then he opened a small refrigerator within the cupboard and fetched tonic water, ice cubes, wedges of lime. His back to Harvey, Quince went on talking as he mixed drinks.

"Everybody has a boss. Isn't that the truth? Years ago, when I was just getting started on my own, I thought I was my own boss. . . . Here, drink this and you'll feel better than you have all day."

Quince handed Harvey a big glass and sat down at the desk holding a glass of his own.

"Everybody has a boss," Quince went on. "So I was on my own. My own boss, I thought. No. My customers were my boss. My employees were my boss, in a sense, because they made me do things I would otherwise not have done. Do you see?"

Harvey wasn't sure he did, but he nodded just the same.

"Cheers," Quince said, raising his glass in Harvey's direction and sipping.

Harvey took a gulp; a stiff drink, he thought.

"What I mean," Quince went on, "is that I wanted to be a trusting person. But I found I couldn't be. So I used to set little traps for the dishonest ones. I would arrange to have stray items left where they could be stolen by those so inclined. A TV set left in a dark corner of a semitrailer, even a basket of fruit behind a forklift on a dock . . ."

Quince paused, smiled, waited for Harvey to show he understood.

Harvey nodded and drank. He was starting to relax now. His arms, no longer wet with sweat, were settling into the chair.

"And I—we—have done the same thing with our goods recently. I mean the items we have been leaving with you, for safekeeping in your yard before transfer. Do you follow?"

Harvey nodded. He still felt uneasy, but Quince's voice was smooth, soothing, and Harvey was reassured because Quince was confiding in him. Harvey started to take another gulp from his drink, but he held off. Better to pace himself; he was feeling it already.

"Some time ago, we thought we detected the tiniest bit of pilferage. Of course, even a little bit here and there adds up when we're dealing with something this valuable."

"Mmmm." Harvey was grateful for the way the drink had taken the edge off his nerves, but the slight dulling of his senses had made it harder to follow Quince. Harvey was aware of the red light still blinking at the edge of his vision.

"We—I mean myself and my real boss—we have discussed this problem at length. At first, we suspected . . ." Quince paused and looked at Harvey, smiled. "You."

Harvey sat up with a jolt; some of his gin and tonic sloshed out, running in a cool rivulet from his wrist to his elbow.

Quince chuckled and his eyes brightened. "I said *at first* we suspected you. Then, after we talked it over, we realized how little sense that made. I mean, you have always been so careful and reliable. We have paid you well. And you and I have toasted each other at Chowder's, as friends."

"Friends . . ." Harvey felt a great relief from what Quince had just said. And he was becoming more and more relaxed.

"And if it wasn't you, then who? We asked ourselves that, over and over. Then we wondered—as crazy as it sounds—could it be those two young people?"

Again Harvey was startled. "You mean . . ."

"Yes, those two with the Pearson. Kevin and Yvonne. Their behavior has changed lately. They're supposed to be splitting up, yet when they bump into each other—such a small town—they seem to be in love. Surely you've noticed."

"Mmmm."

"What if that is all a charade? we asked ourselves. I mean, suppose they are faking their estrangement. She's a quick study; we know that. He's a newspaperman, smarter than he acts. Do you see?"

Harvey's mind was racing, yet it dare not trip between what Quince was saying and what Harvey knew to be true.

"Do you see? It's brilliant, really. There could hardly be a safer storage place, a safer means of transport."

"I do see." Harvey took another sip. The gin and lime was deliciously cool and slaking.

"And we know they hung around your yard, your shop, a lot when they were using the boat. Always needing to talk about the engine, needing line—needing to pay you for pulling them free of a sandbar. Remember?"

"I remember."

"And we concluded that they had seen something in your garage, probably while you were on the dock. Oh, we don't blame you for that. They saw something they shouldn't have. And then they enlisted someone's help."

Harvey sat upright again, as if jolted by an electric current. An ice cube slipped out of the glass and plopped onto his chair.

"And if it wasn't your help," Quince went on solemnly, "it had to be Tolly's."

"Tolly?" Harvey was bewildered.

"Don't you see it? He is an old friend of yours, an old associate. Yes? If anyone would know how to get into the yard easily, move around the garage easily at night, it would be Tolly. Don't you see?"

"Tolly . . ."

"A lowlife. Forgive me, Harvey. A lowlife, your friendship notwithstanding. He abused your friendship, stole from you. From us. With the help of those two lovebirds. It's so clear."

Harvey fought off the gin haze, thinking as nimbly as he could. Salvation lay just ahead if he didn't stumble. "I'll be damned," he said at last. "Tolly."

"Fortunately, he did himself in with his carelessness and stupidity, saving us a problem."

"Damn."

"And you doubtless meant to head off another problem by following the lovebirds, yes?"

"Yes! Yes!"

"And you were just about to tell us that?"

"Yes! Damn straight." Harvey took a second to think. "I was just gonna call you, when you called me." Harvey took another gulp; the gin and tonic was one of the best he had ever tasted. He felt like he'd had a couple already. Maybe three.

"Good. That only leaves the problem of what to do with them. After we get our goods back, of course."

"You think you'll have to . . ." Harvey couldn't finish the thought. That kind of thing was way beyond what he had bargained for.

"We'll see," Quince said softly. "That will depend."

On what? Harvey was tempted to ask. But he thought better of it. He was not home free yet, and he had to worry about himself before thinking about Kevin and Yvonne.

Suddenly, Harvey remembered the phone call he'd made. Jesus; he would have to get to a phone, somehow. He had to cancel . . . Damn. Could he do that? Would it be better to tell Quince? No.

Harvey was really feeling the gin now. He shifted the glass from one hand to another; it almost slipped from his grasp. He put his free hand up to support his head.

"We'll talk some more," Quince said.

Harvey thought Quince sounded very far away. In a distant corner of his vision, Harvey again caught the red camera light, blinking, blinking, blinking, blinking. . . .

Harvey's eyes closed. The gin glass dropped from his hand, bounced off the edge of the chair, fell to the floor. By the time he was lifted out of the chair and carried to the van he was in a deep sleep.

5

At the Astoria Consolidated Edison Plant the river turned south and narrowed into a sluiceway toward Hell Gate. Yvonne and Kevin had timed their arrival perfectly, but Hell Gate was still no pushover. The water had just a light chop, like shallow rapids dashing over stones, or a mass of snakes writhing under satin, but beneath the surface the treacherous tides ripped at one another and wrenched the boat off course one way, then another. The water eddied and glistened in the sun, almost like quicksilver.

They went under the black steel bow of the railroad bridge. A few minutes later, the Triborough Bridge roared with traffic high above them. They looked up, but only for a moment: Hell Gate had tricked better sailors than they, scuttled bigger boats than theirs since long before the Triborough was built, long before the men who built it were born. Although the big buildings had been visible on the skyline during the whole trip, when Kevin and Yvonne came out from under the Triborough, the city looked like a wall of concrete.

They were in the current, the Pearson hurtling through the water as though it were skidding on ice. Except that they were in control. Kevin kept his hand on the throttle, ready to adjust it if need be. Yvonne had the tiller and her face and body were taut with attention. Damn, Kevin thought, she looks like she was born holding a tiller.

The bow dipped into a wave, came riding up again, then splashed down, causing spray to fly into the cockpit.

"Yes!" Kevin shouted. "All right! Anyone doesn't like this feeling doesn't deserve to be loved by a good boat."

For a moment, she felt the same thrill, and they were together on their boat.

"Hi, Gracie," Kevin said, smiling, as they passed the mayor's mansion on its bluff overlooking the river.

Then they were past Hell Gate and the south-rushing tide gave them new speed. Only a couple of hundred feet away, a constant flow of traffic buzzed along the FDR Drive. It was moving, free of its rush-hour clot.

"There's the Animal Medical Center," Yvonne said. "Hello, all you good people who saved our Tess."

Kevin saluted the hospital. "Good work, folks."

They both remembered how they had worried together all one night while the doctors battled to save Tess from an infection. And the joy of the next day when the battle had been won. Together, then.

Neither of them said any more.

A helicopter dropped down onto the pad next to the Fifty-ninth Street Bridge, churning the air. Yvonne pushed her hair back in place after the copter had passed.

"A lot of new buildings on Roosevelt Island," Kevin said.

"New subway stop," Yvonne said.

Kevin had to think a minute to realize she had answered him. The new subway stop had made the island more accessible.

"Anyhow, she'll make Marty a damn good boat," Kevin said, trying again. But it had only made things worse. He attempted a graceful exit. "Thanks again for the V-8, Vonnie. I mean, that was above and beyond . . ."

"You're welcome, again." Yvonne wanted to tell him to shut his mouth unless he had something new to say; at the same time, part of her wanted to hear him say the old tired things. Sick, sick, sick, she told herself.

This day, the East River was as rocky as a child's bathtub. It took only a few powerboats and a barge or two to churn up the water, because the wave action had no place to go. It slammed against the wall of the FDR Drive on one side and onto Roosevelt Island on the other, not that far away, and the unspent forces rolled back through the water toward the middle.

"Those old ruins, what the hell are they?" Kevin said, pointing to the end of Roosevelt Island. "Looks like an old fort."

"That's what's left of an old sanitarium. Every so often the city talks about tearing it down."

When they had passed the end of Roosevelt Island Yvonne looked east toward Brooklyn. "Look, Kevin," she said. "You can see church steeples towering over the buildings."

"Yeah, and in Manhattan they're walled in."

"Funny, isn't it. So different on one side of the river from the other."

"You want funny? Wait till we get to the Hudson and you can see New Jersey."

"But that's another state."

"That's another world."

"You sound like a New York chauvinist."

"Is that better or worse than a male chauvinist?"

"Either way it means you've got a head like a boulder."

Yvonne liked the tiller, liked the control, the response of the boat to her touch.

Kevin was just as happy to let her steer, and he squinted as his eyes scanned the sun-dazzled water, trying to discern the chop.

"Vonnie, want to steer into that?" He pointed toward a big wave, probably left by a barge and coming at an angle. It wouldn't have come close to swamping them, but the tiller adjustment let them meet it head-on, so that the bow dipped gently and there was no yawing at all.

Yvonne pushed the tiller back, the bow came around, and they headed straight downriver again. "Good eye," she said.

"How's the real estate business this summer?" Kevin asked.

"Okay. Pretty good, actually."

"Think it'll ever get good enough to make you want to give up teaching?"

"Uh-uh. I miss the kids when school's out." Kevin had asked her that before.

"The office run pretty much the same as ever?"

"It seems busier. We do more for the customers. Get them mortgages even. Rosalie's computer system makes it a snap to find houses. That machine could double her business."

"She seems to be doing all right now."

"She is. Look at her cars, the house, not to mention Scotty's. She's a workaholic, but she's always pleasant. She knows what's going on and she praises you to high heaven when something good happens. She's really great."

"Wonder why your mom doesn't like her."

"Mother told me about some gossip once that Mr. Durer wasn't really Scotty's father. That Rosalie had had a long affair with some shady but very wealthy man. Mother thought that the money to buy Dad's agency hadn't really come from the insurance when Mr. Durer died, but from Rosalie's inamorato."

Kevin chuckled. "Glad to hear your mom hasn't mellowed on her world view. What does your dad say about the rumor?"

"Dad doesn't like hearing bad things about people he likes. He sticks his head in the sand and waits for things to blow over."

"I can relate to that."

"Right."

He caught the edge in her voice, but ignored it. "And I'm glad you like real estate."

After a few seconds she said, "Your job is all right?"

"Yeah. I still think now and then—you remember—about transferring out of sports to the regular news side. Maybe someday I'll get off my ass and really do it. Then again . . ."

"Then again . . ."

"This is a good time of year to be covering football," he said. "Wonderful mix of new players coming in, old guys trying to hang on to their jobs, some of them not being able to."

"It sounds heartless."

"In a way it is. But it's . . . what . . . rich. In emotion, nostalgia. At least it can be, if you find the right stories and handle them with some, you know . . ."

"Restraint."

"Bingo. You always were my best editor."

She smiled at the compliment, but if he was dangling bait for an intimate conversation she wouldn't bite.

They had talked God knew how many times about whether he should switch jobs. Kevin kept up with current events (at least he had before his beer intake went up after the split, Yvonne thought) and read history, biography, and politics in his spare time. At least she hoped he was still doing some serious reading.

She remembered that he had liked covering the police beat early in his career, before he switched to sports. And she thought she knew better than he did the deeper reasons he dragged his feet on switching back to regular news.

"I gotta admit," Kevin said, "you were right about my enjoying the role—you know, Mister Inside Football whenever the big-shot editors want to hear sports gossip."

"Told you." She said it lightly, but she hadn't forgotten how he had taken offense before when that subject came up.

"At least the Jets don't play on Thanksgiving this year."

Yvonne knew what that meant. Kevin loved Thanksgiving and Christmas, was always desperate, even if they were fighting, for them to do something special as a couple. He's already angling for an old-fashioned Thanksgiving of stuffing and drumsticks, she thought. He's not getting it from me.

"Hello, Citibank," Kevin said as the distinctive, slant-roofed skyscraper in midtown came into view. "How come you never asked us to be in your TV commercials?"

"We're not rich, that's why."

That exchange left a momentary brittleness in the air, and they tacitly agreed to keep quiet for a while until it dissolved.

They passed the United Nations Building on their right, a power plant with three huge stacks on their left.

"Is that big Pepsi-Cola sign in Queens or Brooklyn?" Kevin said.

"I don't remember."

They passed the ancient sailing ships berthed at the South Street Seaport, passed the cluster of fabric-covered tennis courts, the "bubbles" where some of the city's privileged played. A while later, they saw the buildings where some of the privileged made their fortunes: the towering skyscrapers of Wall Street.

"I keep forgetting," Kevin said. "I think of the big buildings being uptown, except for the World Trade Center. Then I saw the Wall Street buildings from the water. . . ."

"Plenty of yuppies left in the world," Yvonne said. "Don't let anyone tell you otherwise."

"Who was it said, 'Behind every great fortune there is a crime'? Or something like that. You believe it?"

"No. Not entirely, anyhow."

"There, Vonnie!" Kevin said, chuckling as he pointed to a low yellow building squatting near the water's edge. "I almost worked in that building. Remember?"

And so he had: as they went under the Manhattan Bridge, the New York Post Building came into view.

"Oh, right," Yvonne said, warming to the memory despite herself. Early in their marriage, Kevin had tried for a job at the *New York Post*, been disappointed when he didn't get it, and she had been disappointed with him. Then he had got the job with the newspaper on Long Island, and everything seemed to fall into place. For better and worse.

They went between the massive stone supports of the Brooklyn Bridge, heard the whining of tires on the metal grating above. They had been on the boat for several hours and were nearing the tip of Manhattan.

"There she is," Yvonne said. "I still get goose bumps."

"Nothing wrong with that."

Off to their left in the distance was the Statue of Liberty.

"I wonder if I could ever capture that opaque pale green with my watercolors," Yvonne said.

At the tip of Manhattan, they gave a respectful distance to a Coast Guard cutter and a Staten Island ferry so as not to get caught in their wakes. Then they scooted around the Battery and started north on the Hudson.

"According to the charts, the tide should turn soon and push up the Hudson." She smiled smugly.

"A star for the navigator."

"Very funny."

Just north of the Battery, on an unused concrete support abandoned from the heyday of commercial shipping in New York, several dozen nude men lounged, their skin bronze and shiny in the hot midday sun.

"I'll get the binoculars," Kevin said.

Yvonne turned away. "Bastard," she said. She raised her foot in a playful kick aimed at his midsection, then arrested the move halfway through. The moment of mirth had been only that—a moment.

Kevin glanced once more toward the pier, just long enough to see a fully clothed man standing near the edge, looking out at the water. Toward their boat? Kevin couldn't tell.

He felt uneasy. "See that guy?"

"What guy?"

"There. The one with the clothes on."

"I was trying not to look," she said, turning toward the pier. "Okay, I see him. Why?"

"Is he watching us?"

"Why would somebody be watching us?"

"I don't know. Why the hell did Harvey go bonkers?"

"I still don't know, Kevin." She was annoyed that he had brought that up again. "Maybe the guy on the pier was following us in that boat you saw. He's part of Harvey's army of bill collectors."

But Yvonne felt something squirming in her gut. Maybe it was just the incongruity of a man with clothes on amid the nude sunbathers. Why would he be there, at the end of the pier, if not to watch something on the water?

At that point, a speedboat cut rudely across their bow not fifty feet ahead. "Macho bastard," Yvonne said. She turned the boat so the wake wouldn't hit them broadside.

After they rode the chop, they looked at the pier. The man was gone.

"I'm hungry," she said.

Although they were getting help from the tide, they had no time to waste.

"Think we'll make it before tonight?" he said.

"Yes, if the engine doesn't break. Should have just enough daylight to see what we're doing, once we're there. I did some figuring on our speed and the sunset and so on."

"Suppose we have to lay over?"

She thought she detected a little-boy-lost tone in his voice. "There's a place up near Edgecliff. A little marina with a restaurant. I called before we left."

"I don't remember your telling me that." He was hurt.

"I didn't."

Her curtness puzzled him, but only for a moment.

"In case we weren't going to have enough time, I called a friend of mine to see if I could stay overnight while you slept on the boat," she said.

"Oh." He turned his face to keep her from seeing the jealousy he knew was written all over it.

"DeeDee Lockwood," she said, enjoying his discomfort.

A mutual friend. He hid his face to hide his relief.

He ate his lunch slowly, then filled the time with his own sadness as he spelled her at the tiller and watched her lean against the outside of the cabin and close her eyes. She would nap, he knew. He stared with lonely fondness at the gently snoring woman who could hurt him so much, the woman he had hurt so much.

Tonight he would drink nothing. Nothing. That would deny her the pleasure of sulking at him (for that, anyhow), and would make it easier to say good-bye to the boat.

Damn, they had got so used to the boat. They could steer up to the gas pumps as easily as handling a car, usually him at the tiller and her at the bow, because she was quicker with knots. Damn, how Vonnie looked good stepping onto the pier, cleating two lines faster than a lot of sailors could fasten one.

Vonnie was still snoring. When they were first married, she had denied that she snored. Vonnie, I used to love your snoring. Still do . . .

He thought of the time—they had only had the boat a few days—when they had pulled up to refuel for the first time and made fools of themselves in front of everyone within sight. He had had trouble steering, then had come up to the dock way too fast. "We don't have brakes, you stupid bastard," she had shouted, loud enough for fifty or two hundred or a thousand people to hear. Then she had stepped onto the dock and fallen on her ass, and he had laughed at both of them, but only after he knew she wasn't hurt. Then they had both laughed, and told the story a hundred times after that, and laughed again. . . .

Part of the problem was that they had stopped laughing.

A little while later, with Kevin at the tiller, Yvonne woke and went below to use the head. About the time she was due to come topside, Kevin heard her shout, "Damn!" Hand still on the tiller, he stood up and saw a fountain of water spurting into the galley.

"What the hell . . . Jesus, Vonnie . . ."

"It's the sink hose. It's broken," she said. She slipped on the floorboards, just barely righting herself.

"You okay?" he shouted.

"The fitting, it's rotted through. This is serious."

She groped into the jet of water, trying to ignore the gushes of dirty river that soaked her face and hair and T-shirt and cutoffs. There, there was the hole. She grabbed the hose to try to stop the rush, but the hose broke away from the base of the sink. So much water coming in. She pushed her thumb into the tube, but her thumb was not big enough. Then she thought to bend the tube like a garden hose.

"Kevin, throw rags down here. Every damn one we have on board. And head toward shore."

He flipped open a cockpit hatch, pulling out an old sailbag full of discarded underwear and shirts.

"Toss the whole thing down here."

The bag landed next to her, splashing water onto her legs. Yvonne tied a couple of small rags around the bend and hoped that the rubber was not so rotten that it would burst somewhere else.

"Throw down that bucket, too. I'm going to pump the bilge. The damn thing must have been leaking slowly before it started to gush. Water's over the floorboards. I think the bandage will keep us afloat until we can get it fixed," she said. "No way we can go all the way today."

"Goddamn."

"Head for Edgecliff. We'll get it fixed there."

He turned sharply toward shore.

"Here," Yvonne said, hoisting the bucket.

"Why don't . . ." He stopped himself so he didn't sound totally stupid, but not before Yvonne realized what he had been about to say. They had always pumped the bilge into the sink in the galley.

At the marina, they pulled in as close as they could get to a building that looked like a combination storage shed and garage. As soon as they were fast, Yvonne trotted down the pier. Kevin watched her disappear into the garage; he was both annoyed and grateful that she had taken charge, as usual. In no time she reappeared, accompanied by two burly, earnest-looking men in grease-stained work clothes.

Yes, the men said, they had hose to fix the sink, but they wouldn't be able to do the permanent repair until the next morning. Meantime, they could plug the leak securely. For sure, it would hold overnight, as long as they didn't go anywhere.

"We can use one of the moorings out in the river," Yvonne said. "They're cheaper than the slips."

"Save a few bucks," Kevin said.

Yvonne took her overnight bag, went to the women's room and cleaned up. When she was done, she went to a pay phone.

"I called DeeDee," she said, rejoining Kevin. "She's coming over."

Kevin was glad enough to have DeeDee Lockwood join them; he had always liked her—and she was sexy. And having a third person with them for a while might smooth some bumps.

"They did a patch job on the sink," he said.

"The dockmaster said we can tie the dinghy near the end of the pier," she said. "You'll be all right on the boat. I'll probably be up before you anyhow."

"So you can row me out?"

"Right. And I guess you should call your friend and tell him we're not going to make it today. So he's not waiting there all night to buy a boat and we never show up. . . ."

"Yeah, I'll do that." She was taking charge. Again. He was annoyed at her need to super-explain everything to him.

6

I'll take the cheesecake," Yvonne told the waitress. The restaurant was built over some of the slips and had a view of the Hudson River and New York City.

"Speaking of cheesecake," Kevin said, looking over Yvonne's shoulder.

Yvonne turned. What she saw made her feel dirty and unkempt from her day on the boat. "Wow," she said, dusting crumbs from her lap.

Deirdre Lockwood was wearing tennis whites. Everyone noticed her arrival except for a child begging for ice cream and an old woman who was cutting her meat into very small pieces. DeeDee was a long-legged blonde, very much like Yvonne. In high school people even had mistaken one for the other, and sometimes Yvonne and DeeDee would go along with the mistake as a joke. Now, however, DeeDee had lightened her hair to a Nordic platinum and, while Yvonne was lean and slim from exercise, DeeDee was voluptuous, with tan, tight flesh. Her shirt was loose-fitting and cut low over her breasts. The lower curve of her buttocks peeked from under a pleated skirt.

Yvonne waved and she and Kevin stood up to greet her. DeeDee bussed each of them on the cheek.

"Excuse the outfit," DeeDee said. "I just came from a tennis lesson. Yvonne, you should see the instructor. What a hunk."

"You look wonderful," Yvonne said. Inhaling her perfume, Yvonne wondered whether she really had been playing tennis.

"Yeah, you look great," Kevin said.

Yvonne felt a twinge of jealousy as she saw his eyes race up and down. "We're just having dessert," she said. "Do you want some cheesecake, coffee?"

"I could use a diet soda. Dessert is not on my diet. I joined the new diet club Regimes."

"I've heard that's expensive," Yvonne said.

"Yes, but I'm worth it," DeeDee said with a giggle.

Kevin shook his head and smiled, a sort of fawning smile, Yvonne thought as the twinge returned.

The waitress, a chubby teenager, had been gaping at DeeDee. "A Diet Coke?" she said.

When the waitress left, Kevin said, "Wanna bet she screws it up?"

Yvonne turned to DeeDee. "She gave me french fries and I ordered rice, and Kevin had no cheese on his cheeseburger."

"She's probably having trouble with her boyfriend," said DeeDee, flashing a smile that pushed her eyes into little curves and made her look like Marilyn Monroe.

"There you go again," said Yvonne. "Always psychoanalyzing."

"Remember when I was teaching in Port Guinness, you used to call me the shit-house analyst?" DeeDee tossed her head back and laughed a round, full guffaw.

Yvonne thought, that's the DeeDee I know. The natural, fun-loving, raucous friend still lives under this sexpot exterior. I wonder what's happening with her love life.

Just as DeeDee's guffaw had reopened the camaraderie between the two women, it had broken the spell for Kevin. "You still seeing that stiff from Fort Lee? I couldn't stand the way he used to close his eyes when he talked." DeeDee had dated an English teacher whom Kevin considered priggish.

"You mean Josh? I still see him, but he's a bit too tepid for me. Like a tea bag in lukewarm water."

"You always said that tea needed water that was boiling passionately," Yvonne said. That had been one of DeeDee's quirks in Port Guinness. Whenever the kettle in the teachers' room was left to whistle, someone would say, "Where's DeeDee?" because she wouldn't use the water until the kettle was screeching.

"They made fun of me for that at Leonia High too. What an epitaph that would make: She made her tea with passionately boiling water."

"How do you like Leonia schools?" Yvonne asked. "Are you still glad that you left Port Guinness?"

"My unhappiness with Port Guinness, I realize now, was manufac-

almost talked out, tired and content when Yvonne noticed a small boat sliding up next to their Pearson. At least she thought it was the Pearson.

"DeeDee, look. Is that our boat? Where that little boat is next to the bigger one? Out there on the moorings?"

DeeDee looked toward the spot where Yvonne pointed. "I don't remember. Your boat was in that area. But there's frequently some activity out there at odd hours."

Yvonne decided that one of the other boats must be the Pearson. She hugged her arms, realizing that she was chilled. "Do you have a sweater or a cotton blanket?"

"Let's close the doors and go raid the icebox," DeeDee said. "Then I'm afraid we'll have to go to bed. What time do you want to get up? Shall I set the alarm?"

"I never sleep later than eight no matter what time I go to bed. Kevin certainly won't be up before I get to the boatyard, even if he doesn't have anything to drink tonight. Hmmmm, I'll bet I know why those two guys were out by the Pearson, if it was the Pearson."

"Huh? Why?"

"I'll bet Kevin ordered some booze from the kid who runs the tender. Or maybe Kevin had already gone back to the bar and he brought back a drinking buddy to the boat."

"Why didn't he just stay at the bar?"

"You know how budding alcoholics are. They make promises to themselves that they can't keep."

"Do you really think Kevin's an alcoholic?"

"Not yet, but getting close. Frankly, I don't want to be there ___ e goes over the line."

"What are you going to do? I mean with___

"Oh, I've got my health and m___ mputers, actually."

"When did you get converte___ uld undermine civilization as ___ Being around Rosalie and s___ tagious. She's an electronic w___ business, and belongs to a coup___ crochet lessons from one of the___ never could figure how she did___

tured. What I really wanted was to be near Josh. Why else would I have looked for a job only near him? But I'm glad I took the plunge. It has worked out rather well, professionally anyhow. My love life is another story, but I'm not alone in being alone. It's the complaint of the nineties."

Yvonne and Kevin looked at each other and then down at their place mats.

"What's with you two?" DeeDee said.

"We're splitting," Yvonne said.

DeeDee's face drained. "No. You two? The perfect couple? I mean, teenagers in Port Guinness wanted to grow up and be like you. You guys, you had everything," DeeDee protested.

"Times change, people change," said Kevin, hoping to end the conversation by retreating to aphorism.

The waitress returned with a Diet Coke for DeeDee, a cup of water and an envelope of decaf for Yvonne, and a cup of coffee and a saucer of coffee for Kevin. "The last piece of cheesecake is all mushed up. I don't think you'd want it," she said. "And we're all out of the pecan pie. Do you want the ice cream?"

She had got the order right after all.

"I'll have some ice cream," Kevin said.

"Me, too," said Yvonne.

"Make that three," said DeeDee. "I'll run a lap around the tennis court to work it off."

"Diet soda goes great with ice cream," Yvonne said, laughing.

They managed to avoid the uncomfortable until the check came and Yvonne slid fifteen dollars to Kevin. DeeDee, seeing her, began to fish in her purse, but Yvonne put a hand on her arm and shook her head.

"It's okay, I'll get it," said Kevin, pushing the bills toward Yvonne. "I'll let you treat me tomorrow."

He managed that gracefully, Yvonne thought. Then Kevin flashed his great Irish smile, and Yvonne felt her insides melting.

The sun had dropped behind the Palisades when the women rowed Kevin out to the boat. Yvonne couldn't help noticing the way Kevin watched DeeDee climb into the dinghy. Would he call her for a date? she thought. God, I couldn't take that. But I don't own him; I don't have any claim on him. Let go. Let go.

As soon as Kevin was dropped off and the dinghy was out of earshot of the boat, DeeDee looked at Yvonne and said, "I wouldn't. I've been used like that before."

"Mind-reading again," said Yvonne, her smile downcast. "Used?"

"Husbands try to hurt their ex-wives by dating their friends. And women are so keyed in to men's desires that they think the guy was lusting after them all the while. I've been there, Yvonne, and I spent a lot of money on a shrink to learn how to stay out of those messes."

"Really?" Yvonne thought that DeeDee's appearance belied her depth. She wanted to ask her how she could dress like a temptress and think like a sage. She tried. "You look like you're in the dating game. I mean, very soigné—alluring, even."

"You know what Lil says about that? Lil's my shrink. She says this kind of outfit is a power play within the bounds of socially acceptable power."

"No shit," said Yvonne.

"She's good. I think she's wise. You'd like her. But now that I've got you alone, tell me what the hell happened to you and Kev."

DeeDee was easy to talk to, and somehow this time the telling was less painful. The pregnancy, the miscarriage, the bitterness, the blaming, the feeling of being betrayed.

Only when they walked down the pier was the conversation interrupted. There some rough-looking men gaped and pointed at them, and Yvonne thought the men followed them as they walked to DeeDee's car. Damn jackrabbits, Yvonne thought.

An Edgecliff police car drove by and the men disappeared, much to Yvonne's relief. DeeDee was less bothered by the men, probably because she got a lot of attention when she was power-dressing, Yvonne thought.

DeeDee's condo was all art deco, light and airy and furnished with blissful disregard for child- or pet-rearing. Best of all was her balcony, which had a wide-angle view of New York City and a southern exposure. Yvonne could see the Pearson rocking at its anchor, facing northward toward the current now that the tide had changed.

Yvonne and DeeDee sat inside the doors to the balcony sipping white wine and catching up. They hadn't seen each other for a year, the longest they'd been separated. They figured this out by retracing

their lives since they first met in kindergarten. The second-longest time had been when they were juniors in college. DeeDee had spent that summer on campus at Northwestern, avoiding her hometown where her parents were at the plate-throwing stage of separating. That was the year that Yvonne had started to work in her father's office.

"I think you were responsible for my going into real estate," Yvonne said.

"You were headed that way anyway. You were father-fixated," DeeDee said. "Don't blame it on me."

"Shit-house analyst," Yvonne said, and they laughed again. "Let's not lose touch this time. Let's get together regularly, okay?"

"It should be easier now that Kevin and Josh are not taking up so much of our time. We could go hunting together."

"I don't know about that. Seeing you get all the attention wouldn't do much for my ego. We could just do what we're doing now."

"Well, what do you say if I lose a little weight, you gain a little, we both start wearing our hair the same. We could start confusing people again." DeeDee had leaned forward and her face had taken the expression of a child playing make-believe.

Yvonne knew that DeeDee wasn't going to lose weight, but surer still that she herself could not stop her own jogging and exercise. But she answered, "What will it be? Platinum or mousy blonde?"

"Mousy with platinum highlights."

"Where do I get an outfit like that?"

"You buy it off the rack and then spend hours taking tucks there until it falls carelessly in just the right way, hiding the good stuff."

"It doesn't look like you're hiding anything," Yvonne said.

"You alley cat. But I am, I'm hiding my waistline. It's this outfit my bust and my derriere distract from it. the a word of this to anyone, I'll tell everybody that ur bed."

bitch. At least you made me laugh. I haven't la

ave I," said DeeDee. "It's good therapy ed into more laughter, followed by te t up from behind the New York s rina below. They had been sitting

a flawless manicure. Is she crocheting any little things for Scotty and Melba's progeny yet?" DeeDee smirked as she asked the question.

"Ha. Melba and Scotty? No way. Can you imagine the two of them . . . no. No. And I've never heard Rosalie say anything about grandchildren either."

"It does seem rather bizarre to think of Scotty and Melba as parents. But just think of all the new things Rosalie could make. Anyhow, you sound happy when you talk about the computer." DeeDee yawned. "It's probably a good distraction at this point in your life."

Yvonne suddenly realized that she had had a conversation about babies and hadn't thought about her own pain. She was getting better. Grief doesn't last forever.

They had been nibbling Vermont cheddar and rice crackers and drinking soda water at the kitchen snack bar. The blue numbers on the digital clock over the sink had all just blinked from 2:59 to 3:00.

"I'll try to be quiet when I get up tomorrow. You don't have to get up and show me out."

"I'll give you a lift to the marina."

"You'll be a zombie in the morning. It's not that far. I'll walk. Just show me where the towels are and I'll shower tonight. I'll call you next week, and we'll get together again soon. Thanks for everything, really. I missed you."

DeeDee smiled and yawned again. "I missed you, too. Good night."

Yvonne watched DeeDee in her tennis outfit scuffing sleepily toward the bedroom, looking more like the little girl she had known in kindergarten than the centerfold she had become.

7

The ache inside Harvey's head made him afraid to open his eyes—as though the stab of light would make him sick at once. He was waking, much against his will, to a hangover. What he really wanted to do was go to sleep again; he imagined himself slipping down into a deep, blue, cool tunnel of bliss. If he could just go back to sleep, he would stay there until—until?

But the ache in his head would not let him sink into the tunnel. Jesus, maybe he really was drinking too much. His memory had blacked out. He had been drinking with Quince, in Quince's office. He remembered the blinking red light.

The memory roused him instantly. How many drinks had he had? Just the one; that was all he could remember. He hadn't even finished . . .

Bits of recollection darted through his mind like silver minnows, appearing, then vanishing, impossible to hold.

Were his eyes open now? All around him was pitch-black. Was he dreaming?

The last sure thing he could remember was drinking with Quince. Yes, that had really happened; Quince had called him right after—

Oh, Jesus. Holy Christ!

Panic tumbled over panic as Harvey recalled the fear he'd felt while drinking with Quince. No, he had not seemed friendly at all. Wait! Hadn't Quince changed later, become more friendly?

Sure, he had. Quince must have given him a ride home too. Sure, Harvey thought. That must be it. I passed out, and Quince . . .

But suddenly Harvey knew his eyes were wide open and seeing

nothing. He was not home. He was not dreaming! Fear filled him, a beast in his chest.

He listened, caught a pulsing sound. His own heart? No, an engine! He was on a boat! He tried to swing his legs out so he could stand up and explore, but he couldn't move. He was tied! His arms were held close to his body, his ankles bound together.

The darkness was heavy with the smells of oil and tar and rope. In a hold, he thought, on a big boat. He tried to get comfortable, but something stung the end of his nose. Rope, he thought. I have a coil of rope for a pillow, for Chrissake. As he moved, a bristle from the line stuck into his nostril. He shifted his head again. Not a good idea; a barnacle cut the edge of his nose.

Was he dreaming all this? He wished he were, but the smell of the hold, the rumble of the engine, the heave of the boat were too real.

Night, it must be night. They were on the Sound, probably. Or the ocean? How long had he been out? Jesus, where was he going? Why was he tied up? Were they going to . . .? Oh, God. No, don't think about that.

He had learned years ago to keep calm in an emergency. He could postpone pain if he had to. A good sailor learned to do that. Plenty of times, with a purple squall coming up, he had done things right, done them quickly and correctly. He had picked up cuts and bruises—he thought of the time he had gashed his palm open years before, couldn't remember how—but he had been in control then. Now someone else was in control.

Quince! Maybe Quince was near. He almost shouted for him, then changed his mind. Harvey sobbed for a moment, then choked it back. A tear ran down his nose and fell onto the coil of rope in the dark.

His feet were cold. Oh, there was nothing on his feet except his socks. Where were his shoes?

He wondered what time it was. Maybe Chowder's was still open. How happy they must be there, not to be worrying about what was going to happen to them. . . .

No, no. He had to fight the fear, had to keep his head. He had some things going for him. They must need to talk to him, or else they would have already . . . Maybe they would believe him. Quince! Quince had said he understood. Quince would stick up for him.

Over the rumble of the engine he could hear voices. Closer. There was a bang of a door, a sound of metal scraping on metal as it was pushed open wide. Heavy feet now, near his head, and a flashlight in his face, blinding him.

"Up, up," a thick voice said. Huge, strong hands, a pair of them clamped around each of Harvey's biceps, yanked him to his feet.

"C'mon, c'mon," the same thick voice said. The voice belonged to Chuck, the big guy who worked for Quince. Harvey was being dragged now, toward the open door. His right big toe caught on a coil of line; it hurt, but he was afraid to complain.

Out of the hold and into a brightly lit white metal corridor. The boat he was on must be a sixty-five, seventy-footer, he thought.

Into a small cabin the rough hands dragged him. Harvey was set down hard in a gray metal folding chair. The chair was out of place in the cabin, which was carpeted, wood-paneled, and lit softly by lamps next to the portholes on both sides. Quickly and efficiently, Harvey was untied. He felt the circulation pick up in his hands and feet.

He was facing a large dark wood desk whose top held a small lamp and a telephone. Fancy boat, big businessman's boat, Harvey thought. Maybe it belongs to the guy who runs everything.

A noise from behind him. Someone coming into the cabin on soft feet.

"Harvey," the familiar voice said. "I'm truly sorry about all this."

Quince sat down in the chair behind the desk. He wore a dark turtleneck, and a soft smile slightly turned up the ends of his mustache.

"Take it easy, my friend," Quince said. His voice sounded almost . . . sad.

"Quince, I . . . Jesus. What happened?"

"Just relax," Quince said quietly.

The desktop phone rang. Quince put the receiver to his ear but said nothing. Then he nodded. Harvey thought he saw his forehead wrinkle, thought he saw Quince's eyes change, and change again, but he was not sure.

"Right," Quince said. "I'll ask him. Yes, right in front of me now. Right . . . Let you know as soon . . ."

Quince's voice trailed off, and Harvey was bewildered as well as afraid. Quince nodded some more as he listened. After a minute or so he cradled the receiver.

Quince pressed a button on the desk, bent low and whispered into a microphone Harvey couldn't see. A moment later, Chuck entered wordlessly and set a big mug on the desk close to Harvey.

"It's just coffee," Quince said, chuckling. "No tricks this time. Go on, drink."

Harvey picked up the mug, blew the steam away, sipped. The coffee was strong, but even the aroma seemed to help his headache.

"That was some gin and tonic," Harvey said.

Quince smiled, but his eyes remained serious. "And now that you're here, we want you to be alert. Do you remember? We were talking about how those two youngsters were not to be trusted."

"Right. Right."

"And how your friend Tolly was also not to be trusted."

"Right."

"We were talking also about how you were following the youngsters, or having them followed."

"Right . . ."

"Helping us."

"Right, right!" Harvey was afraid, wanted desperately not to be afraid.

"And you want very much for me to believe you."

Harvey opened his mouth but could not speak.

Quince stood up, opened a sliding door to reveal a television set with a videocassette recorder. He took out a box labeled "Port Guinness Sailing Races," took out a videotape and put it in the VCR.

"Watch now," Quince said. A command, Harvey recognized.

The television screen lit up, and Harvey saw himself, sitting in Quince's office.

"Watch closely," Quince ordered. In his hand was a small remote control for the VCR.

Harvey heard Quince's voice coming from the television set:

"Some time ago, we thought we detected the tiniest bit of pilferage. . . ."

"Mmmmm."

Harvey saw himself slumped in the chair, looking uneasy.

The tape went on:

"We—I mean myself and my real boss—we have discussed this problem at length. At first we suspected . . . you."

"There!" Quince said, pressing the remote control to freeze the picture. "See how that question jolted you? See how you splash gin on yourself."

"I was . . . I was nervous, is all." Harvey's throat had gone dry.

Quince smiled with his lips; his eyes were cold. Then he let the tape play.

Harvey saw himself on the screen, listened to his pathetic lies.

"See," Quince said, pausing the tape. "See your eyes there? The facial twitching? See how you are almost jolted upright?"

"I was nervous, afraid . . ."

"With reason."

"Oh, my God . . ."

"Afraid because you weren't telling the truth."

"Oh, dear Jesus."

"Let's watch some more. . . ."

The tape rolled, and Harvey relived the lies about Kevin and Yvonne and Tolly. Watching himself, he saw how childish had been his attempts at deception.

Quince stopped the tape. "Tell me," he said, "did you think we would buy such a fairy tale, even for an instant?"

"Quince, you said—"

"No, *you* said. I gave you bait and you took it. How silly."

"Oh, Jesus. Quince . . ."

But Quince waved his hand, shook his head in disgust. "What kind of man are you, that you would lie about others, put them in danger . . ."

Quince paused, his contempt filling the silence. "Whose idea?" he said at length. "Yours or Tolly's?"

"Tolly's! Tolly's! I mean, oh, Jesus . . ."

"And those kids—they don't have any idea what they're carrying?"

"No, no, I swear. I even tried to get it back—" Harvey realized with horror that he had gone way too far.

"So. We thought there were others. You sent them to try to retrieve what you had planted on the boat for safekeeping. Is that it?"

Harvey was shaking; he put his face in his hands.

"These others? Where did you find them?"

"From Tolly! From Tolly!"

"Ah," Quince said softly.

"Where on the boat is it?" Quince said.

Harvey was wild with fear. He knew, having planted the stuff himself, but he dare not say, because that would be confessing his guilt. "I . . . Tolly, he did it. I mean, he . . . I never . . . Tolly told me he put it on the boat. . . ."

"You're saying this was Tolly's idea?"

"Tolly's! Oh, Tolly's! Tolly's!"

Again Quince shook his head with disgust. Then he got up and changed the tape in the VCR.

At first Harvey thought it was the same tape. The scene was in Quince's office, same wall, same chair. But in the chair where Harvey had sat was Tolly. Tolly alive. Tolly having a drink with Quince. Tolly talking in his Irish brogue, smiling.

On the tape, Quince and Tolly talked in low, lazy tones—about the Mets, about the yacht club where Tolly ran the launch, about boat engines.

Then Quince shifted the conversation, so gradually that Tolly—at least to judge by his face on the tape—did not notice at first. But Harvey, knowing what he knew now, knowing that the Tolly he was watching on the tape was soon to die, felt his skin crawl as Quince kept Tolly talking about boats and engines, then about who was the better mechanic: Tolly or Harvey?

Tolly made a joke, but he looked uneasy in the chair.

Quince's voice on the tape changed to a lower, more serious tone. "Do you think Harvey is sometimes a little careless?" he asked.

Tolly sat up straighter in the chair. "Careless?"

"Careless. You know, not attentive enough about details. Little things."

"Little things . . ." The light in Tolly's eyes changed. He didn't like the way the talk was going.

"Yes. I've been wondering if he's careful enough about things entrusted to him. You know?"

On the screen, Tolly looked up, wide-eyed. He was looking right into the camera, and Harvey saw that he was startled, just the way he himself had been.

Quince went on: "You and Harvey have been very helpful, but lately

we've been wondering a little about Harvey. Whether he's getting
careless. Or . . ."

Tolly raised his glass to drink, but the glass was empty and his hand
shook and the ice cubes rattled in the glass. Tolly coughed, but he
couldn't cover the sound of the clinking ice.

"Am I on candid camera?" Tolly said, laughing in a wooden cackle.

Quince let the joke lie like a stone.

Tolly looked confounded, still fighting the plunge into fear.

"Come on," Quince said to Tolly. "You're a friend of Harvey's, but
haven't you noticed how careless he's become?"

"Yeah, yeah, I have." Squirming now.

"But you haven't become . . . careless?"

"No. No."

"But Harvey has?"

"He . . . maybe. Oh, Jesus."

"Harvey said you're the one who's become careless. Or even—"

"No! Harvey's a liar. It was his . . . Oh, Jesus."

"You see?" Quince said to Harvey. "I didn't tape Tolly soiling
himself in his fear. That would have been degrading. And I erased the
later tape, the one in which he says you were the one. The tape that
shows Tolly sucking booze and engine fumes."

Harvey's jaw dropped. "You were there. You . . ."

Quince pressed "rewind," then "erase." For a long time, the whir of
the tape was the only sound.

"Quince, please. You gotta believe." Harvey sobbed.

"Believe? Who to believe? And if one doesn't know who . . .?"

"Quince, listen. We've been friends. 'Member all the times I fixed
your engine for nothing? Remember the Mets game we went to? You
gotta help me this once." Tears and snot ran down Harvey's face, but
he was beyond humiliation.

Quince's eyes seemed to soften for a moment. "I can help you," he
said quietly. "I can."

"Quince, I won't forget."

Quince took a pint bottle of gin from the desk, took off the top, gave
it to Harvey. "Drink," Quince said.

Harvey took a long, hot gulp, then a deep breath. If he got out of
this, he would never, ever . . .

"Of course," Quince said, "you must tell us the names of the others."

"Ernesto and Felipe. You know them two—"

"Ah," Quince said. "And they followed the two young people?"

"They followed. I can get in touch with them, get them to see you—"

"That won't be necessary. Drink some more."

"Quince, you said you could help me. You promised."

"Drink."

Harvey took another gulp. "Please. You said—"

"I am helping you, amigo. Drink."

"Quince!" Harvey took a swallow.

The desktop phone rang. Quince put the receiver to his ear and listened for several seconds. "Yes," he said finally. "Yes . . . No, we're sure. . . . Yes, as soon as possible. Ernesto and Felipe next. Yes."

Quince cradled the phone and looked at Harvey. "We're going to put you back on your boat," Quince said. "We've got it in tow."

"*Annabelle?* So I can take my own boat home?"

"Yes, you're going home in your own boat."

"Quince, I don't know how—"

"Save it."

The door to the cabin opened and three men came in: Chuck; another big man whom Harvey had seen from time to time around Quince's trucks; and a third, smaller man. Harvey thought his bowels might give.

"Quince! You said—"

Big, strong hands grabbed Harvey by the biceps and dragged him out to the corridor. They shoved him roughly to the floor, one big man stretching Harvey's arms up over his head. Then Harvey saw the other big man holding Harvey's own pair of chest-high waders, the ones with the suspenders. They had been taken off *Annabelle,* he thought.

The corridor was all white, and Harvey could feel the gin.

Quince knelt down next to him. "Open wide and drink, amigo," he said. "Drink as much as you want. It's the only choice you have left."

Quince held the bottle to Harvey's mouth. Harvey opened and took a swallow; the gin was warm. He wanted to ask Quince if Quince could please, please fix things up just one time, for the sake of friendship.

Harvey started to plead, but another dose of gin went down his throat, some of it the wrong way. Harvey coughed.

Harvey continued to cough as one big man held his arms back over his head and the other began to jam the waders onto his legs. The man forcing the waders on was rough, Harvey could feel his toes being twisted and pinched by the rubber. He tried to ask the man to be more careful, but he wasn't done coughing. The man strained and puffed; he had the waders on up to Harvey's knees now.

"Please. Please, Quince," Harvey managed to say before coughing again.

The man who had forced the waders onto Harvey's legs said something to the other big man, who reached over Harvey's body and pulled the waders up the rest of the way, pulling the suspenders into place across the shoulders. One of the suspenders snapped across Harvey's face, stinging his nose. The men hadn't done that on purpose, but they didn't care either.

The big men pulled Harvey roughly to his feet. Now Harvey wasn't sure he could stand on his own, there in the white corridor. He could feel the gin. . . .

The men held him there. If he could just talk to Quince alone, as a friend. Quince was still holding the gin bottle.

"Quince . . . Quince . . ." Harvey's words did not come out right.

"Shhh, amigo," Quince said softly. He held the bottle to Harvey's mouth again. "Take some more. Please."

Quince put the neck of the bottle in Harvey's mouth, and he took a gulp of hot gin. He was getting drunk. No, he couldn't get drunk; he had to make Quince understand, had to make him remember all the times they had been friends.

"More." Quince put the bottle into Harvey's mouth again, but this time Harvey shook his head violently. He spit out the gin. He had to make Quince listen to him.

One man was chewing gum, harder and harder, as if he were watching a porno movie, Harvey thought.

"Aaargh . . ." Harvey could not believe he had made that sound. It didn't even sound like Quince's name.

The door to the outside was opened. Harvey could smell the water and salt air. As the big man steered him through the door, Harvey saw that they were on the Sound, which shone with moonlight. They led him to the stern, where Harvey saw that his *Annabelle* was tied alongside. *Annabelle*'s engine was running softly, at trolling speed.

Quince stood on *Annabelle*'s deck, still holding the bottle of gin. The big men half lifted, half pushed Harvey over the gunwales of the bigger boat, onto *Annabelle*. Then the big men themselves stepped nimbly onto Harvey's boat.

"Do you want some more gin, amigo?" Quince said.

Harvey screamed. He wanted to beg, but the sound that came from his throat was not human. He would tell! He would! He tried to make the sound come out right, but his tongue was dead.

"Put him over," Quince said.

The big men lifted Harvey and dropped his legs into the water. They let him down slowly, allowing him to claw for the gunwale of *Annabelle*. Harvey felt the water, cold and heavy, filling his waders. He could feel the weight on the suspenders. Why couldn't he make Quince hear him?

Harvey was barely able to hold on to *Annabelle*, his waders were so heavy.

"All set," Quince said. Harvey saw him step back onto the bigger boat, saw that the big men were holding *Annabelle* close to the bigger boat with a hooked pole, saw them lift the pole away, felt Annabelle slowly pull away, at trolling speed.

Harvey could not hold on, he knew it. His only chance was to keep cool, keep cool, keep cool. Get out of the waders, out of the waders, and stay afloat. . . .

A light was trained on him from the bigger boat. They were still close enough. Maybe Quince would hear, would change his mind. . . .

Harvey could not believe the sound that came from his throat, an animal growl that rolled across the water.

His fingers came loose and he fell into the water. Harvey thrashed, wanting to stay up long enough to plead to Quince one last time.

Harvey screamed across the widening expanse between the boats. It wasn't agonized vocal cords that made him stop screaming—Harvey had enough terror to scream forever, despite the pain—but the water that rushed into his nose and throat.

He was under now, sinking, still able to see the light playing on the water, but sinking. He clawed at the suspenders, got them loose, and tried to roll over to get the waders above him. He had to cough; bubbles jetted from his mouth, and then the water rushed down his throat. He couldn't roll over, but he knew it didn't matter.

Harvey was in total blackness, no longer able to see any light. He tried to remember the prayers from his childhood. He had a long way to go before he hit bottom.

8

As always when he slept on the boat, it took Kevin a while to settle down. With the tight quarters, the low headroom, plus the gentle motion of the Hudson as it crept beneath his feet toward New York Bay, the whole task took about twice as long as it would have on land.

He arranged the cushions on the port side of the V-berth (Yvonne had always slept on the starboard side), propped the hatch open an inch or so, and opened the tiny starboard porthole halfway. That way, he figured, he would get a gentle breeze through the V-berth without a draft blowing right over his head.

Then he shut the door between the V-berth and galley (Yvonne had always preferred to have it open, liking the feeling of openness, but the door sometimes swung back and forth, which usually woke him up); took off his shoes, slacks, and shirt; and tried to get comfortable. For starters, he pulled a sheet over himself.

God, he was tired. No wonder: Starting the day with a hangover, then the thing with Harvey—what the hell had that been about, anyhow?—then the trip itself.

At least he felt good about not having had anything to drink. Zip, zero, nada. Nothing. Good. Maybe Yvonne would respect him more in the morning.

The drinking was no small thing to Kevin. He could stand the thought—no, the fact—that he drank too much sometimes, even the fact that the sometimes were too often lately. What he couldn't stand was the notion that he was hooked. He had to be able to go a whole day without a drop. Well, today he had. Call it penance, he thought. No, call it not being a drunk.

He got his head comfortable on the pillow and breathed deeply. The sails, the anchor line, faint aroma of bilge, brine. A good smell, a boat smell.

He shifted his arms and head. One of the wrists smelled like Yvonne's skin lotion. He had always liked the smell, the way it blended with the smell of Yvonne.

Then he thought of how DeeDee had smelled. He had picked up a wisp of her perfume, found it interesting—no, arousing. Not that it took much to make her attractive to him. God, she was sexy.

Yvonne's smell on his wrist made him fight off the fantasies about DeeDee. Vonnie, the things I do for you.

He wondered if his sense of smell was keener without alcohol in his blood.

His father had never been able to face up to himself about the booze. Jesus, the Irish. It was true what they said about the Irish, at least in his family. Poor old bastard. Always the red face, and for the longest time the boy Kevin had thought it was because his father worked near the furnace in the mill, worked real hard to buy him shoes and braces and ice cream. Or maybe his face had got redder as the years went by. Probably.

The Hudson slid along under him, its timeless rhythm rocking the boat up and down, up and down, gently.

So many things were clearer, looking back. On Sundays, after church, Kevin's father often poured himself a glass of wine. Years later, Kevin understood why his mother frowned and turned away when he did that.

Later, it was whiskey in the morning on Sundays. There, that was the big sign. When his father switched to whiskey instead of wine on Sunday mornings. A gradual thing. As Kevin recalled it, his father preferred whiskey on cold winter Sunday mornings. And his father loved Christmas, which was always like a Sunday no matter what day it fell on. And Christmas was cold. Perfect for celebrating with whiskey. . . .

And the fireplace. His father had loved that. A glass of whiskey in his hand, he'd sit in his easy chair in front of the fireplace. Kevin remembered the reflections in his spectacles: flame from the fireplace, lights from the Christmas tree.

The river went by underneath, sometimes slapping gently on the boat. Funny, but the sound of the river and the hiss of the fireplace on Christmas morning seemed to be one. . . .

Kevin started. Had he been asleep? Yes, but not for long. One arm was a little numb. Okay, it would not take him long to doze off again. He was tired, tired. He pulled the sheet up to his shoulders, gave himself up to the motion of the river.

Probably the saddest thing was that his father wasn't sharing when he sat by the fireplace, sipping whiskey. Never just one whiskey . . .

He was shutting people out, that was the thing. It had taken Kevin a long time to figure that out, and he still didn't have it all straight. And never would. His mother had died before he could talk to her about it. If he ever would have.

The river rocked him up and down, the river that had flowed by for thousands of years, millions of years. . . .

Kevin sifted out some of the bad stuff, thought of a house full of Christmas smells, sausage and bacon and pancakes and warm whiskey and the fireplace, all the way from Christmas Eve to late on Christmas Day, and sitting in front of the fireplace, waiting patiently for a standing rib roast. . . .

He and Yvonne had had some things like that. Kevin reached out to touch her, touched only emptiness. He started awake again. Not there, she was not there. He had started to dream.

Christmas had ended in disaster. He'd gone to the Jets party, telling Vonnie and himself that it went with the job. All right, he'd come home with more than a few drinks on his breath and some lipstick on his face. The lipstick had been from holiday kisses, nothing more. Well, only a little more: any man would have enjoyed getting kissed by that girl in the ticket office. But it had never been like Yvonne suspected.

He and Yvonne had had a terrible fight, a watershed kind of fight, looking back on it. Okay, he should have stayed home, especially with her pregnant and worried. But she had been wrong to suspect him.

Maybe they would lie near each other, next to each other, again. Maybe, maybe not. He couldn't do anything about it tonight, so he might as well shake off the sadness and go to sleep.

He shifted his arms again, put the wrist with her smell on it right next to his face. He could almost feel her arm over him as the eternal river cradled the boat gently up and down, up and down. . . .

He zeroed in on a good memory and held it, caressed it. A memory of a night just a few years ago. They had been so happy.

Beautiful memory of a beautiful summer evening. No races that night. He had come home early from the Jets' practice, it had been a light day, and they had just packed a bottle of chilled white wine and some crackers and fruit and cheese and gone sailing.

Some sailors swore that late summer was the best time on the Sound, that that was when the breezes came in just right in the late afternoon, filling the sails and bearing the smell of the sea but not stirring up the water.

What a beautiful sail they had that day, that evening. God, if he could have known how precious that would become, he would have savored it so much it couldn't get away. . . .

Ah, but it would have. Had he started to dream? No, no, he was remembering what had really happened. . . .

Oh, right, they had taken Tess along on the sail. He had always worried she would jump overboard or something, and Yvonne had always dismissed that worry, saying the dog wasn't dumb, and anyway, she could swim better than he could.

That night, Tess had lain down between them in the cockpit, utterly content, putting her head first on one set of feet, then on the other. And Kevin and Yvonne had sailed, leisurely, leisurely, not bothering to tack very often, and hardly ever jibbing because it took more work. They had sipped wine and eaten fruit and cheese and crackers, tossing a cracker to Tess once in a while, and watched the sun dapple off the purple water. And sailed back in time to get the boat moored before dark, and gone home sober enough to make love. . . .

Kevin tried to focus on how things had changed, thinking if there were any steps he could just retrace to fix things.

Kevin fell asleep, thinking about Yvonne, imagining that the smell on his wrist was really Yvonne herself, sleeping on the starboard side of the V-berth. He could almost hear her snoring.

He didn't know how long he had slept. At first the bump, bump, bump was part of a dream of a night on the boat, of him and Yvonne. Then he came up out of the dream, slowly, coming to the surface from a great depth. The bump, bump, bump was still there. The dinghy,

Kevin thought. The boat had shifted in the current, and now the dinghy was bumping against the side.

No. The dinghy was tied up at the pier. He and Yvonne had decided that, hadn't they? He was coming up from the dream faster now, near the surface of wakefulness. Bump, bump, bump.

Kevin thought as hard as he could. Yes, the dinghy had been left at the pier. Yes, that was absolutely real, that had happened, no dream. And he was awake now, no dream, the sweat pouring off his chest, his heart pounding in his ears like a hammer.

All he could hear over his heartbeat was the bump, bump, bump against the side of the boat. No dream, no dream.

And the thump of a foot above him, on the deck, and the feel of the boat heeling slightly for a moment with the weight.

It was not a dream.

Still in the bunk, he propped himself up on one arm, the arm shaking from the strain and his fear. Footsteps above him. No, he was not dreaming this.

He blinked, hard, hoping to see that it was daylight, hoping that the steps were just Yvonne's, that she had come back to the boat.

No, no. Pitch-dark outside, still deep in the night. Not Yvonne's footsteps (he knew her footsteps), but a man's. No, more than one man. Above him, a pant leg had brushed against the partly opened hatch.

Kevin thought he should try to pull his pants on. No, he could swim better without them. . . . But he might need his shoes if he had to move around the boat at all, if he struggled.

But he was afraid to move. He lay there, breathing as quietly as he could, listening to the footsteps. His arm was getting tired of supporting his body. Slowly, he let his body back down on the bunk. He lay there, trying to control his breathing, trying to hear over the thunder of his heart.

Voices. From above, in whispers. Speaking Spanish. Whispering.

Jesus, were they whispering because they knew he was on board? No, no, that made no sense. They had to be whispering because they didn't want to arouse anyone else nearby. How near? Probably no one within a few hundred feet, at least no one who could help him. No one who could come in time to stop the men from braining Kevin, or cutting his throat.

As much as anything, Kevin feared the thought of his throat being cut. Years before, covering the police beat, he had known firsthand of throat cuttings, and they had chilled his stomach like nothing else.

The footsteps went aft, stopping about where the galley hatch was. Spanish voices again. Kevin wished he had studied Spanish. No, maybe it was better if he didn't know what they were saying. . . .

There, the sound of the galley hatch being slowly opened. A thump as a foot came inside the galley, landing on the first step, then a louder thump as both feet landed inside. The water around the boat sloshed slightly, and there was a bump against the side again. Must be their dinghy. Another thump, another foot landing on the first galley step, then a louder thump as two more feet landed inside. The water sloshed again, the dinghy bumped the side.

If Tess were with him, she would have barked by now, maybe scared them away. Or maybe they would have killed her. Jesus.

Muffled whispers in Spanish, shuffling feet, tapping and banging. They were right out there, just a few feet away. Kevin pushed up on his arm again; through the crack at the bottom of the door between the galley and V-berth he could see flickers from a flashlight.

If they were looking for something, they would come into the V-berth. Kevin forced himself to sit up. He slowed his breathing and, still looking at the crack at the bottom of the door, he reached behind him. On the shelf, right next to the porthole, he found a foot-long winch handle. It was for trimming the big jenny, which he and Yvonne had almost never used, and it was steel. Yes, a good weapon. He would crack someone's cheekbone or wrist or knee before he would let his throat be cut. . . .

He strained to hear their whispers, even though he understood no Spanish.

"Key . . . key . . ." one of them said. English now, Kevin thought. A key for the ignition? Jesus Christ, they want to steal the goddamn boat. The ignition key, with the tiny red plastic buoy attached, was in a drawer in the galley, along with some miscellaneous junk. They could find it if they looked hard enough.

Kevin strained to hear, strained to keep his own breathing quiet. He tried to put himself into the minds of the intruders: If they started the boat, would they come into the V-berth? Maybe not, maybe there would be no reason.

He might have a good chance of getting away, once they started up. Even in broad daylight, the mast partly cut off the view from the cockpit. At night, he might be able to climb out of the hatch and slip over the side without their seeing him.

He waited for the sound of the drawer being pulled open, expected at any moment to hear them dump the contents, looking for the key. They did not seem to be moving around too much.

Maybe they just wanted to steal some of the equipment. A lot of sailors lost their fenders to thieves. No, if that was all they wanted, they would look in the hatches up in the cockpit, the logical place for fenders, and in fact where the fenders were. . . .

Kevin heard one of the men breathing hard, cursing. There was the sound of wood scraping against wood. Jesus, they were trying to take out the steps that led to the galley, the steps that also served as the engine cover.

Yvonne would be furious with him for letting someone come and steal the battery, or maybe steal the whole engine. . . . Maybe they wouldn't come into the V-berth. Oh! Maybe they had been watching, had seen them go ashore together and had not seen him come back. So they figured the boat was empty, with no dinghy tied alongside.

He gripped the winch handle tight. The first guy to come into the V-berth would get smacked real good—on the wrist, on his face, in the balls.

He heard the puffing and wood scraping and cursing. They were having just as tough a time as he always did getting the steps pulled off.

More muttering in Spanish.

From outside, getting closer, sounds of a powerboat, maybe a thirty-five-footer. It was a few hundred feet away, but Kevin could hear voices and laughter.

"Hey, you asshole, you fucking asshole . . ."

A splash, from about wherever the powerboat was. A bottle thrown into the river?

"Eat it. . . ."

They were drunk, whoever they were. Kids, maybe. In their twenties, at the most. Great help . . .

Silence in the galley; the Spanish guys were listening too. Jesus. For a moment Kevin wondered whether he should just stand up, pop his head through the hatch and holler as loud as he could for help. No. He had a better chance trying to defend himself. At least he was sober.

Another voice, older, not drunk, from over where the powerboat was: "All right, shut the fuck up, unless you want to be in deep shit."

Oh! A flickering blue light; Kevin could see it reflected on the water. Police boat, a police boat! Stopping a bunch of drunks. Now, now he should stand up and holler like hell. No bullshit, no worry about whether it was macho.

Only, before he could decide to do that, Kevin felt the boat rock as the intruders scrambled topside, rock some more as they scrambled into the dinghy, one of them cursing as he cracked a knee or an ankle, as he and Yvonne had each done a hundred times. Whispers in Spanish, the slopping sound of water around the boat as they paddled away in the dinghy, away from the sight of the police boat, Kevin thought—but how far away?

"You take the wheel and take this goddamn thing home right now," he heard a policeman say to someone in the powerboat. "Rest of you, shut up and stay shut up till you're home. Got it?"

The silence was broken after only a moment as the powerboat, its passengers quiet and chastened, chugged by.

At last, Kevin had the courage to look up through the hatch. He caught a glimpse of a white T-shirt in a dinghy just before the dinghy disappeared into the darkness.

Should he shout for the police? A "Yo!" started to form in his chest, but before it could reach his throat the police boat's engines roared.

He was alone again, still standing up in the hatch. He stared a long time into the darkness, praying he would not see the dinghy reappear. Everything was quiet. At last, he went below again.

Kevin was still in a praying mood. He prayed that God would tell him who the people on the powerboat were, so that he could send them a case of beer. Make it two. . . .

Then he prayed some more, this time that God would lead him to the intruders, in broad daylight, so that he, Kevin, could smash their skulls with the winch he still clutched in his fist. The intruders had made him feel less of a man.

Slowly, the feeling of violation ebbed, leaving him with questions: Who were they? What the hell did they want?

Since his boyhood, the deep of night had always been a time for feeling afraid and helpless, either after nightmares or if he couldn't sleep at all. Now, after the day with Harvey and the strange boat and the man on the pier, his night fears had him staring into an abyss.

He longed for Vonnie, and a drink.

He wasn't sure if he slept for the rest of the night. Maybe he did: he would suddenly find his mind wandering, and not be able to recall what he had been thinking about, or trying to think about. Mostly, Kevin just lay in the V-berth, still gripping the winch handle tight, just in case.

His mind churned with dread, relief, elation, bewilderment, shame at the terror he had felt. He could sort the feelings out later. All he wanted was to get through the night.

He heard the birds start up while the sky was still blue-black. By the time it was dawn, the birds were doing a raucous chorus. Then it was full daylight, though still a long way to go before most people got up. Kevin's back ached, and his hand was sore from clutching the winch handle.

At last, he heard people stirring nearby, in boats and on the pier. Then there was the sound of a dinghy—them!

No, Yvonne. It was Yvonne.

"Kevin?" she called, bumping the dinghy gently against the boat.

He stood up and looked through the hatch.

Disgust in her face. "You look like hell," she said. "I thought you weren't going to drink last night."

9

After Kevin told Yvonne that he hadn't had anything to drink the night before, that his life might have been in danger because of a boarding party, she said she was sorry.

"Last night I did think I saw men around the boat," she said. "Then I thought I must have mixed up our boat for someone else's. Or else . . ."

"Or else I must have been taking on a cargo of beer."

"It did cross my mind."

Kevin took a deep breath. "I can understand how you might have thought that."

They ate the bagels and oranges and drank the coffee Yvonne had brought.

Kevin thought the bagel tasted fine going down, but it sat like a sinker in the cold mist of his stomach.

Yvonne thought that she had made an honest mistake. She had often seen that bedraggled face in the morning. But this morning, when she got a whiff of his breath and smelled only the vapors of morning dragon and not the overworked-liver exhaust, she believed him. She wanted to start the day all over again and hear again about the intruders.

"Nice morning," she said.

"Hmmm."

It was. The river was slow and calm and there was no traffic yet. Across the water, they could see cars crawling along the West Side Highway.

"I called Rosalie last night and reminded her about Tess. Just to

82

make sure that automatic feeder and water dispenser are working. You did tell me you got hold of your friend last night?"

"I got Marty's answering machine. He checks it all the time. I told him we'd be along today."

"Maybe we should report it. Those men boarding the boat last night."

"Hmmm. Well, what can we tell the cops?"

"Just that. They were trespassing. What did they want? And why was Harvey . . . ? Oh, I don't know, but we should tell someone."

"Well, they were scared off. So what could we say?"

"Tell me what you're really thinking."

Her bullshit detector's working again, he thought. "Well, under those new Coast Guard regs, I think we have an illegal head. . . ."

"Kevin, the police don't give a shit. Why don't you want to report it?"

"Okay, if you want to. But I'm not sure on the registration, exactly. . . ."

"What does that mean?"

"I don't think we're up to date. I guess I didn't renew it last time. I might have let it slide. . . ."

"You might have? You mean you did." She knew the feeling; she had let some things slide too. They'd been over that ground, left so many footprints in it, that she couldn't tell for sure how things went.

"Suppose we'd been stopped in a routine check. They do that, you know."

"Well, I figured the odds were against it."

"Right, you know all about odds. . . ."

He sipped his coffee and said nothing.

She hadn't meant to say that. "Okay, I know what you mean."

"We can talk about it some more. We've got a ways to go."

"Did you lose on the Jets game?"

"Twenty. Just a friendly bet."

"Jackass Jets . . . they should have stayed in New Jersey."

He was grateful for her friendly allusion to the game and his betting, and she was pleased that he had picked up on it.

They motored to the pier and checked in with the repairmen. The sink would be done in about an hour.

"I showered at DeeDee's," Yvonne said. "I'll wait for you in the coffee shop. You'll need quarters for the shower."

"Tell me the truth, Vonnie. You must miss me. Who do you have to boss around?"

Yvonne shot him a stern look. "I should have let you get to the shower, stand there naked, and realize you didn't have any quarters."

"There are worse things that could happen to a man."

"Yeah. Being bossed around," she said.

"Or not being bossed around."

"Go wash the stink off." She was smiling.

"Yes, dearest." Kevin saluted.

Yvonne decided to call Rosalie again. Rosalie would have checked on Tess by now on her way to the office. Yvonne wanted to hear something about Tess, how the dog missed her or whatever.

"Yes?" Rosalie answered.

"It's Yvonne. Sorry to bother you again, but I just wanted to check on my doggy."

"Yvonne! We're fine here. Tess was sleeping when I arrived at your place. Did you tell me last night that you were staying in Edgecliff?"

"Yes, at DeeDee Lockwood's. Do you remember her from Port Guinness?"

"No. I don't think so. A friend of yours?"

"You'd remember her if you saw her." Yvonne thought Rosalie sounded preoccupied. "We almost sank yesterday."

"Sank?" Rosalie said, sounding more interested.

"A stupid sink fitting gave out. Anyhow, uh, did the food and water dispensers work okay?"

"Like a charm. I may get them for my little Peon." Peon was Rosalie's little Shih Tzu.

"And will you look in on Tess on your way home tonight? Or if you can't, will you ask Melba? I think we should make it back today, but it may be late."

"Of course. I'll peek in on Tess."

"I'll bore you with our adventures when we get back."

"Adventures? I can't wait."

Yvonne was about to say good-bye, but she had an impulse to vent some anger. "You know, that damn Harvey thinks he's so terrific with engines. If you see him before I do, tell him he should look at sink fittings, too."

"No telling when that'll be, hon. Listen, I gotta run. Take care."

"Time to get going, I guess," Yvonne said, taking the bowline off the pier cleat. The repairmen had finished, and Yvonne had picked up the scores of little clippings and snippets they'd left behind.

Kevin had the engine going. He swung the boat out into the river, feeling the tide fighting them a little. It would slow them up a bit before it turned.

"I'll take the tiller if you want to take a nap," Yvonne said.

That sounded good to him, though he was far too wound up to sleep. He stretched out, getting his back as comfortable as he could against the cabin. "Vonnie?"

"Hmmm."

"I was scared out of my mind."

"You were right to be. Funny they didn't look in the V-berth."

"I figure they just wanted to steal the boat. I heard them muttering and swearing, looking for a key to start the engine."

"Lucky you took it out of the ignition."

"Jesus, suppose . . ."

"The really lucky thing was that the police boat came by. I still think we ought to report it."

"A few hours from now, the boat won't be ours anyhow."

"What about Harvey? Could he have sent them to steal it?"

"I was just thinking about that. Doesn't sound like him, does it?"

"He wasn't himself yesterday morning, either. And what about that boat we thought was following us?"

"I don't know. Hell, maybe Marty Diehl talked about the boat, and someone decided to steal it. It is a classic."

"We're getting paranoid, Kevin. Let's stick to what we know. Somebody was on the boat last night, and we should tell the police."

Kevin recognized her tone. It was the one she used when she was sure she was right.

"Well?" she persisted.

"You're tough. Steel and ice."

"What?"

"You. You're steel and ice."

"No, Kevin. Not steel and ice, just common sense." She wondered if he'd ever really known her. The cringing, frightened child that she became after the baby was gone. She hadn't even known herself. How could he know?

"Okay, we'll report it."

"Call the New Jersey State Police," she said.

"Hey, Yvonne, maybe you should call. You know what you want to say."

"You were the one on board. You talk to the cops. You're the ex-police reporter."

"And you're the one who wants to report it."

"Yes, and is this some kind of blackmail? If I want it reported, I have to do it myself?"

"I give up. You win, I'll report it."

"Good. Is that all the fight I'm getting out of you?"

He looked in her face. There was a smile playing at the corner of her mouth.

"Bitch," he said, laughing.

Several miles north of the George Washington Bridge they saw a marine-supply place on the Jersey side of the river. Actually, it was nothing more than a wooden pier on which rested a small shack, a couple of gasoline tanks—and a telephone booth. Yvonne told the attendant, who was clad only in cutoffs, that he could top off their fuel tank.

The inside of the phone booth was decorated with obscene graffiti. The phone book had been partly shredded, so it ran from *C* to *Y,* but Kevin was able to look up the Jersey State Police. The Hudson River station answered after a single ring. The officer asked for a description of the boat, took down the hull number, and to Kevin's relief asked nothing about the registration date.

Kevin told him about the men coming on board, explaining that he had been sleeping in the V-berth and had stayed hidden until a police boat scared off the intruders.

"You did the right thing," the officer said. "No sense confronting them. You can always buy a new boat."

"Right."

"We have had some electronic equipment stolen off boats recently. But you say yours doesn't have any fancy stuff?"

"No. Too much money."

"Hmmm. If you do find anything missing, just let us know. Then you can report it on your insurance."

"Thanks."

Kevin told Yvonne what the officer had said.

"Did he say any boats had been stolen?"

"No, just electronic gear."

"Well, at least we reported it."

Kevin shook his head. "Goddamn Harvey anyway. All the money we paid him over the years, and he couldn't even check out the sink fitting."

"Goddamn Harvey is right. We know we're not terrific mechanics. That's why we pay him."

"Suppose the sink fitting had waited until we were way upriver, when it was almost dark."

"Blub, blub, blub."

"We'd still be holding onto the mast."

The image made her laugh.

But Kevin was still boiling. "I'm gonna call Harvey and ream him out."

"Give him a jab for me."

Kevin got quarters from the pier attendant and went back to the phone booth. He expected the phone to ring five, six, seven times, which it often did when he called the boatyard. It meant Harvey was down by the pier, or fussing on a boat. Kevin hoped Harvey was as far from the phone as possible; let him get pissed.

Kevin's pleasure at imagining Harvey's annoyance gave way to frustration when no one answered. He let it ring a few more times, finally stopped counting and hung up.

"Figures," Yvonne said. "He probably doesn't get enough of Chowder's at night. Needs his beer in the daytime now, too."

"Yeah, well, I'm not even that bad."

She smiled at the little joke.

"I almost feel like calling Chowder's," Kevin said.

"We can tell him off later. If we want to bother."

"Yeah, and if we ever get another boat, we're not gonna keep it at Harvey's."

Kevin wished he hadn't said that, but Yvonne ignored it. She had the engine running and motioned for him to uncleat the bowline.

Yvonne pulled away from the pier, then gunned the engine. Some spray splashed into the cockpit. Kevin liked the feel of it on his face, liked the look of it on Yvonne's shirt.

It was coming closer, Kevin thought sadly. The time when they would no longer have the boat. When they weren't even "they."

Kevin propped himself up, his back against the cabin. Maybe now he could nap. The pier with the shack and phone booth grew smaller. Kevin saw the pier attendant talking to two men. Was it his imagination, or did the attendant point at the boat?

"Vonnie, look. Those guys back there."

"What?"

"I think they just pointed at us."

"It couldn't be that the whole world's after us, Kevin."

"They pointed. I saw them."

Yvonne studied the pier. The men were just standing there now. Then her eyes followed the line from the dock past their boat, looking for something else that the men could have pointed at. A buoy? An apartment building on the opposite shore? "I don't know, Kevin."

Kevin felt stressed out; nerves and lack of sleep could do that, not to mention the whole thing with Vonnie. If it hadn't been for the guys on the boat last night, the world wouldn't seem dangerous at all. Would it?

A sensation came over him like a chill—as cold as ice, or the edge of a razor.

"Kevin, look."

Yvonne's voice startled him. Still at the tiller, she pointed upriver. Kevin swung around and saw, in plain view but still a good distance away, a dozen or so sailboats—no, two dozen. Maybe more.

"Racing," Yvonne said.

The sun was poised to start its slow descent and reflected dazzlingly on the whites and reds and blues of the sails.

"Neat," Kevin said.

"We'll have to be careful we don't get in their way," she said.

"We're just about at the widest point of the river. We can give them plenty of room."

"I hope your friend is there to meet us."

"Well, if he isn't, I'll just call him again. Marty doesn't live that far away." Besides, Kevin thought, Marty was the one he owed the twenty bucks to because the Jets hadn't covered.

"Want to take her for a while?" Yvonne said.

"Sure."

He slipped into the rearmost part of the cockpit and took the tiller. Instead of sliding over, Yvonne went forward, feet skipping nimbly along the gunwale and her hands grasping the rails along the top of the cabin, to the bow. She sat down, just aft of the pulpit, pulled her knees almost up to her chin and wrapped her arms around her legs. When spray hit her face, she realized her skin was hot. Tension. As if there weren't enough just being with Kevin.

Just a few days before, he had suggested they get back together. How could he think, after all that's happened, that we could just start over? she thought. He's living in a dream, a childish dream, as if he could go confess to a priest, say a few Hail Marys, and all the sins would be erased. She felt a little sorry for him, though, baring himself, asking for another chance. But children did that too, to get what they want.

She had to manage her own separate life, tend to her own wants and needs. She didn't want to be half of a relationship; she wanted to be whole, not swallowed up.

She took a few deep breaths, stomach-breathing, trying to relax, to refocus. Work, the office, working with the young couple who were planning to have a child and wanted to buy a house in Port Guinness even though they only had enough money for half a house. Handyman special, they said they wanted.

Rosalie had advised Yvonne to stop wasting time on them. Impossible, she said. Rosalie kept an eye on the bottom line. But the search had made Yvonne something of a guru of low-priced houses in Port Guinness. Another extra had been getting to know the computer listing system. Many of the other sales people, especially the older ones, were paper-bound.

Funny, Yvonne thought, about her conversion to electronic record keeping; how tentative she had been at first, how afraid, every time the

coming to a large basinlike area of water at least as big as a football field, the piers lined with boats.

"Vonnie, hang a couple of fenders off the port side."

She scrambled back to the cockpit, got a pair of the rubber bumpers out of a hatch and in no time had them dangling over the side, protecting the widest part of the boat.

Not seeing Marty Diehl anywhere, Kevin pulled into an empty area of the pier. They could tie up there for a few minutes and not be in anybody's way. There were no boats within a couple hundred feet.

As they drew near, Kevin threw the engine into reverse and the Pearson nestled to the pier as gently as if he'd used brakes. Yvonne stepped out and tied a line onto a piling, fore and aft.

"Well?" she said.

"No Marty."

"Why don't you call him, and I'll stay here."

"Okay. Right. Let me just rest a minute, okay?"

"Okay."

He leaned back, either too tired to be sad or too sad to be tired, he wasn't sure which. Jesus, the least Marty could have done is send someone. . . .

Kevin could see all the way up the pier, to where it intersected with a wide walkway where eight or ten piers connected. Big marina, Kevin thought.

He started to stand up, brushed his knee against the gearshift sticking up from the cockpit floor, reached down to pull the shaft out, then thought the hell with it. God, he was tired.

Three men were walking toward their boat from the other end of the pier. Marty's friends? Kevin wondered. One was Kevin's size, although more muscled; one was smaller; and one was much bigger, taller. Sunglasses, dark hair, jeans and T-shirts.

Yvonne's back was to them; she was looking at Kevin now, puzzled that he wasn't getting out of the boat to call Marty Diehl.

"Vonnie, I think we have company."

She turned and looked down the pier, and when the three men saw both Kevin and Yvonne looking at them, they smiled and waved. Most boaters wear cutoff pants on a day like this, Kevin thought.

"Maybe they're friends of your friend," Yvonne said.

"Maybe."

Yvonne caught the uncertainty in his voice, looked into his face with alarm, stood up to face the approaching strangers. Kevin stood up too. His legs felt rubbery.

"Hi," the tall one said. Phony attempt at heartiness, Kevin thought. They were at the end of the pier now; no room for Kevin and Yvonne to get off the boat, no other boaters nearby.

"Hello," Kevin said. He tried to sound casual, at ease, but knew his voice hadn't made it.

"Nice boat," he said. "You're looking to sell, right?"

"How'd you know?"

Yvonne spoke up. "Did Marty Diehl send you?"

"That's right, Martin Diehl sent us."

No, Kevin thought. Marty is never anything but Marty.

"He asked us to look over the boat and be sure it was okay," the big one continued. "He couldn't make it himself."

No, Kevin thought. Marty had seen the boat; he didn't need to have it inspected again. And no way he would have missed the meeting, not when we're friends, not when I owe him twenty bucks from the Jets game. . . .

For a moment, Kevin wished the three strangers weren't wearing sunglasses, so that he could study their eyes. Then he thought it was just as well he couldn't see their eyes, and just as well he was wearing sunglasses too. Because they could have read the fear.

"He couldn't make it himself?" Kevin said. He couldn't keep the fear out of his voice.

Without bothering to answer, the big stranger stepped onto the boat—heavily, clumsily, and without waiting for an invitation—and his unsmiling companions stepped aboard after him, causing the Pearson to slosh and bob. Kevin wondered if two of them were the men who had boarded the night before. How did they know where to meet them?

"Let's all sit down," the big stranger said.

Kevin didn't like the way they sat on the side closer to the pier; he felt like a prisoner. He was.

He and Yvonne sat down. She slid close to him.

"Friends of Marty?" Kevin said, his voice a frightened croak.

"Take a look below, Tony," the big stranger said.

The man named Tony went below clumsily. Kevin and Yvonne

heard him open the door to the V-berth with a bang. Thump, thump, clang, thump as cushions, life jackets, and winches were tossed unceremoniously into the galley.

"Kevin," Yvonne whispered, sliding closer.

"You're not really friends of Marty Diehl," Kevin heard himself say.

"No shit."

From below, the thumps and clunks continued.

"Tell your friend that gear's expensive," Yvonne said.

Kevin couldn't believe his ears. He had always admired her courage, knew how it would usually get the best of her fear, but this was ridiculous.

"Tell him yourself," the big stranger said.

Before Kevin could stop her, Yvonne stood up, planted her hands on either side of the opening to the galley, swung her legs up and over the threshold and dropped below—gracefully, as always.

"Stop that, goddammit!" she shouted.

"Tough bitch," the big one said, chuckling softly.

From below, more thumps and clunks, and voices:

"I said, stop that."

"Fuck off, lady."

"I'll scream bloody hell."

"Better not," the man below said, "unless you want your dickhead husband all cut up."

As if on cue, the small man sitting next to the big one pulled up a pant leg and took something from a leather sheath on his calf. Kevin heard a click, saw the blade gleam in the sun. Long, silver blade. Cut a man's throat as easily as a lamb's. Kevin felt sick in the stomach. He thought he might faint.

"We can cut you, cut both of you, and be out of here before anybody knows," the big stranger said.

"Want to see if we're right?" the man with the knife said, chewing his gum with a fierce energy.

Kevin did not want to see if they were right, especially when he saw Yvonne's face looking up from the galley, her face contorted in pain.

"Kevin, he's got my arm. . . ."

"Don't," Kevin said—a plea, not a command. God, please don't let this happen. "Please."

"Tell us where, or we tear this fuckin' boat apart," the big guy said.
"Tear you apart too," the man with the knife said, his chewing gum
snapping.

Kevin looked around; they were a galaxy away from people who
might help.

"Where?" the big stranger said.

"Where what?" Kevin said. He could not bear Yvonne's face.

"Ow . . ." Yvonne said.

"Where is it?"

"Ow . . ."

Vonnie, his Vonnie, was being hurt. Could this really be happening?
As if in a nightmare, Kevin saw the man step across the cockpit to the
galley hatch, pull a roll of wide adhesive tape from a pocket and wrap
a couple of strips roughly around Yvonne's mouth. Hurting her,
Kevin thought. Hurting Vonnie. Her eyes were wide with fear and
pain.

"Take her to the bunk and have some fun," the big stranger said.
"Me next."

Yvonne's face disappeared as she was spun around and shoved
toward the bow.

"Please," Kevin said. "Just tell us what you want. Please." He
would give them anything, anything, if only—

From below came the sounds of scuffling. The V-berth door banged
once, twice. Yvonne was fighting him off.

"Don't," Kevin said. "Tell him don't. Please . . ."

"Where?"

"Where what, for Jesus's sake?"

"Go ahead, Tony. Think up something new."

Louder scuffling from below. "Mmmm . . ." Yvonne was trying
to scream through the tape; Kevin couldn't bear the sound. He stood
up; the big stranger and the knife-holder stood up too. The blade
flashed near Kevin's face.

"Wanna bet we can cut your neck open before you can holler?"

"No . . ."

Kevin moved slightly, trying to get away from the blade. His leg
brushed against the gearshift handle still sticking up from the cockpit
floor. The big stranger and the man with the knife were looking below,

their eyes momentarily diverted from Kevin, wanting to see what their friend was doing to Vonnie, his Vonnie.

From below, more scuffling, louder. Yvonne still fighting. How much longer could she fight? "Mmmm . . . ."

Kevin bent slightly at the knees, grasped the handle of the gearshift and pulled it free. Good, heavy metal, about the length and weight of a tire iron.

Yvonne and the third man twisted and struggled in the V-berth. He had tried to pin her arms, to hold her down, but she had struggled free. Whenever he seemed to have her under control and reached to unzip his trousers, she would lunge again. He kept looking over his shoulder as if he were wondering whether the other two were watching. Yvonne's head was pounding with exertion and something else, an animal response, a closing off of the usual channels of thought. She kicked and scratched and pummeled, ripped at the man's clothing. Her rage was unstoppable, but he was stronger than she and she was tiring. She couldn't get her breath with the tape over her mouth. She started to tear at the tape, and he had her, her arms pinned behind her back.

The men were still looking below; the man with the knife was resting his right arm—his blade arm!—on the roof of the galley.

Kevin started his swing from as far back as he could, bringing the metal shaft down in a long, smooth arc that ended on the hand that held the knife. The crunch was followed instantly by a shriek of surprise and pain and a second later by a metallic clatter as the wicked knife fell to the floor of the galley below. The man who had lost his knife and the use of his hand in the same moment crumpled to the floor of the cockpit, whimpering.

The other one came at Kevin, knocking him back against the gunwale with his weight, then sprawling on top of him as Kevin lay on the bench of the cockpit. Kevin held on to the gear handle as hard as he could, but he could get no room to swing. Kevin kept squirming with his arms and legs; he knew he had to keep the big man from getting steady on top of him, because if that happened the man would smash his face with a single punch, crushing his mouth and breaking his teeth or driving the bone in his nose deep into his brain.

The man whose hand Kevin had smashed stood up clumsily, still whimpering, then he collapsed again, his movement tilting the boat just enough to send Kevin and the big man sprawling to the floor of the cockpit. Kevin rolled over, got to his feet, still holding the gear handle.

The man who had dragged Yvonne forward started to climb up, his face bewildered. Kevin saw his hands. No knife, no knife. He hadn't picked up the knife from below. Before the man could climb up, Yvonne appeared behind him (her face wild with anger, like Kevin had never seen, not even in their worst fights!), the masking tape dangling from her cheek, a winch handle in her hand.

The winch handle was almost as long as a hammer, and about the same weight. Kevin wondered if she would have the stomach to use it. He only wondered for a moment, because Yvonne brought the winch handle down on the man's head, not hard enough to knock him cold but hard enough to gash his scalp open, so that when the man stumbled up from the galley he was dripping blood all over the cockpit and holding his head with both hands.

The man whose hand Kevin had smashed lurched to his feet, stumbled from the boat onto the pier, almost falling into the water and tilting the boat enough so that the biggest stranger lost his balance for a second as he came at Kevin. He started to get up again, but the boat tilted yet again as the man with the head wound followed his companion to the pier, and the biggest stranger was down on his hands and knees, coming at Kevin like a crab and growling in fury.

Kevin had no time to think, but didn't need it. He still remembered *"Take her to the bunk and have some fun. . . . Think up something new. . . ."* He remembered Yvonne's pain and his anguish, his shame at not being able to help her.

Kevin brought the metal shaft down again. It glanced off the side of the big man's head, splashing more blood into the cockpit, then spent the rest of its force on the man's upper back. The man groaned, and Kevin stepped to the farthest corner of the cockpit.

"Kevin?" Yvonne said softly.

Kevin didn't think his legs would hold him. He could smell his own sweat. Like an animal . . . The big man was getting to his feet again. God, he's strong, Kevin thought. Have to hit him again. Bleeding all over the place.

"C'mon, Chuck," the gum-chewer said, still holding his hand.

The big man stood up, stepped onto the gunwale and scrambled up onto the pier. There he took off his shirt and pressed it against his head, as the man Yvonne had hit was doing. The man with the smashed hand pressed it against his chest with his other forearm.

A couple of hundred feet away near the other end of the pier, a knot of boaters had gathered. They watched, not knowing what to do. The three bleeding men backed away as Kevin waved the gearshift handle. Yvonne stood behind him, holding the winch.

"Get away from us," Kevin said. "Get away. . . ."

"You're as good as dead," the big man shouted back.

Kevin's heartbeat pounded in his ears; he breathed in great gulps. He felt exhilaration from the victory, rage over what they had planned to do to Vonnie, his Vonnie, who sobbed even as she started the engine and untied the lines from the dock—clumsily, her hands trembling.

"Come on, Kevin. Put the gearshift in. We're getting out of here." She had pushed the boat a couple of feet away from the dock.

The three strangers had recovered, even the one with the broken hand, and started toward them again. The two with the head cuts were still stanching the blood with their T-shirts. Now Kevin was waving the winch handle.

"We're going to kill you next time," the big stranger said.

"First we cut you like bait," said the one who had had the knife.

The knife! Kevin jumped below, picked the knife off the galley floor, scrambled topside. "With what, creep?" Kevin screamed, holding the knife in the air.

"Kevin, stop it, for God's sake."

"With *what?*" Kevin tossed the knife into the water. It splashed like a fish and sank.

"You should have kept it to show the police," Yvonne said.

Several from the crowd of boaters started uncertainly toward the three bleeding men. The three turned their heads toward the crowd. "Help us!" Chuck shouted to the crowd. "He's crazy! Attacked us for no reason. Must be on drugs. Look what he did. . . ."

"He's a liar!" Kevin yelled. "They came after us!"

Chuck was cooler now. Still holding his T-shirt to his head, he turned to the onlookers. "That guy's drunk."

Someone in the crowd spoke up. "Do you want us to call an ambulance?"

"There, you see?" Yvonne said to Kevin. "Those people believe them. They're the ones who are bleeding."

Another voice in the crowd: "Harbor patrol. Someone call the harbor patrol."

"What the hell are they doing?" someone else said. "Get the number of their boat."

Yvonne backed the boat into the channel, hoping that she wouldn't hit a high spot and run aground. The dinghy bumped against the side.

It's in the way, she thought; the dinghy will slow us down. Get rid of it.

One hand on the tiller, she untied the dinghy and let it drift.

"They'd believe us. We have the proof that this is our boat—" Kevin stopped, remembering that the registration had expired. Did that matter?

Yvonne shifted into forward and gunned the engine. She steered toward the river. She could hardly hear the engine over the pounding in her head. Escape. Please let us escape.

Kevin looked over his shoulder. The three were watching. They said they would hunt us down. Jesus, why?

But for now, he and Vonnie, his Vonnie, had beaten them. "I love you, Vonnie."

"Get up on the bow," she said through her teeth. "Make sure we don't hit any rocks."

He stumbled forward. He did feel love for her. But he felt something else too. He felt savage, triumphant.

"Ha!" he shouted as loud as he could. Jesus help me, he thought. It was almost worth it, worth the pain and fear, just to swing the gear handle and draw blood.

10

Yvonne cried and cursed as they reached the Hudson, steering across the chop left by a freshening breeze, the kind of breeze that would have elated them if it had been another time, another place.

Kevin's heartbeat had slowed, and he looked back toward the channel entrance. Nothing. He scanned the bank, the trees, the shadows. They were there. He was sure. He knew they were watching.

Speedboat! The noise of the churning screws came up suddenly, from rear port side. Kevin could see two men; the third must be crouched down—waiting to blast them with a shotgun? Jesus . . .

"Vonnie."

"Oh, Kevin. God."

He pulled the gearshift handle out of its hole again. He wished he had not thrown the knife away, they would have a better chance with the knife. God, please, don't let this happen. . . .

As the speedboat came near, it suddenly slowed—out of pure courtesy, it turned out. The driver smiled and nodded and his companion waved as they passed, then sped up.

Yvonne let out her breath.

Kevin was so relieved that he vowed never to say, or think, an unkind word about speedboaters again.

"Kevin, look. Back there."

Another speedboat had appeared at the channel mouth. It was just a speck, but getting bigger, aiming for them as if drawn by a laser beam on the Pearson's stern. The speedboat was gray, low to the water line, sinister. This time, Kevin had no doubts.

"Vonnie, maybe we just want to head for the Westchester shore in a straight line."

"No way we outrun a speedboat."

"Jesus, then what . . . ?"

"Get below, fast. Bring up the jib." Her voice was controlled, the way Kevin remembered it when she was sure what to do. "We can't outrun them, so we won't try," she said. "We're going to be part of the sailboat race. They're all about our size. We'll blend in. Stay out here all day if we have to."

Kevin jumped below, stepped through the pile of cushions, life jackets, winches, and other gear left by the goons, and scrambled up topside with the sailbag.

"We can do it," he said, more with hope than conviction.

"Hurry, Kevin."

"You got it, kid." He would not let her down this time. Kevin went to the bow, banging his knees as always, to rig the jib.

The racers were between them and the speedboat. Now they were close to one end of the racecourse. As he knelt on the bow his knees rested on part of the sailbag to keep it from rolling overboard; that had happened once, and she had hollered at him as she fished the sailbag out of the water with a boat hook. . . .

As he fastened the jib hanks to the forestay, he could hear the luffing sails of the race boats as they tacked around the marker.

Yvonne had taken the engine out of gear to let the boat drift as she hoisted the mainsail and let it luff in the wind.

"Yo!"

Kevin looked up and recognized the boat and its cargo of drunks from before.

"Yooo!" Kevin hollered back. "Yoo! Yes, this time, yes!"

"Yoooo!"

"Kevin, goddammit. Don't act crazy, just hurry up!"

"You got it, kid."

He did not feel as cool as he tried to sound, not nearly. As he finished hooking the hanks, he was surprised to see that his hands were bleeding from scratches that he couldn't remember getting. Yvonne was back at the tiller now, trimming the main. Kevin stepped up next to the mast to hoist the jib.

"Get on the windward side, Kevin, or the sail will blow you overboard," she said.

"Shit," he said.

The speedboat was a hundred yards or so away, closing fast, sleek and menacing as a serpent.

Kevin hoisted the jib, willing his hands not to fumble with the halyard. The sail luffed momentarily, then filled with a thump as Yvonne pulled in the sheet. Kevin scrambled back to the cockpit.

Under sail.

"Hey, mister. You can't just barge into a race. . . ." A sober voice, serious sailor, from a small sloop just rounding the marker. Kevin and Yvonne had just blocked their wind.

"Sorry," Kevin said. "Buy you a beer later."

"Yooo, fuck him. He's not drinking." The inebriate again—a sailor more like Kevin.

"Kevin."

He looked to where Yvonne had pointed with her head, off to the starboard. A hundred yards or so away, the gray speedboat idled, riding the chop.

"Watching us," Kevin said.

"I'm not sure it's them."

Kevin had to squint; the speedboat was between them and the sun. He blinked hard but it didn't help. One moment he could see the speedboat, the next moment gray spots danced in front of his eyes.

"Jesus," he said.

The speedboat looked like the one he had seen yesterday, near the Throgs Neck. But he couldn't be sure. He squinted again; the men in the speedboat looked dark-haired, dark-faced. Or was it just the sun behind them that made them look like that?

"I can only see two guys," Kevin said.

"That doesn't mean anything. They might've left the one with the bad hand. Or one of them might be below. And even if it's not them, it could be part of the same gang."

"Damn."

"Hey, you racing or not, you people? Either get out of my wind or fall off, okay?"

"Sorry."

"I don't know why you want to cut in late anyhow. It won't mean anything."

"Actually," Yvonne said to the sailor, "it could mean a lot." Then she turned to Kevin. "Here," she said. She tossed him a fresh orange T-shirt to replace the sweat-soaked gray one he'd worn all day.

"Do I smell that bad?"

"Yes, but I don't care. Crouch down and change your shirt. Make it harder to spot us."

Kevin did so. God, she was sharp.

Without taking off her own pale-blue top, Yvonne pulled a yellow one over it. Then she put on a floppy boat hat, tucking her hair up in it.

Then she began to cry again. "Those bastards."

Now they were not just one boat on the water but one of a score or so of sloops racing, more or less, around a triangular course. A couple of the boats had distinctive traits—a hull of firecracker red or royal blue, say—but most, like theirs, were silver or gray or somewhere in between. Anyone following them could easily lose track.

"Vonnie." He put his hand on her shoulder.

He could not tell if he was any comfort to her. It was the same helpless feeling he had had when she lost the baby.

"Anything I can say?" he asked hoarsely.

"No."

There was no rebuke in her voice. He moved away from her and pulled in the jib sheet.

The boat heeled a little and picked up speed.

"Kevin?"

"Yeah?"

She nodded toward where the speedboat had been. It was gone now. Gone where? And did it matter at all?

They caught a good cross-river breeze and let it take them down the course on a starboard tack, close-hauled. They had always liked sailing close-hauled, feeling the wind coming at them and the boat heeled over.

"Yoo!" It was the drunk hailing them again. But this time the elation had gone out of Kevin. The feeling had been triggered by fear and adrenaline anyhow, and had been closer to horror than he cared to think about just yet.

"Yooo . . ."

Kevin waved at him halfheartedly and looked back at Yvonne. She had stopped crying, but her face was swollen and her lower lip was trembling. Kevin bent over to put his head in his hands and saw that they were shaking violently. He put his right hand against the gearshift and squeezed as hard as he could. He remembered what the men had said, about hurting Vonnie, and the sounds of her scuffling with the man below, and he wished for all the world that he could swing the gearshift at them again. The man who had been below with Vonnie was the only one he hadn't hit. God, if you don't do anything else for me, just give me the chance to splatter his brains. Okay?

Jesus, Kevin thought. What the hell kind of prayer is that?

"Ready about," Yvonne ordered.

"Ready." Damn, she was a sailor to her marrow.

Yvonne swung the Pearson smoothly around the marker and let the boom swing across the cockpit and out over the port gunwale. Kevin trimmed the jib, and they were heading back up course.

"Look at all the boats," Kevin said. "Pretty."

Yvonne said nothing.

The boat with the serious sailor, the one whose wind they had blocked out, passed them without so much as a wave. Serious sailor, Kevin thought. Fuck him.

"I don't see the speedboat anywhere," Yvonne said.

"Good. I've had enough for a day. Or a life."

"The leading boats are heading downriver a little and cutting over to the Westchester side. We'll follow along and tie up wherever we can."

"Do you believe this shit, Vonnie?"

"I don't know what it means, but I know we can't handle it. And I told you I never trusted Harvey."

"That's right, you didn't."

"And what about your friend?"

"No, Marty's okay. Just a sportswriter, like me. He can't be in on all this. But what's it all mean?"

"They were looking for something. On this boat."

"What? And where? No place to hide anything. We're not the *Queen Elizabeth,* for Christ's sake. Maybe they wanted the boat itself."

"No. Something else. Soon as we tie up, we call the police."

"I'm gonna call that goddamn Harvey—"

"The police. First thing. We tell them everything we can remember. Everything."

They were downriver now, on the other side of the Tappan Zee. The leading boats were passing under a banner strung across the entrance to a channel on the Westchester side. "Tansytown Boat Club Annual Late-Summer Sailing Races," the banner read.

Kevin saw a gray speedboat bobbing up and down near the channel entrance. Them! He was about to say something to Yvonne when he took another look and saw that a man standing up in the speedboat was holding a clipboard and writing something down. Oh, a race official. Of course, for God's sake.

"For a second I thought that boat there—"

"Me too," she said.

The man with the clipboard wore a straw hat, dark glasses, and a T-shirt that said "Tansytown Yacht Club." As the Pearson passed near him, he smiled like Bert Parks and said, "Race number?"

"We're not racers, not officially," Kevin said. "We just want to put up here for a while if that's all right."

The man with the clipboard stiffened and his smile took on an edge, as though he were dealing with social inferiors. "Keep to your right down the channel," he said. "You can tie up at the pier that says 'Guests.' We have reciprocal privileges with some clubs in the area. You'll have to talk to the dockmaster." The man said that as though he was absolutely certain they couldn't possibly belong to any decent club in the area, or anywhere else.

Kevin dearly wanted to tell him to fuck off, but he thought the better of it. They had barged into a race, and they looked like a couple of bums. At least he did.

They tied up at the guest pier between a couple of ketches that were worth fifty or a hundred thousand dollars more than their boat. Kevin got a bucket, filled it with water from a faucet on the pier, and rinsed the blood out of the cockpit. Yvonne took a sponge and finished the cleanup, then had second thoughts.

"Should we have left the blood alone?" she asked. "We're throwing all the evidence into the Hudson. The blood, the knife."

"Maybe. I don't know." Now he half wished he hadn't thrown the knife away.

Kevin and Yvonne agreed that maybe it was good to be parked in such exclusive company: security would be tighter with these expensive boats around. Wouldn't it?

Then how come two men with mean hard looks were walking down the pier, each carrying a satchel, coming right for their boat? They were about Kevin's size, sun-burned, with muscles in the arms and shoulders like he only dreamed about. . . . Eyes like lasers, mean. Jesus.

"Vonnie." He grasped the gearshift handle again, but his arm felt weak.

The men stopped in front of their boat. No one around to help, the whoops and laughter of the racers far away . . .

Kevin and Yvonne looked up at them. Kevin started to pray, hoped that it still counted because he hadn't been to church for so long. The men were tough-looking; sun blisters around their lips, no doubt used to pain, used to dishing out pain. . . .

Still frowning, the men unzipped their satchels. This can't be happening, Kevin thought. Our Father Who Art in Heaven . . .

One man took a metal canister out of his satchel and tossed it in a graceful arc toward Kevin. Kevin brought his hand up just in time to catch the can of beer as it bounced off his chest. It was cold, with bits of ice clinging to the metal.

"You catch better than you sail," one man said, breaking into an ear-to-ear grin. "Welcome to the Tansytown Boat Club."

"How about you, ma'am?" the other man said.

"I can use one," Yvonne said, smiling.

One of the men, it turned out, was the dockmaster, the other a race organizer. They came on board, spoke admiringly of the Pearson Ariel, looked puzzled when Kevin and Yvonne said they were planning to sell it, but didn't press the subject. About halfway through the beer (which tasted so good Kevin knew he could never give it up completely), Kevin and Yvonne began to tell about the boarding party and being followed.

"Cops. You wanna talk to the cops," the dockmaster said. "Drink up, and I'll take you up to the office. By the way, my name's Mel."

"Kevin."

"I'm Steve."

"Yvonne."

Then still another voice, a woman's, from the stern of one of the ketches: "I love your boat. We used to have a Pearson."

"Thank you," Yvonne said.

"Aw gee, never forget her. Great boat." The voice belonged to the husband of the woman on the ketch. Both had come up from the galley and were sipping gin and tonics and smiling.

"We've had a good time on her," Kevin said. He figured the man to be ten or twelve years older than he was, the woman that much older than Vonnie.

A little girl appeared from the galley of the ketch. About nine or ten years old, face like both her parents, freckles and braces.

That should be us not so far down the road, Kevin thought, and he wondered if Yvonne was thinking the same thing.

She was.

The people on the ketch exchanged pleasantries with Mel and Steve about the race and the weather and sailmakers. Then the woman said, "Have fun with that Pearson, you two."

Treating us like a couple, Kevin thought. That doesn't make it so.

Mel and Steve led them up the pier to a small office crammed with charts and boat equipment. They had felt safe leaving the Pearson untended; the people on the ketch promised to keep an eye on things, and Mel and Steve said they would watch it. As they sat in the office, Kevin and Yvonne felt safe for the first time in hours.

Kevin dialed the State Police, told them the bare bones of what had happened. The officer on the phone said he and Yvonne should stop at the office and fill out a report, and Kevin said there was no way they could do that because they didn't have a car with them. Then Kevin gave him a few more details—about the knife, Yvonne's near rape, how they'd fought off the men with gearshift handles and winches, cracking heads and hands, and the officer's voice changed. Now he takes us seriously, Kevin thought.

The officer told Kevin they should stay at the boat club, stay out of sight, and he would send an investigator pronto.

Next, Kevin dialed Marty Diehl and was relieved when the man and not his machine answered.

"Marty, what the hell happened?"

"Damn, Kevin, I thought the deal was off; I mean, there was a message on my machine."

"A strange, Spanish-sounding voice?" Kevin asked.

"How did you know?"

"A long story. Do you still have that voice on your answering-machine tape?"

"Uh, no, it's already erased. Funny thing is, when I got the message I was relieved, because I was having second thoughts about buying a boat this late in the season. . . . Um, you still want to sell it?"

" 'S okay, Marty," Kevin said. "We can talk about it later."

Yvonne understood enough just from Kevin's end of the conversation to know what was going on. They shook their heads, swore together and laughed.

"Can't afford to keep the boat and can't get rid of it," Yvonne said.

"Maybe we're not supposed to sell it," he said. But he didn't want to go any further with that line.

"We don't have a ride either," she said.

"We'll rent a limo," he said.

They shared a laugh over that.

"I was impressed with you back there," she said.

"Yeah, well, ditto. Double ditto."

They talked about calling Harvey but decided not to until their tempers had cooled.

They got up to leave the office and go back to their boat when it occurred to Yvonne to call the police in New Jersey again, to tell them about the boarding party and ask if they had any leads.

Kevin dialed and got the same man he'd talked to earlier. The man said Kevin's and Yvonne's recollections might be very important, and that the New Jersey police would be comparing notes not only with the police in New York State but with the local police in Edgecliff as well.

"Why is that?" Kevin asked.

"Because an Edgecliff woman was beaten and tortured and her apartment was ransacked earlier today," the officer said.

"A woman tortured? Her apartment in Edgecliff ransacked?" Kevin said, thinking he sounded like Donald Duck.

Yvonne felt the blood drain out of her face.

"You know the name?" Kevin asked.

"Not being released at this time," the officer said.

"Deirdre Lockwood," Kevin said, telling him rather than asking.
"You know her?" the officer said.
"We know her," Kevin said.
Yvonne's knees buckled and she sank to the floor. Who would do that to DeeDee? A boyfriend? A jilted lover? The tennis instructor? Then Yvonne knew. "I should never have stayed there. It's my fault." Yvonne sobbed. "Poor DeeDee."

11

Kevin sat in the cockpit, listening to the sobbed curses, shuffling and thumps in the galley.

Thump, thump, thwack as life preservers, winches and charts flew onto the galley floor.

"Something . . . something . . ." Yvonne said between sobs.

"Vonnie . . ."

"Shut-UPPP!" she screamed.

"Let's wait for the police, Vonnie."

"The hell with the police." Sob and choke. "My friend is lying mangled in the hospital. And there's something someone wants on this boat."

"Please, Vonnie."

"Please what? Please don't make you feel uncomfortable? Please don't cry about DeeDee? Please just be quiet and don't disturb you or anyone else? Please be reasonable in the face of violence? Please what? Please who? Don't PLEASE me, goddamn you. If we weren't splitting up, if we didn't have to move the boat ourselves . . . It's the boat. Something on this boat."

"It's just a boat. Just a boat." Kevin felt a hundred years old.

"Then why did those animals threaten us? Why did that gorilla drag me into the V-berth . . . ?"

Almost suddenly, Yvonne sat down on one of the galley benches, gave one last, racking sob, and began to cry more quietly. He sat stiffly, wishing that he could cry, could wash out some of the pain the way she did.

Kevin peeked below. Over Yvonne's heaving shoulders he could see

110

into the V-berth. She had emptied it out, right down to the triangular cushions. As he watched, Yvonne took a deep breath, went up into the V-berth as far as she could and knelt on the bare fiberglass, feeling with her fingers along the edges, right up to where the anchor lay in the bow.

"Nothing," Yvonne mumbled. "Men on the boat in the middle of the night. Boats following us. Leaking sink hose. Rapist. Men on the boat with a knife. Asking us where. Where. DeeDee hurt. What's happening? Why us? Why me? Oh, poor DeeDee. Why her?"

Yvonne went back into the galley and sat down again. "Kevin." A change in her voice now.

Kevin looked down into the cabin and was taken back in time to the day he saw Yvonne in the hospital right after the miscarriage. Her face was the same, full of pain, swollen with tears, and infused with a strange expression, more than grief and pain. It radiated betrayal, defeat, distrust and loss, maybe a loss of hope.

The police would arrive soon, Kevin knew. God, he hoped he and Yvonne didn't have to talk to them a long time. All he wanted was to go home. Home? He caught himself thinking of the house he and Yvonne had shared. No, no time for that.

"I'm sorry, Vonnie. Can I do anything for you?" He realized those were the same words he had used that day. That day when she had looked this way. Everything had gone wrong from that day on. Could he do better this time?

"Kevin," Yvonne said again, "tell me about last night when the boat was boarded."

Kevin was about to protest. Why go over the same ground? But maybe it would help her. Hadn't he just asked if there was anything he could do?

"The goons looked below," he said. "They didn't find anything, but that's where they looked. And a key. They were looking for a key. Maybe they didn't want a key to the ignition but a key to the topside hatches."

Kevin went below, stepped around Yvonne's legs and opened the drawer near the V-berth. He took out the keys, then went topside again. Kneeling, he opened the port and starboard cockpit hatches, then the stern hatch. Each side hatch had about as much space as an old-fashioned steamer trunk, the stern hatch about half that. The side hatches held fenders; the port one also held sponges, brushes, a spare plastic bucket. The starboard hatch had coils of extra line. The stern hatch held spare life preservers (one, for a child, they had left there for someday) and a hose.

Kevin took out each fender, felt the rubber cylinders one at a time. He half expected to find that one or more had been slit open, then resealed. Of course, a perfect hiding place. A boat that hasn't been used all summer, sitting out in the water. Harvey, you prick, I gotta hand it to you. I didn't think you had it in you.

The fenders were untouched, as were the life jackets.

Yvonne watched as Kevin searched, following his hands. He had nice hands, strong broad palms and long squared fingers. He had a capable way of moving them.

A key? "Kevin, didn't you say they were speaking Spanish?"

"Yes, most of the time."

"'*Aquí*,' they were saying, not a key, A-Q-U-í, it means 'here' in Spanish."

"Here? That means, Jesus, that means they knew where they were supposed to look."

"And that's why they didn't look in the V-berth. It wasn't in the V-berth. Where did they mean when they said 'here'?"

"Shit, I don't know."

"What about the mechanics who fixed the sink fitting? Maybe they found something and kept it."

They looked at one another and shook their heads.

"Too . . ." said Yvonne.

"Farfetched," Kevin added.

"Something still . . ."

"Doesn't make sense," said Kevin.

"You're finishing my sentences," Yvonne said, almost smiling.

"Maybe that means we're back on the same wavelength," Kevin said.

Yvonne looked away as they heard the sound of street shoes on the pier. They looked up to see two men: one tall, young, and uniformed; the other a little older, heavy, wearing a rumpled suit.

"I'm Detective Guardino," the man in the suit said, perfunctorily showing his credentials. He looked into the boat, frowned when he saw the debris in the galley.

"My wife was looking for . . . whatever."

The detective nodded, almost imperceptibly, to the trooper, then said, "He'll stay with the boat. Why don't we go inside."

The detective sat them down in the boat-club office, took out a notepad. "You saw Miss Lockwood when you were in Edgecliff?"

"Just me, not him," Yvonne answered. "I left her this morning around seven."

The detective looked puzzled for a moment and wrote in a notebook. "You weren't together, the two of you?"

"Kevin stayed with the boat," Yvonne said, irritated that her life was this man's business.

"We were taking the boat up the Hudson to sell it," Kevin said.

"Two men came on board the boat at Edgecliff," Yvonne said. "While Kevin was on it."

"At night," Kevin said.

"Then three men boarded the boat over at the Haviland marina," Yvonne said.

"Forced their way on," Kevin said. "One guy had a knife. They tried to beat us up—"

"What do you mean, *tried*," Yvonne said angrily. "We had to fight them off. One of them tried—"

"Whoa, whoa," the detective said. "My circuits are getting overloaded."

"Well, ex-CUSE me," Yvonne hissed.

The detective put his notebook down, sat back in his chair and smiled. "I know this is tough," he said gently. "I've got to take you through this, believe me."

And he did take them through it, all of it, starting with their departure from Harvey's the morning of the day before. The detective at first seemed plodding, dull, but before long they realized he was just being absolutely meticulous and thorough.

They told him how they had timed their departure to give them time to get to Hell Gate. A non-sailor, the detective was interested in hearing how the timing of the current had to be considered. The detective asked them what kind of unusual things had happened.

Yvonne listened as the investigator asked questions and Kevin answered most of them. Maybe the detective was an old-fashioned

male chauvinist (like most cops, she thought), or maybe he was just
more comfortable interviewing a man (which maybe amounted to the
same thing), but most of the detective's questions were directed at
Kevin.

Yvonne didn't feel like making an issue of it. For one thing, she
thought she was a bit more strung out than Kevin who, after all, hadn't
had to fight off a sexual attack. (Not that she could resent Kevin too
much, after the way he had smacked that bastard on the hand. . . .)
Then, too, Kevin had been on the boat when the two men had come on
board during the night.

Something about that still didn't sit quite right with her. What the
hell was it?

Yvonne found herself taken up with the puzzle of what had
happened to them in the last day and a half. She was glad for the
mental exercise.

As a girl, she had been good with jigsaw puzzles. She could look at
a tiny piece of a puzzle and see how it might fit into a larger whole;
sometimes she had seemed able to see the bigger picture from the hints
in the fragments. Sometimes, two pieces that seemed to belong very
far apart, or to have no connection whatever, were joined by one piece.
Then all the other pieces fell into place.

She let Kevin go on—his reporter's recollection was pretty good, in
all fairness—but she interrupted from time to time to add something.
She especially wanted to make it clear that DeeDee wasn't a hot
number. She thought she had noticed a leer when the cops talked about
DeeDee. The cops seemed to want to connect DeeDee to all that had
happened to Kevin and Yvonne.

"She's a good person, DeeDee," Yvonne said. "A teacher. You can
check all you want to and you won't find her involved in drugs or
anything like that."

Some things Kevin and Yvonne agreed on: Harvey had acted strange
when they took the boat; they had had the feeling—no, more than
that—of being followed, once, twice, or three times. Of being
watched.

"Chowder's," Yvonne said.

The detective looked at her uncomprehendingly.

"We were at Chowder's the night before last," Yvonne said.

"A well-known seafood restaurant and bar in Port Guinness," Kevin explained.

The detective nodded and kept his eyes on Yvonne.

"We were there—and so was Harvey!" Yvonne said. "So was half the town, for God's sake. I mean, there were a bunch of people who knew we were moving the boat."

"They thought there was something on the boat," Kevin said. "I mean, the guys in Haviland, the ones who tried to . . . well, one of the first things they said when they climbed on the boat was, 'Where is it?' Or something like that."

At that point, Yvonne told the detective that what Kevin had heard as "key" might have been Spanish for "here." The detective wrote something in his notebook.

"We don't know where 'here' is," Kevin said.

"Wait a minute, Kevin," Yvonne said, waving for everyone else to shut up. "If the guys on the boat last night were saying 'here' in Spanish and the bastards at Haviland were saying 'where' in English . . ."

"Then there's five guys who're after us because of something on our boat," Kevin finished.

"Five . . . that we know of," Yvonne said, swallowing hard.

The door to the office opened just then and the uniformed trooper stuck his head in. "Nothing yet," he said. "Maybe we'll have to haul it out of the water and look at the bottom."

"I guess we shouldn't complain too much," Kevin said, "but you never asked us if you could search our boat."

Detective Guardino smiled and spoke softly. "You gave me every reason," he said. "I checked your boat number through the computer. Registration's expired, so officially I had every reason."

"Goddammit, Kevin," Yvonne said.

"Pardon my French," Detective Guardino said, "but I don't give a shit about the registration. I'd like to find out why someone beat up on your friend."

Kevin realized he had only glanced at the detective's badge. "Who're you with?" Kevin asked.

"Bergen County, New Jersey, prosecutor's office. I wasn't just interested in searching your boat for . . . whatever. If you had had any of Miss Lockwood's belongings . . ." The detective raised his eyebrows suggestively and shrugged his shoulders.

"Look," Kevin said. "I'm a newspaper reporter, for *Long Island*. I, we, don't need any special treatment, but if you'll just check us out . . ."

"We will. But I wouldn't worry. I can tell what kind of people you are."

"Chowder's," Yvonne said. "A lot of it starts, somehow, with Chowder's. And Harvey, he was there the other night, and yesterday morning he acted really weird."

"We'll definitely talk to him," the detective said.

The door to the office opened again and the uniformed officer entered. "Nothing yet," he said. "Looked in all the hatches. There seems to be some recent repair work under the sink . . ."

"A fitting broke," Kevin said. "Yesterday, near Edgecliff. That's why we stopped, in fact—all the water gushing in."

"If it hadn't been for that, maybe . . ." Yvonne said.

"What about the steps that lead down to the inside?" the trooper said. "They seem to wiggle. That storage space under there, or what?"

"Just the engine," Kevin said. "Matter of fact, the guys that came on last night, I think they were trying to pry the steps up when a police boat came by."

The two investigators looked at Kevin for more explanation.

"See, they were looking around the back, sort of whispering. I think they were yanking at the steps when a police boat came by to quiet down a boatload of drunks."

"And they left right after that without looking under the steps?" the detective asked.

"Yeah, and I'm sure of that, because they would have made a lot more noise if they'd pulled the steps out. We never look under there because we aren't mechanical at all. . . ."

Kevin stopped and looked at Yvonne. Something clicked between them.

"That's where 'here' is," Kevin said quietly. "Under the steps, near the engine. We can't even get the steps up ourselves most of the time without scraping our fingers."

"Harvey has done all the engine work for us," Yvonne said. "I mean, all of it."

"And we haven't used the boat this summer at all," Kevin said.
"Because we haven't been together."

"Have a look," the detective said to the trooper, who hurried off.

Through the small office window, Kevin could see that it was getting dark. He was exhausted, hungry, depressed. Needed a shower. "What happens now?" he asked.

"We'll figure out how to take care of you for the night," the detective said.

"We don't have a way to get back to Long Island," Yvonne said. "Oh, Tessie!"

"The dog," Kevin explained.

"It might be a good idea if you didn't go home tonight. You got on the wrong side of some bad people. You know that. I think you should stay up here tonight."

"In Westchester?" Yvonne said.

"I know a place," the detective said. "Small and clean. Out of the way but not far from the New York State police. They've used it to put up witnesses. They keep a good eye on it. You couldn't be safer. I'll see that you're looked after."

The door to the office opened, and the trooper came in, holding up a plastic-wrapped package the size of a large sandwich bag. "White powder," he said. "Not talcum."

"Afraid we'll have to impound the boat," the detective said. "The New York cops are taking statements at the marina. They'll work with us on this. And the feds will want to know about it too. You got any overnight stuff on board, better get it. I'll see about the motel."

"We'll have to call about the dog," Yvonne said, thinking how much she missed Tess.

"We'll have one of the Port Guinness officers look in on your dog, Mrs. McNulty. We'd rather you didn't call anybody tonight. We don't want anyone to know where you are."

Later, when Yvonne was in the shower at the motel, she wondered why she hadn't asked the trooper to give them separate rooms . . . adjoining rooms. Then they could each have a bed. She didn't intend to share a bed with Kevin, but she wanted him to be nearby. Then she thought of DeeDee. She wanted to see her and explain what had happened, to tell her how sorry . . . DeeDee. Beaten. Left in a puddle of blood. Her lovely white rug. Bloody. Yvonne wondered if she would be able to sleep, and if she did, what horrible dreams would run riot through her head all night.

Kevin sat slumped in a plastic chair, listening to the shower running. A couple of times he thought he heard sobbing sounds. He would not intrude on Vonnie's pain, but he would share if she asked him.

Suddenly he remembered: He was supposed to work the next day, covering whatever news came out of the Jets' practice.

No way. He dialed the newsroom switchboard of *Long Island* and told the clerk he wouldn't be in the next day because he was sick (not far off, considering how he felt). He was surprised that his call had gotten through, and wondered how thorough the cops were, since they hadn't made sure no calls could be made from the room.

Yvonne emerged from the bathroom, trailing steam and fragrance of skin lotion. Her eyes were moist and her hair was wrapped in a towel.

"Me next," he said, grabbing clean cutoffs, underwear, and T-shirt. In no time, he was under the shower. The hot water made his bruises feel better and lessened his tension, if not his melancholy.

Yvonne was lying on the bed, her hair still wrapped, watching television when he came out.

A knock at the door made Yvonne sit up; the towel fell off her head.

Kevin went to the door, looked through the peephole and saw the strong, protective face of the trooper.

"It's him," Kevin said. Kevin opened the door, and the trooper entered with a cardboard box that contained several large bags and one small one.

"Provisions," the policeman said. He unpacked two loaf shapes wrapped in foil ("steak-and-cheese sandwiches, best I ever ate"), two containers of salad, a large bag of french fries—and a six-pack.

"I'll get some ice," the trooper said.

Kevin and Yvonne unpacked their food hungrily.

The trooper put some ice in the sink, added water and submerged the six-pack like a guy who had done it before. "You're all set," he said.

"Thank you," Yvonne said.

"You've got a friend in the press from now on," Kevin said. "What do we owe you?"

"You're dining courtesy of the great Empire State," the policeman said. "Don't open your door to strangers, and dial this number if there's any trouble. We'll be checking on you every hour or so all night."

That's why the phone is working, Kevin thought. "Will you want to talk to us tomorrow?" he asked.

"Probably. Detective Guardino will call you. We'll pick you up in the morning."

The trooper smiled, waved good-bye and left.

"I think he likes us," Kevin said. "Thinks we're lost, or something."

"He's not wrong."

Kevin took two cans of beer from the sink, opened them and handed one to Yvonne, who did not protest. He took a huge gulp. Then he opened the small bag the trooper had brought, opened the bottle of iodine and, with unsteady fingers, dabbed some on the scratches that crisscrossed his hands, elbows, and knees. There were more than he had realized. One of his shoulders ached; he had noticed it only after squirming as he applied the iodine.

He opened the rubbing alcohol, got a washcloth and slapped some on his shoulder. Instantly, he yelped with pain.

"Take your shirt all the way off," Yvonne said, getting up from the bed. Standing over him, she said, "You have a dirty, nasty scratch there—look, blood on your shirt—in the middle of a big bruise. Hold still. . . ."

For a moment, the sting of the iodine was more than he could handle. He felt nauseous from the pain and from the mingling smells of food and medicine. He thought he was going to faint.

"Thanks for fighting so hard," she said.

"You're welcome. Let's not do it again for a while. . . ."

She took the iodine and alcohol to the bed and began dabbing methodically. Kevin was about to offer to help, but he thought it might sound too much like a come-on.

"I called the paper. Told them I wasn't coming in tomorrow. I didn't tell them where we were. I figured that would be okay with the cops."

"What about DeeDee? We've got to go see her." That was as far as she could get without choking up.

"They didn't even tell us what hospital she was in."

"Oh, God. I hope they didn't do any . . . anything permanent."

"We can't do anything tonight."

Yvonne looked at him sharply but said nothing.

They went back to their meals; in no time, they had each drained a beer and wolfed down half their sandwiches and most of the salad and french fries.

Kevin fetched two more beers. He took his time on his second, but he was still done before Yvonne had taken more than a few sips. He would hold off on his third; maybe wait until Yvonne was asleep.

In fact, Yvonne was feeling drowsy. "Kevin?"

"Yeah, Vonnie?"

"Is it okay if I take the bed?"

"Sure, Vonnie. Sleep well."

Kevin saw that Yvonne had put her head back on the pillow. Her mouth was open slightly. Sleeping, he thought. He went over and picked up the beer can resting against her thigh. Still some left. He drained it.

He went to the window, pulled the curtain just enough to see into the parking lot. Nothing. He checked the lock on the window, secured the chain, checked the door. Finally, he took another beer from the sink.

Kevin turned off the light and lay down on the plastic sofa, which wasn't quite long enough to accommodate him comfortably. Then he began to think night thoughts. He thought about what had happened since yesterday and even more about how he had messed things up.

Yvonne felt herself falling. That feeling of falling, an endless fall . . . What's at the bottom? Nothing . . . No, DeeDee's there to catch me. . . . It's not DeeDee; it's a man with a knife. I can't get away.

"Help," she tried to say. But it came out as a groan as she edged her way toward consciousness. It was a dream. Where was Kevin? In the bathroom. In the bathroom with the baby. No, no baby. She opened her eyes and stared at the unfamiliar walls.

"Where . . . ?"

"You were dreaming," Kevin said.

"Uh." She mumbled, thinking she was telling Kevin about the dream.

* * *

Detective Guardino sat on the edge of the sofa, smiling between his clumsy stabs at small talk and trying to show concern for their feelings. But his impatience was so transparent that Kevin and Yvonne hurried through the coffee and juice.

They tossed their meager baggage into the rear seat of the police car, where it acted as a divider.

They rode in near silence through the near perfect late-summer morning. Guardino took them across the Tappan Zee Bridge, from which they could see dozens of boats on the gleaming Hudson.

Once into New Jersey, Guardino took several serpentine roads with easy familiarity.

"I live not too far from here," he said, seeming to read their thoughts.

They passed comfortable middle-class homes with tidy lawns and flowers and children playing out front.

Kevin and Yvonne looked at each other.

"Do you believe this shit?" Kevin said quietly.

Understanding at once, she shook her head no. Yesterday, they had shared fear and danger. Today, they envied the people they passed, people who weren't being chased and menaced. People who were still together.

The hospital was a huge, sprawling complex of buildings built in stages over the decades as northern New Jersey's population grew. It took Kevin and Yvonne almost five minutes to go from the reception desk to the wing that housed DeeDee's room, where a nurse sat outside a closed door marked "I.C.U."

The nurse, who looked barely out of her teens, was sandy-haired and freckled. "May I ask who you're here to see?" she said, looking at Kevin.

"We're here to see our friend DeeDee Lockwood," Yvonne said.

"All right. Since this is an intensive-care section, I'll have to ask you to put on gowns and to please limit your stay to fifteen minutes. She is under sedation right now."

They helped each other into the pale-yellow gowns that tied in the back. The nurse put Yvonne's bag on a shelf and asked them to scrub

"We're in a motel in Westchester."

Yvonne blinked and looked toward Kevin. His feet rested on one arm of the couch and his head was tilted up at the other end. She patted the bed next to her. "You can sleep here," she said. "Stay on your own side."

His pride told him to stay where he was, but comfort won out. He slid under the covers near the edge and breathed a deep sigh. "This is better," he said.

She turned on her side away from him. Wide awake now, she thought. She wondered how she would get back to sleep, tried a few deep breaths, remembering her Yoga class. Before she had finished the third breath she was asleep. Deep in the abyss, this time.

Kevin looked at the space between them and took a little of it. Maybe they could try once more, if the ground rules were different. He would go to a shrink, therapist, whatever, if Vonnie wanted him to. He would do it. "I still love you, Vonnie," he whispered into the dark.

12 _____

Yvonne started to wake up first, comforted by Kevin's arm draped over her shoulder. Then she blinked. What was he doing? Then she realized she had flung one of her legs over his. Had they made love? No, she didn't think so. She didn't know whether that made her relieved or sad.

As she started to move away, Kevin stirred. Still half asleep, he patted her shoulder as he always had. Then he opened his eyes wide.

"Uh, sorry," he said. "I tried to stay on my own side."

"So did I," she said, pulling her leg the rest of the way back.

An embarrassed quiet settled over both of them. They were relieved when the phone rang.

"Good morning. It's Detective Guardino. How're you doing?"

"We've both been better, thanks," Kevin said.

"I don't doubt it. Listen, we arrested three men last night. Or I should say the police in Fort Lee did. We think they're the three who messed you up."

"*All right!*" Kevin said. Then, covering the phone, he said to Yvonne, "It's Detective Guardino. They think they got the three guys."

"Do the police think they're the ones who beat up DeeDee?" Yvonne asked.

"Tell me more," Kevin said into the phone.

"There was a traffic jam at the George Washington Bridge," Guardino began.

"Do they think they're the ones who beat up DeeDee?" Yvonne asked again.

". . . just a usual traffic jam at the bridge this time of year,"

Guardino went on. "Some people had taken enough notice of the big tussle at the marina to get the license number of the van the three left in . . ."

"Kevin."

". . . after they saw the blood on the guys. . . ."

"Just a second," Kevin said. Then, to Yvonne. "I'll give you the phone, I won't let him hang up."

"Some witnesses called the police at Haviland and they put out a bulletin, and there we were. They're not charged in the assault on your friend, but we're looking at that."

"Do you think we're safe now?" Kevin asked.

"We'll need your cooperation," the detective went on, in an evasion Kevin would have picked up at once even if he hadn't got used to talking to cops from his days on the police beat. "As I said, we're pretty sure they're the three who messed you up. One of them has a badly injured hand. . . ."

"Yeah, well, I'm not sorry."

"Right. Anyhow, I'll pick you up in a little while. Don't go out the room till I get there."

"Tell him we haven't had breakfast," Yvonne said.

"We haven't had breakfast yet," Kevin said, this time glad Yv had butted in.

"I'll swing by with coffee and juice."

"Then what?"

"Then down to Hackensack, where my office is. Also w Bergen County Prosecutor's office and jail is. Some more que ask you, then we can see about sending you home to Lor After you look at a lineup, of course."

"Just a minute, Yvonne wants to talk to you," Kevin s

"Do you think these are the guys who broke into DeeD Yvonne asked.

"As I told your husband, Mrs. McNulty, we're loo possibility, checking your friend's apartment for pr anything special that you'd like for breakfast? I don't w the room till we get there."

"You mean we're not safe yet?"

"We don't want to take any chances."

"Okay, but we want you to take us to see DeeD

their hands. "If you have a cold, we'd like you to wear a mask," the nurse said, pointing to a binful of plastic bags.

"No colds," Yvonne said.

"Then you can go in now."

Inside the room, another nurse sat at a desk crowded with clip-boards, folders, a telephone, and a copy of a women's magazine. The nurse sipped a diet soft drink through a straw, looked up and smiled.

Kevin and Yvonne recoiled for a moment at the sights: a teenage boy lying flat on his back, his head wrapped in a cocoon of white bandages, his arms in casts by his side; an old woman, tiny and bird-thin on her pillows, apparently unaware of a much younger woman sitting by her side, gently stroking her hand; a girl of five or six, eyes closed and mouth open in sleep, her entire torso swathed in bandages.

And over to the side, DeeDee.

Kevin pulled the curtains on either side of the bed; then he and Yvonne sat in metal folding chairs next to her.

"Jesus Christ," Kevin whispered.

"I think she's asleep. How could anyone do—" Yvonne's voice broke.

DeeDee Lockwood's head lay nestled in pillows. Around the edge of the bandages they could see that some of her hair was missing; they could see that part of her head had been shaved so the doctors could stitch the deep cuts, and in some places her head looked raw, as if some of her hair had been yanked out.

DeeDee's eyes, the lids swollen and purple, were closed. A thick white pad covered her entire forehead, and gauze two inches deep was taped over her nose. Thick pads were also taped to her cheeks. Her lips were swollen and cracked. As she breathed in and out, the thin transparent tube that led from the nose gauze to a bottle by the bedside moved ever so slightly.

Kevin wanted to say something but couldn't.

Tears formed in Yvonne's eyes. "I don't know whether to wake her or not," she said quietly. She shook her head slowly. "She's alive, at least."

"Hmmmm. I'm alive. I am." DeeDee had opened her eyes, which were red where they should have been white.

"DeeDee, it's Yvonne and Kevin. You're safe. We love you." Yvonne squeezed her friend's hand.

"Hi, DeeDee," Kevin said.

"My nooose," DeeDee said with a wheeze. "They broke it. . . . It hurt a lot when they broke it. . . ."

"Oh, DeeDee," Yvonne said.

"Cut me . . . too. But the nose hurt so bad . . . cuts didn't hurt so much."

"Animals!" Yvonne said.

"No. Animals are nice." DeeDee's swollen lips turned up at the corners.

Yvonne squeezed her hand harder and felt DeeDee squeeze back.

"Cheeks cut . . . bad. I had a dream about . . . about the knife . . . silver knife. . . ."

"Don't worry, DeeDee," Kevin said, glad that he'd smashed the hand that had wielded the knife.

"You're safe now. Safe here," Yvonne said.

"Safe . . ." The purple lids closed, and Yvonne felt DeeDee's hand relax.

"Asleep," Kevin said.

"That's okay. We'll sit here for a while and let the cops wait."

"Not . . . asleep." DeeDee's eyes opened again.

"You fooled us," Yvonne said.

"Fooled you. . . . The men . . . thought I had something . . . thought you . . ."

Yvonne and Kevin looked at each other and shared a realization. "I'm sorry, DeeDee. I didn't know they were following us. . . ."

"Kept asking me . . . hitting me . . . 'Where's the stuff . . .?' Coc-aine stuff . . . How I know? I never, ever . . . You know where stuff is?"

"I didn't know yesterday, but I do now." Yvonne gripped her friend's hand tight again. "But don't worry. The cops got those guys."

Huge tears oozed from under the purple eyelids.

"Dirty bastards," Kevin whispered.

"Know . . . what?" The puffed-up mouth formed a smile again. "What?"

"Finally gonna get . . . that nose job I wanted. . . ."

Yvonne and Kevin laughed out loud at that. The form on the bed shook with laughter too.

"Good for you, DeeDee," Yvonne said.

"Maybe a face-lift . . . no more wrinkles . . . Good?"

"Good," Yvonne said.

"Did me a . . . favor." DeeDee's mouth turned up even more in a smile. Then in an instant it turned all the way down again, and tears streamed down her cheeks.

"Goddamn Pollyanna," Yvonne said, crying too.

" 'Nother good thing."

"What's that?" Yvonne said.

"They make good tea here."

Yvonne and Kevin laughed again and the nurse came over to the bed. She checked DeeDee's tube and held her wrist for a few seconds. "We can probably put you in your own room tonight," she said, patting DeeDee on the arm.

DeeDee winced.

"Sorry," the nurse said. "I didn't know they got you there, too. I'll check it after your friends go." The nurse turned to Kevin and Yvonne again. "Her mother is asleep on a couch down the hall. Do you want to see her?"

"No. Just say hello for us, would you?" Yvonne said.

"Sure thing," the nurse said, glancing at her watch.

"Our time up?" Kevin asked.

" 'Fraid so," the nurse said. "I'd let you stay longer, but the cops want to talk to her later and I don't want to tire her."

"I'll talk . . . to cops," DeeDee said.

"They'll be here later," the nurse said. "After you rest."

"We've got to go now," Yvonne said.

"Bye," DeeDee said. Her eyes closed and her head rolled to one side and she fell into a deep, peaceful slumber.

"Welcome to Hackensack," Detective Guardino said.

He opened the car door to let them out. "Follow me," he said.

Without thinking Kevin took Yvonne's hand and she welcomed the clasp for a moment. Then they both realized what had happened and let go.

They followed the detective down a cold cement corridor. Near the end, he steered them into a room with two rows of theaterlike chairs and a wall almost totally filled by a window that revealed a lighted stage.

"Just like on the TV cop shows," Detective Guardino said. "We can see them, but they can't see us. Now, you folks are gonna have to view separately."

"Huh?" Yvonne demanded. Though not afraid, she liked the idea of having Kevin next to her for this.

"So a defense lawyer can't claim the identification was tainted in any way," Kevin said.

"You got it."

"I'll go first," Kevin said.

"Mrs. McNulty, could you step outside just for a moment."

Yvonne stood outside the door. Far away, down the end of the cold corridor, were sounds of office machines, telephones, and bureaucratic mumblings. People sounds. They made her feel safer.

The detective pressed a button on the wall and spoke into a screened microphone. Kevin heard the muffled sound of a door opening and closing. Four sullen men shuffled onto the silent stage from the right, stopped, turned and faced the window.

"Second from right," Kevin said. "He was the one with the knife."

"Take your time and be sure," Guardino said.

"It's him. End of discussion."

Kevin saw that the man had a graying bandage on his right hand, and that he seemed to be trying to hold his hand behind him. For a moment, Kevin was sorry he had crushed his hand.

"I'll have them turn to their left and right, one by one," Guardino said.

"Suit yourself. It'll still be him."

Kevin smiled reassuringly at Yvonne as he came out, and she smiled back as she went inside.

"Just relax," Guardino said. Yvonne thought he had a good protective manner.

Yvonne heard the faint sound of shuffling steps. There, on the stage, was the man who had had the knife.

"Second from left," she said. "Where are the others?"

"We have two more groups."

When the second group came on stage, Kevin felt a rush of anger that made his head throb. There, the very first one, was the one who had hurt Vonnie.

"Number one. He's the one who . . . you know, my wife . . ."

"Be sure."

"Number one, goddamn it."

Yvonne had to bite her lip. "That's the one who . . . the one I had to fight off."

"Number three, step forward, please," Detective Guardino said.

"I know who he is," Yvonne said, barely keeping control.

"Turn to your left, please, number three." To Yvonne, the detective said gently, "Take your time."

"Never mind," Yvonne said, steel back in her voice. "Let's do this right."

When the man stepped forward and turned to his left, a blood-crusted gauze pad was visible just below the top of his head.

"That's where I hit him," she said. For a moment she felt, not guilt, but . . . sorrow, as though the act of wounding the man—justified or not—had tainted her soul.

"Second from right is the leader," Kevin said as the third group came on stage.

Kevin tuned out Detective Guardino's words as the man Kevin had picked out stepped forward, turned left and right, then stepped back.

It was him, no doubt about it. What bothered Kevin was that, while the two men he had picked out in the earlier lineups had seemed sullen and defiant, their leader looked scared.

"Pardon the filth," Detective Guardino said, ushering them into his small one-window office and nodding toward an overflowing waste-basket and a desktop full of files.

"We've already seen the real filth," Yvonne said.

"Did we pass?" Kevin asked.

"Flying colors, both of you. Of course, we switched the order of the men in each lineup. . . ."

"In case we were comparing notes, you mean?" Yvonne snapped.

"Have to do it that way," Guardino said.

"Who were the other men in the lineup?" Yvonne asked.

"The usual catch of drunk and disorderlies," Guardino said. "Plus a couple of our undercover officers."

"Tell them they fit right in," Kevin said.

"So . . . we'll give you a ride to the GW Bridge. Nassau County will give you a ride from there."

"Well, we could take the subway to the LIRR," Kevin said, not sure whether he welcomed the ride in a police car.

"You've been through a lot," Guardino insisted. "Least we can do is give you a ride."

Guardino flashed a small smile, but Kevin's arm hairs told him it was partly for show.

"We, uh, want you to watch out for yourselves," Guardino went on, eyes downcast in embarrassment. "Depending on the progress of the investigation, we might need you."

"Depend on it." It was a new, officious voice, belonging to a man in a gray suit and pale-blue shirt. He was linebacker-tall and strong, clean-shaven, close-cut hair, handsome, grim.

A fed, Kevin figured at once.

"Special agent Bleucher, Drug Enforcement Administration," the newcomer said.

Kevin was about to extend his hand, but something in special agent Bleucher's manner stopped him. "I'm Kevin McNulty," he said.

"I'm Yvonne." She, too, was put off.

"I need to go over your story with you, step by step," Bleucher said. His voice was cold and infuriating.

"How long will this take?" Kevin said, voice rising in annoyance.

"As long as I need," the federal agent said.

Screw you, Kevin thought.

"We have needs, too," Yvonne said. "Like getting home to Port Guinness and getting our lives back to some kind of normal."

"I understood you were separated," the fed said.

"So?" Kevin challenged. He looked at Guardino, who stood near a window, posture and expression apologetic.

Sure, Kevin thought. Guardino believes us, and this guy isn't sure, and Guardino told him everything he could about us and feels bad about it. Which he should, because we trusted him. Ah, we're the ones who should feel bad, Vonnie and me. For trusting.

"So," the fed said, picking up the challenge, "I'll ask what I need to ask, and if I need to ask again, and again and again, either because I don't like your answers or I need more information, I will. Understand?"

Kevin was furious. He felt as if he'd been slapped. He knew if he tried to put his rage into words he'd blow it by sputtering.

Yvonne had always been able to articulate her anger better, which had given her a big advantage in their fights. This time, Kevin was grateful to her.

"Agent Belcher . . . Bilker . . .?" she began.

"Bleucher," the Fed corrected pompously.

I love you, Vonnie, Kevin thought, knowing her mispronunciation had been deliberate.

"Whatever," Yvonne went on contemptuously. "I'd like to say 'Fuck you,' but I'm a woman, even a lady sometimes, so I won't. I'll just say let's cut right through all this horseshit. We've been threatened, been beaten up, and I was almost—"

"So you say."

"Let me finish. Almost raped. And a friend of ours was badly beaten. We're victims, and you're hassling us. Now, that pisses me off, I can't tell you how much, and if you don't like what I'm saying, I don't really give a goddamn."

I love you, Vonnie, Kevin thought.

"You always kept your boat at the same place on Long Island," the fed went on, like a robot. "Then you suddenly move it. How come?"

"We told the cops that," Kevin said. "We have to sell it. We thought we had a buyer, up in Rockland County. Moving a boat the size of ours would cost five hundred bucks at least by truck."

The federal agent said nothing, and Kevin could tell nothing from his eyes. Kevin looked at Guardino and said, "Didn't you tell him what happened?"

"Sure, he did," Yvonne said. "Mister Federal Agent here is just sizing us up, trying to trip us up, because he's trained not to trust people. If he knew what he was doing, he'd interview Harvey. He acted—"

"We can't find Harvey," Guardino said. "We don't know if he—"

The federal agent's eyes flashed at Detective Guardino, who pursed his lips and looked at the floor. Having lost his secret, the fed went on: "His boat was found circling in the Sound. No Harvey."

"We don't know where he is. Period," Yvonne said.

Kevin felt a chill crawl over his skin. "You have a theory?" he asked.

"We thought you might help," the agent said.

"Why? How?" Kevin said.

The fed said nothing, but Yvonne thought she knew. "They think we might be partners with Harvey," she said. "Partners in crime."

"What bullshit," Kevin said.

"All the same, we can't find Harvey." For the first time, the federal agent had allowed some humanity to soften his voice—too late, Kevin and Yvonne thought.

"We can't help," Kevin said.

"The police told you, I suppose, how weird, belligerent, he was the other morning, when we took our boat away—" Yvonne stopped. Had it only been the other morning?

"You do have a theory," Kevin said. "About Harvey."

"We think he collected a bundle and skipped the country," the fed said, then he shrugged. "So far as we know, you were the last people to see him."

"Shit," Kevin said. "How much more trouble can we get into?"

"You cops better get your act together and look for the real source of the trouble," Yvonne said. "You have one missing, an innocent bystander beat up, and we're just lucky we're not corpses." She was flaming.

"Come on," Guardino said in a gentle, slightly embarrassed voice. "Your ride is waiting."

"Stay in touch," the fed said.

Yvonne shot him a scorching glare.

They were on the Long Island Expressway. Almost subconsciously, Kevin reached across the back seat of the police car and put his hand on Yvonne's. "I remember something you told me once," Kevin said.

"What?"

"That people don't really change. Deep down."

Damn him, Yvonne thought. She had welcomed his hand as a

friendly, comforting gesture. Now, she figured it was a come-on. It was just like him, she thought, to remember one hurtful remark and forget more important things. She had said that thing about people not really changing when he had promised (for the tenth or hundredth time) to cut down on his drinking and cut out his betting.

"I don't suppose you recall anything else from that conversation," she said.

But Kevin was thinking of something altogether different. "I meant Harvey," he said.

"What about Harvey?"

"That fed's theory about him going to another country? It's all bullshit."

Yvonne sat up straighter. She had misread him; now she told him with her silence to go on, for she had never stopped believing in his hunches.

"Harvey's set in his ways."

"Yes?"

"You know. Fart around the boats all day, do just enough work to keep his yard going. Then gin and beer at Chowder's."

"Okay."

The cop-driver picked up his microphone and responded to a radio message. Kevin went on: "That's his life, see? He wouldn't change that much. He wouldn't leave his boat and his boatyard—and Chowder's; he wouldn't leave his social life at Chowder's to go off to another country. Forever and ever. He just wouldn't."

Yvonne let that sink in. Probe, she told herself. "Then why was he acting so crazy? And what happened to us? And him?"

"He was doing something cute. Not planning to run to another country, not that cute. But still something too cute for him. And one thing I know for sure. Harvey is not the boss. There are bigger fish. And I think the cops know that."

Yvonne calculated quickly. "And we upset Harvey's plans, his routine, by taking our boat away. We screwed up his cute little side deal with the drugs. Just by doing something unexpected."

Kevin nodded.

The cop pulled off the highway, stopping behind a car emitting clouds of steam from under the hood. The cop got out and went to talk to the motorist.

Kevin thought about Harvey. He tried to put himself in Harvey's place, tried to imagine what Harvey would *feel*.

Suddenly, Kevin felt a wave of pity. "Harvey was afraid," he said. "He was just so afraid . . . what he needed more than anything was to stop us, somehow. . . ."

"Because once the boat changed hands . . ."

"Good-bye drugs," he said.

"So he followed us—or sent somebody to follow us."

"Harvey was out of luck anyhow, once we left with the drugs. I mean . . ."

"No, no. Listen," she said. "Maybe Harvey was just so afraid that he lied to . . . whoever. And blamed us! Told them we had stolen the drugs."

"Right! That's what I was getting at. If Harvey was really afraid, he'd make up some story to tell the higher-ups he was working for and to cover up his own double-cross. . . ."

"He would tell them he'd found out that we were stealing some drugs and taking them somewhere to sell," Yvonne said, seeing it now with great, sad clarity. "Even if they didn't believe him, they'd follow us and—"

"Board the boat to look for the drugs. And they followed you to DeeDee's, and you left before they got there. . . ."

"They thought I'd delivered drugs to her."

"Yes," Kevin said. "Harvey would say anything if he was desperate. If he was afraid for his life." He paused, felt a chill, remembered his own fear when he had seen the knife. "Who wouldn't?"

"Yes, that fits," Yvonne said.

"A little double-cross would have been Harvey's style, all right," Kevin went on. "Always looking for the shortcut, the easy way. He was just small potatoes to the organization. They used him to run errands, maybe to store stuff in his yard—"

"Of course. A million places to hide things there, and who would look?"

"Then he thought up his little scam. And then he had to lie to save his skin. . . ." Kevin let the thought trail off. He still felt a chill.

The cop was walking back to the car now.

"But . . . who are the people he lied to?" Yvonne asked. "We're not out of the woods yet. Those guys on the boat weren't the bosses either."

"Maybe not."

"If we hadn't upset things by having to take our boat away to sell it . . ."

"See," Kevin said. "I told you we shouldn't have split up."

That joke didn't go over with Yvonne, who was still thinking. "Harvey wasn't figuring on fleeing the country or anything like that," she said. "He was just doing a small-time rip-off. So where is he now?"

Kevin and Yvonne looked into each other's tired eyes. They said nothing, and didn't have to. They remembered DeeDee's face, the struggle in the boat, the gleaming knife.

The answer hung in the silence.

13

Yvonne fell in love with the house all over again when the car drove into the driveway. There it was, hunkered down among the old pines on its narrow slice of land between a couple of four-acre waterfront garden spots.

A plain house, bereft of any artistic aspirations, a functional house. Really a garage and a basement with rooms over them, a rectangle with a deck overlooking the water.

That it was *hers* now, not theirs, and that it was soon to be someone else's didn't keep her from enjoying the moment.

She was remembering some of the parties that she and Kevin had had on summer evenings, parties that had sprawled from the open space that served as kitchen, living room, and dining room down the stairs and onto the rocky beach and into the Sound.

Yvonne was about to mention one rowdy party in particular, when Kevin said, "Remember that party when Scotty went swimming with his clothes on?"

Yvonne giggled, recalling Scotty holding his drink aloft and wading into the Sound. "He didn't go swimming. Don't you remember? He said he was just washing off the gin that he'd spilled on his clothes."

"And then Rosalie called from the shore: 'Gin doesn't stain, Scotty dear.' "

"The look on Scotty's face. 'Mother! Now you tell me!' "

"Then he spent the rest of the evening dressed in an old muumuu."

Their musing was interrupted by the dog's frantic joyful barking.

"I'm going in to see Tess before she has a stroke," Kevin said.

"Ah," Yvonne said, smiling.

Kevin and Yvonne squatted beside the old Doberman as she bumped against them, wagging from her tail to her nose.

"Well, there's one thing we agree on," Kevin said.

"Absolutely." Yvonne smiled, turning her mouth away from the dog to escape the flapping tongue. The dog happily licked on, catching ear, neck, cheek, and hair, then moving on to Kevin.

"Let's give her some canned food, she's been living on the dry stuff for three days. Then I'm going to get out of these clothes. What about you? Do you want to go to your apartment and pick up some clothes and then come back?" Yvonne paused. "I think I'd feel better if you stayed over."

"I would, too."

The cop who had dropped them off had told them to call if they saw anything unusual. He was quick to tell them that the law-enforcement agencies thought they had a handle on what was happening, but just to be on the safe side, there would be a detail patrolling Duck Point Lane for a while.

"Do you still have those old sweatshirts and khaki trousers that I left here?" Kevin said.

"Oh, yes. They're on the shelf in your closet. . . . What used to be your closet."

That remark, the licorice-sweet night, and the Irish in him gave rise to sentimental longings again. "Do you think we could keep the place, Vonnie? I mean, I really liked living here."

"How would we manage that once the divorce is final?"

"Maybe it won't be. And I could live in the basement."

"I'll bet that would impress your girlfriends—living in the basement of the house your ex-wife lives in. Very classy."

No girlfriends, so far, Kevin wanted to say. But that would make him too vulnerable, so instead he laughed. "I guess it would take someone very understanding."

"How about crazy?"

"Anyway. I wish we could think of a way to keep it."

"Maybe we could rent it. I think we could get more than enough to pay the mortgage and make the repairs. But you wouldn't get a chunk of cash now to buy anything else."

"Hmmm. But I wouldn't be living here. That's what I want."

"Maybe you want to buy my half then. But I'm not going to sell out cheap. You'll have to pay the going rate."

"Well, I guess it'll have to be the cellar and I'll give up dating." Kevin laughed again.

"There is the possibility—I know it's remote, but I may have a date at some time in the future. Who's going to want to come to my house with my ex living in the basement?"

"Well, you could go to his place." Kevin was enjoying the joke now, or trying to. "That is, until you got serious. Then you'd have to confess, I guess. But by then he wouldn't be able to live without you no matter what."

"And . . .?" Yvonne was smiling.

"And I could just go on living downstairs and you and your new husband could live upstairs."

"Upstairs, downstairs, eh? . . . Well, there is one advantage that you haven't mentioned yet. We'd both get to see Tess, and we'd have a built-in dog-sitter for vacations."

"That's settled. Now let's map out the showering strategies, for tonight, I mean. You can go first and I'll feed the dog and wash the lettuce, if you have any."

"No lettuce, but some tomatoes and cucumbers. And some red onion. I think they're still edible. I have some Italian sausage in the freezer, and I can make some pasta in the machine."

"Great. I'll make the garlic and oil for the pasta, if you have those. . . ."

"Of course. You start on the cutting. I'll pick up where you leave off."

Yvonne started toward the bathroom, but turned back toward the living room. Kevin watched her happily, wondering what she was doing. When she returned to the kitchen area, she was carrying something behind her back.

"Here. Open this and let it breathe."

"Right! . . . Jesus! It's that great Chianti! Yahoo!"

"Don't shake the wine!" Yvonne said, turning again toward the bathroom. "And try to make this enough, instead of having five beers afterward."

"Four, then."

They had finished eating and were cleaning up the kitchen when the phone rang. Kevin gathered from the one side of the conversation that he heard that it was Rosalie and she was coming over. He would rather have had Yvonne to himself, Rosalie's dog-sitting and all the help she gave Vonnie notwithstanding.

"Rosalie wants to hear our adventures. She said she'll give me a brief computer lesson, too. Just enough to get me started while she has the time. Maybe I could use a dose of everyday life just now." Pause. "But I hope she doesn't stay too long. I'm starting to feel whipped."

"Me, too," Kevin said, meaning that he hoped she didn't stay too long.

"The computer is still in the box it came in. I guess I'd better start unpacking it."

"Wait for Rosalie. She'll probably know what to unpack first and save you a few steps."

"True. Okay. I won't desert you in the kitchen."

"That wasn't why—"

"Just kidding."

Rosalie drove in the driveway before the cleaning up was finished.

"What did she do? Call from her car?" Kevin said.

"She only lives down the road."

"She couldn't walk from her bedroom to her garage in the time she took to get here," Kevin said.

"I'll grant you that—in that big house of hers. But maybe she called from the kitchen."

"The car. I'll bet you."

"Never mind betting," Yvonne said.

Kevin stopped speculating on where Rosalie had called from and started wishing that there weren't little buzz words like "bet" that could open the doors on so much bad feeling.

Rosalie swept in, trailing chiffon and preceded by bundles.

"This is for Tess," she said, putting down a bag on the dining-room table, "and this is for you two. Tell me that you haven't had dessert yet." She watched Kevin and Yvonne shake their heads. "Wonderful. I've brought profiteroles. Just zap this in your microwave for a minute and a half," she said, giving Yvonne a jarful of chocolate sauce.

"Will you join us?" Yvonne said.

"Is the Pope Catholic?" Rosalie laughed. "Just don't remind me of all the money I pay my nutritionist . . . until after I'm done eating."

"What is this dessert?" Kevin asked.

"Profiteroles," Rosalie said in her best French accent.

"Oh, well, now that you say it in French . . ." Kevin said.

"You remember . . . we had them at Chez Susanne," Yvonne said.

"Am I in heaven, or what?" said Kevin.

"Not heaven, must be what," Rosalie said. "But tell me about your adventures."

As she said that, Kevin felt Rosalie's hand on his forearm. As he looked into her eyes, which were clear and wise, measuring him, she squeezed his arm and smiled slightly.

Yvonne had put the sauce in the microwave and was getting out three dessert bowls when she heard Tess bark.

"She wants to come in again, Kevin. Besides, Tess hasn't had the treat Rosalie brought."

"I'll get her as soon as we finish dessert," Kevin said.

Yvonne looked impatient, exasperated. "Dish out the dessert, I'll get the dog. Then we'll fill Rosalie in on everything."

"Okay," Kevin said. There were some commands he felt didn't need obeying. Sometimes Yvonne was just plain bossy. "Rosalie, you can pour on the sauce."

Yvonne was already on her way down the stairs, wondering why she was so pissed. Was it such a big deal? Did the dog have to come up right away? "Coming, Tess." Yvonne thought she heard the dog whine. She opened the door to the run, but the dog was not at the opening. Yvonne opened the door wider, and to her horror the dog was lying on her side, still.

"Tess! Tess! Oh, Tess!" No, God, not this too. Yvonne started toward the animal, afraid of what she would find, when she was caught from behind roughly and pulled back out of the pen.

She wheeled around and felt her dinner pressing up against her lungs as she was confronted by two figures. Bright ski masks, one yellow, one fire-engine red. Goggles around the eyes. They pointed guns at her.

"Shut up. Get up the stairs," one of them said in a thick whisper.

This time, we'll die, we can't be lucky enough to live through something like this again. I'm going to go through what DeeDee did,

Yvonne thought. She decided she had nothing to lose by screaming. But the bigger of the two was ready for her and had covered her mouth before the scream could form. He had big arms and smelled of musk under the detergent smell of a bright-yellow jacket. It's washable, she thought. Yvonne briefly wondered why she was taking note of all this. It would be futile this time, she was sure. His hand smelled of something she had smelled before. Somewhere. What was it?

Kevin was startled to hear so many footsteps coming into the house—two people? three? Where was Vonnie? There was Vonnie, her face pale and pleading, shoved roughly through the kitchen and into the living room by two creatures from a nightmare.

"They killed Tess," Yvonne said, starting to cry.

"They what?" Kevin said, talking a half-step toward them. But his courage was gone, replaced only by childlike terror, even before he saw the guns, before a gun butt smashed into the side of his face.

He went down hard, toppling a standing lamp as he fell, the glass crashing into pieces as it struck the wall. He knew the kick that went into his ribs was a hard one, but he already had too much pain to feel the difference.

From way above him, far away, he heard the sounds of slaps, then screams that were quickly muffled. Vonnie had screamed, then Rosalie. Then Kevin heard only the muffled gagging sounds the women made as they tried to scream.

Another slap, then another, and Kevin recognized somehow that it was Rosalie who was trying to breathe her pleas for mercy through some kind of cloth gag.

Then other slaps, one, two, three, closer—Vonnie!—and Kevin prayed. Don't let them kill Vonnie.

Unable to get off the floor, worried that he would choke to death on the food that threatened to rush into his throat from his stomach, Kevin turned his head and managed to look up. All he wanted to do was plead, to tell them that they could have anything they wanted, but they already knew that.

It was a mistake for Kevin to look, because the next moment he saw a shoe grow large, blotting out all the light, as the tip of it rammed into his nose. Kevin heard a loud sob, as near to a scream as Vonnie could get, before everything went dark for him.

* * *

Yvonne had been pushed down roughly onto the couch and had scrambled to an upright position. A yellow kerchief had been tied across her mouth, cutting the corners. It, too, had the familiar smell. It made her retch.

Her arm ached where the bigger man had twisted it behind her back. Her faced burned where it had been slapped repeatedly. Her head was pounding with fear and the tourniquet-tightness of her kerchief.

Why haven't they killed us yet? she thought, and at the same moment thought of the dog. Oh, Tess. Poor innocent baby.

And then she saw the shoe crash into Kevin's face and saw his eyes roll back and the blood gush onto the carpet. And she gasped, sobbed, choked.

Poor Kevin. He's as much an innocent baby as Tess. Have they killed him? Oh, Kevin. Live, please. She stared at the blood. So much blood. Will he bleed to death? Let it clot; oh, let it stop. Could she clot it by staring at it? Could she will the blood to stop? Was he still breathing? Will he choke to death on all the blood?

As she stared she felt her left eye closing. She could not keep it open. Then there was more blood. Hers. Dripping onto her shirt. And the big horrid face was looking into her other eye. The moment seemed to last forever. Yvonne could no longer hear what was said. Only the pounding, pounding, rushing blood. And then the room began to spin and she fell, spinning, down, down.

When Kevin regained consciousness, it was like coming to the surface through a hundred fathoms of pain. At first, he heard the faraway sounds of furniture being shifted and bumped, of heavy feet trodding carelessly through the house.

Vonnie's gone and sold the house, Kevin told himself. The movers are here and they're taking everything away.

No, that wasn't right.

He tried to breathe deeply, to wake himself up, but the blood going into the back of his throat made him gag and cough. Then he remembered.

Kevin opened his eyes, saw a saucer-size bloodstain on the carpet near his face. My blood, he thought, mine.

He listened carefully, tried to think through the pain. The heavy footsteps were far away, in another room. Slowly, he raised his head. There was Rosalie, tied to a chair, a towel around her mouth. Her eyes met his: Be still, they told him, be still and pray that they go away.

Kevin shifted his head, every little movement filling his face with pain. He wondered if his nose had been broken.

There, there was Vonnie! Tied to the sofa, her head rolled to one side. Oh, Jesus, is she dead? They had hit her. One eye was swollen shut. Her puffed, reddened cheeks glistened with tears.

Kevin's lights went out again.

Yvonne heard a voice pierce the darkness. A man said, "They're both out."

Another voice whispered, "Can it."

"They can't hear." The voice shifted to a whisper. "You got it, boss."

Yvonne decided to play possum and maybe groan a little. No sense giving them any more reason to hurt her, she thought. She remembered Kevin and all the blood pouring from his nose and wanted to open her eyes again. "Aannhh," she moaned, then listened. Footsteps, going away from her. More steps—in the bedroom, in the kitchen, then down the stairs. Heavy footfalls going down the stairs. A few seconds later footsteps coming up, lighter steps. Yvonne groaned again and lifted her head, trying to open both eyes and having only one respond.

The smaller intruder, wearing a pink jacket, was carrying the TV through the kitchen and heading toward the stairs. Thieves. Here. After all the other—drug dealers, thugs—now thieves. Why here? With all the fancy neighbors. Why us? She was about to protest with a grunt through the gag, but she caught Rosalie's eye.

Rosalie shook her head slightly and knitted her brows, as if to say, "Hush."

When Kevin started to come to again, the footsteps were much louder, more rapid. Just like the movers, he thought. When they're near the end of a job and a place is almost empty, they can move around faster and there's less to absorb the sound.

Wait. These aren't the movers.

"Couple of TVs, a camera with a long lens . . ."

"A microwave. Cheap model, but what the hell. Niggers in Queens will love it. Hear that?"

Was the voice talking to him? Kevin wondered. It didn't matter; he couldn't answer, could barely open his eyes into slits that saw only the carpet fiber, close up, with his blood on it.

Heavy steps from the small bedroom. "Bingo!" a voice said. Sounds of heavy cardboard being ripped open. "Lookit. A computer. Brand new!"

"We'll find a Wall Streeter who wants a bargain. Get a thou for it, I bet."

As he drifted in and out of awareness, sometimes stopping in the station of half-consciousness with the noises that seemed to come from a dream, Kevin felt profoundly sorry. He had heard a lot of stories about burglaries in the posh communities of Long Island. He had even reported about them for his newspaper. Some of the bigger houses in the better neighborhoods—their owners were often the ones hardest hit. There had been cases of men and women tied up, beaten, abused, forced to watch as their homes were emptied. Sometimes even . . .

Kevin felt profoundly sorry for those people; he was one with them now.

"Hell of a computer," he thought he heard a voice say. "Never been used, still in the box."

Good, Kevin thought. Maybe that will make them happy and they'll leave. He was beyond wishing for anything else: just let them leave, he prayed.

The heavy footsteps were close now. He was afraid they would kick him some more as he lay on the carpet. If they kick me again, I'm probably going to die, he thought. This is what it's like.

"How you feeling?" a voice from above him called. "Want some more?"

Kevin tried to say no, tried to plead, but all he could manage was a moan. Should he try to crawl toward the wall to gain some protection? No, if they wanted to, they could just drag him back into the middle of the floor and break every bone in his body.

Besides, Kevin realized, his hands were tied behind him. Something seemed to be cutting into his wrists; a belt, perhaps.

"We're going now," said a cackling whisper above Kevin.

"Are you happy we're going? Are you happy?"

Kevin moaned.

"Good. Now you won't have so much furniture to worry about if you move."

"Let's go," the other voice said.

"Should we work them over again, just for the hell of it?"

"No. We did enough. C'mon."

And then, quickly, they stomped out the back door, slammed it loudly and were gone.

Kevin sent up a prayer of thanksgiving. He was alive, Yvonne was alive. He wasn't crippled; he knew that because he could move his arms and legs.

He didn't know how much time went by. He was awakened by the motion of someone loosening the belt that bound his hands behind his back.

"Kevin . . . oh, Kevin, Jesus . . . Kevin . . ." Vonnie's voice, right behind him and above. Oh, she was the one, she was the one loosening the belt. "Oh, Kevin . . ."

His hands were free. Something wet and cold on his forehead, and on the back of his neck. Cold and good. Something wet and cold on his face now, being rubbed gingerly around his nose. Now he could focus on the carpet fibers just in front of his eyes.

Kevin raised his head, put it down again in dizziness. "Vonnie," he said.

"Kevin, oh God. Kevin."

The police, Kevin thought. Got to call them. He pushed up with an arm; yes, he could make it through the pain now, nothing broken. Vonnie held his other arm; she was already standing, and she was helping him to his feet.

Kevin looked at her face, bruised and swollen. "Oh, Vonnie, Vonnie. Jesus Christ."

"They're gone. They're gone."

"The police! Goddamn them, I gotta call—"

"They're on their way," Rosalie said. She was standing in the doorway to the living room. One side of her face was reddened, but she had fared better than Kevin and Yvonne.

"Rosalie got loose first, then she undid me," Yvonne said.

Kevin put his arm over Yvonne's shoulders, and she put her arm around his waist. Together they stood, sharing a sense of violation.

"After all we've been through," Kevin hissed through bloody lips. "Fight off a bunch of drug dealers, a friend of ours gets beat up, and the police back home can't even keep us safe. . . ."

He had to stop, because he was close to tears. Yvonne was already crying, her head resting on Kevin's shoulder. Kevin fished out his handkerchief, thought of offering it to Yvonne, then thought he had better use it to dab his bloody nostrils.

"Thank God we're alive," Rosalie said.

They looked at her. Her eyes, even after what they had all been through, were cool and wise. Never had she seemed so formidable to them.

Yvonne remembered the sight of their Doberman, lying on her side. "They killed Tess," she said.

Those words almost made Kevin's knees buckle. In his terror and pain, he had forgotten. "I loved her. I did," he said.

Kevin stumbled toward the back door. After all the dog had meant, he had to see her, had to bear witness to her suffering, had to tell her how much she had meant. Even if she couldn't hear.

He had tears in his eyes by the time he walked out the door into the sweet-smelling night. The tears blurred the light from the moon and stars, making it hard for him to focus on the backyard. He bit into his already sore lip to keep from crying too much (he didn't care if Yvonne saw him, but he didn't want Rosalie or the police to see him). He tried to steel himself for the sight of the dog's body by breathing deeply, but that hurt his ribs.

And then he heard Tess's gentle, friendly whine.

"Tessie, Jesus! Tessie."

She limped toward him from the end of the run, favoring a rear leg. But her tail was wagging, her tongue flicking at his face as he knelt. She was alive, alive, alive.

Kevin turned his head. "Vonnie!" he shouted toward the back door. "Tess is okay!"

But Yvonne had already seen. She was rushing toward the dog, feeling no shame at all in her joyful crying as she knelt.

The dog scrambled to lick one face, then the other, its tail wagging furiously. Then the dog began to lick tentatively at Kevin's shirt, where some blood had caked.

Yvonne grinned. "She's not sure she's supposed to like that."

"Blood is blood, isn't it, old girl," Kevin said, rubbing the dog behind her ear. "She was limping. Something's the matter with one of her back legs."

Yvonne and Kevin examined the dog's hind quarters and found a small puncture. The dog shied when they touched her near the wound.

"Did they shoot her? Is that a bullet wound?" Yvonne asked.

"Easy, girl," Kevin said, pressing the flesh on the dog's flank. "There's something sticking out of here. A tranquilizer dart."

"Bastards."

"Hey, you two," Rosalie called from the back door. "The police are here."

14

It was barely light and the birds had set up their usual morning chorus when Yvonne opened her eyes. Her left one was open today, the swelling having subsided. Another day . . . She sighed, thinking that she was lucky to be alive and hearing the birds. And in the next moment, she was angry and resentful and wondering why Providence had picked her to dump misfortune on.

The police had treated the robbery as if it were an isolated incident, but she was not convinced of that. Too much of a coincidence, she thought. Especially with so many bigger houses nearby. The cops had an answer for that, too: "But they all have security systems, Mrs. McNulty." As if it's my fault that my house was robbed, because I don't have a security system. And then that crack about Kevin and me being split: "They may have been watching the house and knew you were living alone."

To hell with that. Anybody could see I wasn't alone yesterday. Rosalie's car was in the driveway; they couldn't come up with an answer to that. And then all the rigmarole filling in this law-enforcement agency with this piece of information and that bunch of cops with this other item that they didn't know about. You'd think we were the crooks. They ask a million questions and then ask them all over again. "Who's DeeDee Lockwood?" "What's her connection to the drugs that were found in your boat?" "Why were you motoring to Haviland Marina?" "What were you doing in Edgecliff?" "How long have you known Harvey?" When was the last time you saw Harvey?" "Did you know Tolly?"

Tolly. I wonder why they were asking about Tolly. His death was an accident. He was a marina gofer all the years I knew him. It seems he was around the water forever. Even when I was a kid, when we'd go down to Chowder's for supper, Tolly was around. He always looked the same. So did Harvey. Harvey. They say he's missing. That no one has seen him since we left in our boat. Yvonne was wrenched from her thoughts by a noise in the kitchen. Her heart started to pound, and Tess, who had been sleeping at the foot of the bed, lifted her head, sniffed, and wagged her tail. "Oh, it's Kevin," she said, relieved. He had roused himself early from the sofa where he'd spent the night, and she was thankful for his presence.

She dragged herself up, feeling pain in her arm and in her back, neck, and legs as well. "They really did a job on me."

By now, Tess was whining at the bedroom door. She wants to see Kevin, she thought. She misses him.

Yvonne slipped her feet into an old pair of scuffs and pulled on a cotton robe. When she opened the door, Kevin was standing there, about to knock. "The dog wants to see you, but don't get her too excited or she'll pee on the floor."

"Good morning to you, too, Attila," Kevin said. "I'll put her right out. C'mon, Tessie girl."

While Yvonne brushed her teeth, she giggled. "Attila," she said, remembering that Kevin used to call her hon, and then later Attila the hun.

She looked in the mirror at her battered face as she washed her hands. Her eye was still puffed and was turning black. A shiner, great. She tried to remember where she had put her dark glasses. The rest of her face seemed to have come through without much bruising. Not so her arms, though. They were splotched with blue, red, and some yellow. Then she looked at her legs, which were somewhat less marked than her arms, and she thought back to the rough handling the men had given her.

When she got to the kitchen, she saw that Kevin had been up for a while. The coffee was perked, peaches were sliced for cereal, and bread, butter, and jam were at the ready next to the toaster. She smiled at Kevin, who looked as if he had been waiting for just such a smile. "It's nice to have you here. I feel spoiled," she said.

"I think you could use a little spoiling right about now," he said.

"Tell you what. I'll spoil you a little. How would you like some Newburg tonight?"

"You've made my day. It's almost worth all the trials."

"Not really."

"No. Not really. What the hell has been happening? Have you got any ideas?"

"I was wondering this morning why those guys put on such elaborate disguises."

"Maybe we would have recognized them without the masks."

"As I was coming to, I heard one of them talking in a normal voice. He said, 'They're both out.' But he rolled his *r* a little. Then the other one told him to can it. Then he went back to his whisper and he called the other one 'boss.' "

"Boss? Hmmm. Do you remember anybody built like one of those guys? You're always good at checking out the way people are built. Your old figure-study classes may come in handy now."

"It's hard to remember anything except the bright colors. I remember that the big one smelled of musk and something that I've smelled before, but I can't remember where."

"Musk is everywhere. But what was the other smell? Lighter fluid? Cleaning fluid? Weed killer?"

"I don't know. I'll remember when I smell it again."

"Those jackets were beauts, too. Hot pink and canary yellow. You'd think the cops would have noticed a couple of people decked out like that. The cops said they were right at the turn into Duck Point Lane until they got the call to come to our house after the robbery. If they went by, the cops should have seen them."

"If they went by? If they didn't pass the cops, they came from another house on Duck Point Lane or from a boat or from a plane. And where's our stuff? Where's their car? And why us? I don't buy the cops' explanation that they picked this house because there's no security system, and because I live alone."

"They arrested the three who worked us over at Haviland. Maybe these two were the guys that got on the boat that night in Edgecliff." He corrected himself at once. "No. The guys in Edgecliff spoke Spanish. All I can remember from last night is the bright colors. And the pain."

"Yes, but was there anything about—are you sure these were

different guys? Is there anything at all you remember? A voice print in your brain, perhaps."

"All I got was a footprint on my face."

"Well, if the ones last night were different from the ones on the boat at Edgecliff . . ."

"Then we've got two more guys to watch out for. Terrific . . ."

They nibbled at their food halfheartedly, each chewing carefully to avoid the sore spots.

"At least if we have Newburg tonight, we don't have to chew too hard," Kevin said.

"How is your poor face this morning? All things considered, you look pretty good."

"All things considered is right. I did look in the mirror this morning, so you can cool it with that blarney. You're not the Irishman."

"Well, you are recognizable."

Kevin laughed. " 'Recognizable' is not the same as 'pretty good.' Ouch."

"Don't tell me. It only hurts when you laugh, right?"

"Right. I guess I'm lucky that nothing is broken. Not even my nose, which used to break at every football practice."

The police had given them a ride to North Shore Hospital the night before, where the doctors and nurses in the emergency room had greeted them with inquisitive looks and professional sympathy. Rosalie had declined the policemen's offer, saying she would go to her own doctor.

"What happened? What happened?" Kevin and Yvonne had been asked several times by the ER people.

"Burglars," Kevin said finally, just wanting them to shut up.

"Really?" a middle-aged nurse said.

Suddenly, Yvonne understood. "We didn't beat each other up," she said. "This isn't domestic violence, okay?"

Kevin and Yvonne winced as their wounds were cleaned and bandaged. Then they had X rays. The best news was that Kevin had no broken ribs.

A young doctor studied Kevin's face, pressed around his eyes, managed to hit all the sore spots with his fingers. He told Kevin to put his head back and shined a pen-sized flashlight up his nose.

"Well," the doctor said cheerily, "it's not broken. But you did sustain some trauma to the nostril tissues."

"No shit," Kevin said.

The police had driven them home. With painkillers from the hospital, Kevin and Yvonne had even managed to sleep fairly well. They had had their nightmare before closing their eyes.

"Kevin. If that was not a regular robbery, what was it? And what were they after?"

"If it wasn't a regular robbery, I guess it was an irregular robbery."

"Be serious."

"Okay. Hey, do you realize that they didn't take the VCR? Our friends in law enforcement didn't notice that last night."

"What?" Yvonne got up and went into the living room. There, on the shelf under where the TV used to be, was the VCR. "They had to unplug the TV from it to take the TV. And yet they didn't take the VCR. Strange." Yvonne put her hands on her hips and stretched her back. "Oooh. I am so stiff. What I need is three days in a hot tub."

"When we make up the list for the cops and the insurance company, we'll mention the fact that the thieves didn't take the VCR," Kevin said. "You know, they didn't bother with any of the kitchen appliances except for the microwave. Do you think that's strange, too?"

"I don't know. Maybe kitchen stuff is harder to fence. But we can tell the cops that, too. Let's see, there's the toaster, the mixer, the food processor, the blender, the pasta maker, the ice-cream maker."

"They mustn't have spent much time in the kitchen at all. Some of this stuff should be fenceable. They took fairly cheap stuff from the bedroom. The clock radio, for instance, and the little TV, and your Walkman, for Chrissake."

"You're right. They were pretty selective. Maybe their fence gave them a list. Maybe they were after something that they knew was in the bedroom. Jesus! Suppose someone stashed drugs here, too!"

"Who? Nobody's been in the house but you and me. Even Rosalie didn't have a key when she was feeding the dog."

"Okay. No drugs stashed. But what then?" Yvonne walked back into the bedroom and came out again. "You're right. They did a pretty thorough job on the bedroom. They got my new computer before I even took it out of the box. There must have been four or five boxes of stuff with the computer."

"Yeah," Yvonne said. "We were pissed at him, but we never would have wished this on him."

"Mmmm. At least you're in the clear now. And the DEA guy won't be bothering you anymore."

"The prick," Kevin said.

"You mean agent Belcher? Bilker?" Yvonne said.

"Bleucher," Guardino said, chuckling. "I was wondering if you mangled his name on purpose."

"What about our boat?" Kevin asked.

"It'll be released before too much longer."

"Is that real time, or federal-government time?" Yvonne asked.

"It won't be tomorrow. A month, maybe. Meantime, the Port Guinness people say they have some good leads on your house burglary."

"Terrific," Kevin said without enthusiasm, for he knew from his newspaper experience that the police were usually closer to solving a [cri]me when they had *one* lead, not several, and that when they had a [goo]d lead they didn't talk about it.

["U]h, just one other thing," Guardino said.

["Y]eah?"

"[Th]e Port Guinness police would, uh, appreciate it if you and your [wife] wouldn't, you know, say too much about what happened. I mean, [the] whole thing in general, but especially . . ."

"[Espe]cially the part about how we had the shit beat out of us and our [house trashed] while they were guarding us."

"[Yes]. They're pretty upset over this. I mean, really upset. [If you were] to read . . ."

"[Don't worry]," Kevin said. "I just write about pro football this time [of year. Noth]ing about violence and drugs."

"Could the cops be right? That the burglary was unrelated . . ."

"I hope they're watching Duck Point Lane better than they were yesterday," Yvonne said, agitated. "Look, the guys on the boat are in custody. When they boarded, they were looking for drugs. They were looking for drugs at DeeDee's too."

"If these guys are part of the same gang, what are they looking for? And why didn't they question us?"

"Where are the cops today?" Yvonne said, getting up again and going to the bedroom window, which looked over the driveway and toward the road.

"Do you see them?" Kevin hollered from his perch at the kitchen table. It hurt him to move despite the fact that he had no broken bones.

"Not yet. Oh yes, there they are. Parked right next to the driveway." Yvonne was on her way back to the kitchen. "Maybe we should tell them it's all right to use the conveniences . . . offer them some coffee."

"Do you mind if I just sit here?"

"You hurt, don't you? Do you want me to get you some of the pain pills?"

Kevin nodded. The pain really was closing in. His chest felt as if it were in a vise. "Would you mind if I took over the bed for a little while?"

"Be my guest."

Kevin got up slowly, grimacing. "Well, I am sort of your guest." He felt terribly old and feeble as he made his way painfully toward the bed. Once he was lying down, though, the pain left him and he felt the tension in his limbs uncoil. The bed felt good. His bed. His and Vonnie's bed.

Two hours later, when Kevin opened his eyes, he thought that he had just closed them a moment before. But then he noticed that the light was brighter and lifted his head to see the clock. But the clock was gone. He seemed to ache less and remembered what he had heard about the curative powers of sleep, thinking that maybe he would nod off again.

No. There were things to do. Got to help Vonnie get the list ready. No clock. What time was it? He sat up gingerly, expecting the pain to pounce on him again, and was relieved to find it much less intense. He felt almost cheerful.

"I called the insurance company," Yvonne said as he entered the living room. "They're sending an adjuster out today."

"Were they nice?"

"Pretty much. They asked if we'd called the police, and I told them we had. The woman was sympathetic when I told her a little of what happened."

"Good," said Kevin, heading toward the coffeepot. He noticed as he pulled a cup from the cupboard that he couldn't keep his hand from shaking. By the time he had made himself some toast and poured the coffee, the shaking had subsided somewhat. But he held on to the toast plate and the coffee cup carefully as he walked back across the living room and planted himself on the couch. He saw that Yvonne had swept away the broken glass and had sprayed carpet cleaner where his nose had bled. "Thanks for cleaning up," he said.

Yvonne nodded, smiled a "you're welcome" and sat down across from him. "We're alive," she said.

"Barely," he said. Then he felt a nose nudge his elbow. "Tessie, baby, I bet you came by for a treat."

Kevin held a toast end in his mouth, bent forward and let the Doberman take the toast gently, if somewhat wetly.

"You two," Yvonne said in mock rebuke. "You keep doing that, and the next time we have dinner guests Tess will—"

She stopped, realizing the implications of what she was saying.

Kevin knew why she stopped, but he let her off the hook by continuing to fuss over the dog. "Good old Doberman, you even smell good. At least, I think you do."

"She was limping just a little this morning, but I think she's okay. I called Port Guinness Animal Hospital. They said to watch her for a day or two, but as long as she got through last night, she should be fine . . ."

"Weird," Kevin said.

". . . that it was most likely a regular animal tranquilizer dart. What's weird?"

"Those bastards last night. They pound the shit out of us, take everything we own. Mean, right? But they spare the dog."

"There's no figuring. Just be thankful. . . . But wait! They had to

come prepared with an animal tranquilizer. They knew there was a dog here. They must have been watching the house. Oh, it gives me the creeps to think of someone watching the house."

"But—" Kevin was getting agitated. "Those mugs on the boat would have killed Tess without a second thought. These guys were just playing at violence. But I can't believe it's not connected."

"Tell the cops that. See if they'll listen."

"They're not the greatest listeners, are they? For them, crime unfolds in a certain way. It's like the newspaper business, you know the old line, 'We've always done it that way.'"

And then the phone rang. Yvonne answered it. It was Dete[ctive] Guardino.

"Wait a minute," she said. "We both want to hear this."

Yvonne handed the phone to Kevin and went to the bedr[oom to pick] up the other extension.

"I've got some news for you," Guardino said. "You [know a guy] named Quince?"

"Yeah," Kevin said.

"We just picked him up."

"For what?" Yvonne said.

"The three guys we arrested at the Georg[e . . .] us a lot about him. First one broke, and [then the others found their] voices. Quince ran a cocaine warehous[e . . .] a lot of Long Island."

"I never liked him," Yvonne sai[d . . .]

That's right, Kevin thought. Sh[e . . .]

"Our boys tell us Quince ma[y . . .]

"Well, where is he?" Kevi[n . . .]

"We think we know abo[ut . . .] Sound for him," Guardin[o . . .]

Yvonne felt a twist [. . .] happened to him?" [. . .]

"The three guys [. . .] waders on," the [. . .]

"Oh, Lord," Y[vonne . . .]

"Jesus," Kevin sai[d . . .] used to take care of our b[. . .]

15

The sports department was in the far corner of the newsroom. As Kevin walked around the perimeter of the battleship-sized floor, he looked straight ahead so that his eyes would meet as few eyes as possible. He longed for the days when the news floor reverberated with the staccato of typewriters. The noise created shields of privacy. Two people could talk without being overheard ten feet away, and a person could walk through the newsroom almost unnoticed.

But the typewriters had been replaced by green-glowing terminals and the soft clickety-click of their keyboards and their gentle hum.

Kevin felt almost naked. He was scarcely halfway to his desk when he heard the voice.

"Jeez, Kevin, what happened to you?" The voice belonged to Carol (Kevin didn't remember her last name), a clerk who Kevin thought was cute (though too young for him) and always greeted cheerfully.

"Long story," he said. "Tell you soon. Honest." He was brusque, and when he saw her feelings had been hurt he added, "Had a little boating accident."

Kevin kept walking. He reached the safety island of his desk, scanned the morning paper, read his messages. Good; they were all routine. He was not in the mood for surprises.

Kevin saw a reporter colleague walking across the room toward him, curiosity all over his face. Kevin picked up the phone, pressed it against a sore ear, pretended to take notes as he listened to the dial tone. He was psychologically strung out, and he wasn't ready for questions about how his skin had got to be all puffy and scratched and bruised and where had he been the early part of the week.

The insurance adjuster had been sympathetic and helpful and told them they would get a check within a couple of weeks. But Kevin and Yvonne had to figure out what to buy with the money, now that they had two households. Which was in itself depressing for Kevin.

Marty Diehl was still waffling on whether to buy the boat, once it was out of impoundment.

Yvonne was still upset about DeeDee Lockwood; she was unable to forget the image of her in the hospital. Neither could Kevin.

Worst of all, Kevin was going to go back to his own apartment tonight, an apartment that was adequate for his needs and was not that uncomfortable. Except that it had no dog, no style. No Vonnie.

He put the phone down and opened a brown interoffice envelope; the message inside was from Bruce Dunning, the competent but unflamboyant sports editor: "Kevin, welcome back. Hope you had a nice vacation."

Kevin paused, laughed ruefully to himself. He had told his editor he needed the time off for some urgent personal business, not a vacation. It was Wednesday, five days since they had taken their boat out of Port Guinness. God, that was a long time ago. Kevin had told his editor originally that he needed extra time because he had to sell his boat. The editor had looked puzzled, and Kevin had told him quietly that he and his wife were splitting and he just had to have the time. The sports editor had said, "Sorry to hear that; take all the time you need." There was hardly a newspaper editor alive who wasn't familiar with marriage problems.

Kevin read on: "Joe B. is honcho today. I told him you could do a story on what's wrong with the Jets's secondary—other than the fact they can't stop a passing attack."

Kevin knew at once which one of his sources to tap. He would call Chili Wilkins.

Chili Wilkins was a retired, now legendary defensive back of the Jets, one of the few in football who had managed to star in what were almost two different eras. He had been great several years back, when the defensive backs were allowed to bump the receivers quite a bit, and had starred after the bumping rules were tightened.

The more recent rules placed a higher premium on speed and finesse. Chili Wilkins had made the transition, had been a perennial all-pro, would no doubt be in the Hall of Fame.

"God gave me speed and grace as well as strength and courage," he had said. "Why shouldn't I be able to change my style?"

After retiring, Chili Wilkins had settled in Great Neck, a few miles west of Port Guinness, and opened a Chevy dealership. He was hard not to like, partly because the NFL's public-relations machine regularly featured him on its nostalgia films at halftime, partly because he treated people right.

Kevin thought he was one of the nicest people he had ever met in sports, and he was that way without being either arrogant or self-conscious about being black. Or so Kevin thought, having filtered it all through the prism of his Irish, quasi-Catholic prejudice.

He shook the depressing thoughts out of his head, or tried to. And he dialed.

"Chili Wilkins Chevrolet."

"Kevin McNulty from the *Long Island* sports department. Is Chili in?"

"Please hold."

"Chili Wilkins speaking."

"Hi. I have a sixty-five Corvair with dogshit on the tires and I'd like to trade it in for a new Pimpmobile with bucket seats."

"Kev-IN, you dumb honkie! How are you, my man?"

"Surviving." Kevin was glad that the racial humor was out of the way; his heart wasn't really in it, but Chili always expected it of him. "What can I do for you, my man?"

"Got a few minutes to talk about pass coverage?"

"Why not."

Kevin asked a few questions, told Chili that he had bet and lost on the Packer game. Chili chuckled, then started to talk, smoothly and easily.

Chili had always been great with the quotes, and Kevin took down his words (or at least the ones he was sure he'd want to use) on his computer. His fingers flew in easy clicks, and the lines piled up on Kevin's green screen.

"Hold one sec, Chili." Kevin pressed the "store" button, so that everything he had taken down to that point would not vanish if there was a power failure or a thunderstorm, or if the computer coughed just for the hell of it. "Okay. You were saying?"

"I was saying there's no substitute for the great speed. You have it or you don't, man. The great speed. You can't really coach somebody to do forty yards in four point three if God wants him to do it in four and a half."

"Okay, I already know, but say it for the reader. Two-tenths of a second can mean something?"

"Man, *one*-tenth of a second can mean something. Can mean *everything*. Say I let myself get a little flabby. Say I let myself get *old*; it happens, man. So I lose a tenth—a half-step. That's the difference between my body being next to the receiver's, with my hands pretty level with his but still all legal, and my being that little bit farther away from him, enough so he can get his hands higher than mine. You dig?"

"I dig."

"Put it simple, man. At that level of competition, that fraction is everything. God gave some of us the great speed, but it never lasts. Just like youth. You know anyone who's faster at thirty than he was at twenty-five, all other things being equal?"

"No."

"Course not. Trick is to hold on to your speed and quickness as long as you can. You do that by conditioning and discipline."

"Right." Then Kevin felt his instincts kick in, and with it a question he had not planned to ask. "Do you think any of the Jets might have, you know, another kind of problem?"

Pause. "This is on deep background, man. Okay? I mean, file it away to use another time."

"Right."

"Good. So far, from what I hear, the Jets are clean. There's ways to get around the drug-testing, but I don't think they have to. They're clean."

"Good. I didn't lose my bet on somebody's high."

"Right. Only white stuff they use is foot powder. I know some guys on other teams ain't gonna hold on to their God-given gifts too long. But far as I know, the only thing wrong with the Jets is they're too slow."

"Too slow. Okay."

There was a silence on the phone; Chili's choosing his words carefully, Kevin thought.

"Trades are more complicated now than they used to be. I mean, the coaches won't say that, except way off the record. You think a coach is gonna say, 'We'd like to have so-and-so, he's got the speed, loves to hit, but we hear he snorts a line every chance he gets'? Shit, no."

Kevin sensed that Chili Wilkins had more to say. He waited.

"See, I hear a lot 'cuz of who I am and where I am. I mean, Great Neck is close enough to Queens so I know plenty about what goes on. With some of the brothers. And not just the brothers. And I hear things from people, once they trust me, you know? From addicts and users. Because of the work I do in United Way, counseling and all that."

"Right."

"Ummm, Kevin. I'll tell you something if you don't press me on it. Okay?"

"Okay."

"There was a guy, not with the Jets, a big-name star who retired at the end of last season. Said he wanted to go out while he was still on top."

Kevin had a file-card memory for retirements, trades, the waiver list and such. "I count three, maybe four guys who fit that description."

Chili Wilkins chuckled. "Good. I'll let you guess which one I'm gonna tell you about. Anyhow, he gave some bullshit about not wanting to wait until his knees went."

Kevin's mind raced: the part about the knees made it likely Chili Wilkins was talking about a running back or wide receiver. Kevin almost said something, but he stopped himself, remembering his pledge not to press.

"You listening, Kevin? It wasn't his knees at all. It was his nose. Next time you hear about this guy, it'll be when he's in drug rehab. Or in the slammer for dealing coke big-time. Or . . ."

"Or on a slab in a morgue."

"You're not hearing this from me. When the drug tycoons in Colombia declared war on the government down there, that should have opened everybody's eyes. Finally."

"To what?"

"That the drug business is like a separate nation. With its own army, its own treasury, its own foreign relations."

Kevin longed to tell Chili about his and Yvonne's ordeal, to share something with him, but the police had advised him to say as little as possible. Now he wondered how much he dared say, to anybody.

"The police arrest a few people and grab a basement full of cocaine, but so what? The whole thing is like wild berries."

"Wild berries?"

"I can tell you weren't raised in the country. You pull up a plant, chop out some shallow roots, but there's still a root growing down there, real deep. And it springs up somewhere else."

"Hmmm."

"The cops can grab up everything that shows, but it doesn't help in the long run. Because what *doesn't* show is still there. And it starts the bramble all over again."

"You know anybody like that?"

"I don't know who they are. I just know they are. I've said enough, Kevin. Just don't bet on the Jets till they get a couple of cornerbacks who're about two-tenths faster over forty yards than the ones they got. Simple as that. Listen, I gotta sell some cars. Take care."

Kevin thanked Chili Wilkins and said good-bye. After hanging up, he shivered for a moment. Wild berries?

"Kevin, how are you?"

Kevin looked up to the easygoing face of Joe Boles, the assistant sports editor. "Hi, Joe."

"What happened?" Joe Boles said.

Kevin took a deep breath; tell him and be done with it, Kevin decided. "A couple of guys invaded our house the other night. They beat the living shit out of us and ransacked the place." Kevin's voice almost broke.

"Oh, God. Is Yvonne all right?"

"Yeah. She's banged up too, but we're all right."

"Did the cops get 'em?"

"Not yet."

"Is there anything I can do?"

"No. Thanks." Kevin appreciated the kindness, but he wanted to change the subject. "I just got done talking to Chili Wilkins. Some pretty decent stuff. Nothing world-shaking but okay."

"Five or six hundred words?"

"That's about right."

"Good. You don't have to hang around too long today."

Before walking away, Joe Boles brushed Kevin's shoulder lightly with his hand, and for a moment Kevin was more full of emotion than he wanted to be.

Needing a break before he started writing, Kevin walked to a corner where there were machines for sandwiches, coffee and soft drinks, a small table and a few chairs. He bought a root beer and sat down at the table.

"How's it going?" a voice over his shoulder said.

Jesus no, Kevin thought. But he said, "Hi, Landon."

Landon Brice was the paper's Pulitzer Prize–winning investigative reporter. He was—there was no denying it—a gifted journalist: a brilliant writer as well as a tireless, ingenious fact-finder. He was highly intelligent, widely read, deeply knowledgeable about the inner workings of governments and courts from the village to the national level. He spoke a couple of languages and was an excellent cook. And he had enormous confidence in his abilities.

Kevin admired him grudgingly, but couldn't feel warm toward him. They had never socialized, even though Brice's house was just a few miles from Kevin and Yvonne's.

"Wow! You got the license number, I hope." Landon Brice chuckled.

Kevin felt the heat rush to his face. He was annoyed but said nothing; he could not match Brice's repartee even when he was in top form.

"You okay?" Brice said more seriously, as he sat down with his coffee.

"Surviving."

Landon Brice nodded solemnly and locked laser-bright eyes on Kevin's. "What happened?" he asked.

"Some guys beat us up the other night. After drugging our dog."

"Us?"

"Me and Yvonne. And a friend."

"Where?"

"Our house."

"Robbery?"

"They cleaned us out. Almost."

Brice whistled and shook his head. "And they worked you over while they were doing it."

"Sure did."

"Did they have guns?"

"Yep."

"Cops ask you a lot of questions?"

"I guess. I don't know. They're gonna talk to us again tomorrow." Suddenly, Kevin realized he was being interviewed. That was Landon Brice's way: he had to know everything, and he had an uncanny way of making people open up.

Brice frowned. "It's puzzling, in a way. No offense, Kevin, but isn't your house one of the smaller ones around Duck Point?"

"The smallest."

"So what were they doing in your place?"

"I didn't ask."

"What did the cops say?"

"They gave us some shit about not having a burglar alarm. The other thing is, I haven't been living there lately. They might've figured Vonnie was there alone."

"Ah. But you happened to be there the other night. With a friend."

"Yeah. You ask more questions than the cops." At first, Kevin had found the telling cathartic, but now he was tired of being interviewed.

"You're lucky you're alive," Brice said quietly.

"I'm really strung out," Kevin said, pausing to sip his root beer.

"Is there more?" Brice said, sounding like a confessor.

Kevin took a deep breath, let the air out slowly and began again to talk. He told about waking up to the sounds of men on the boat that night while he was in the V-berth and how terrified he was, about DeeDee Lockwood, about the struggle at the Haviland Marina and how he was both thrilled and sickened when he hit the thug's hand with the gearshift, about the discovery of the cocaine.

Brice nodded, stopping Kevin now and then with a question, and he listened. He listened.

"This guy Harvey. He's still missing?"

"Bottom of the Sound, the cops think."

"Why do they think that?"

"Because the guys arrested in New Jersey told them."

"Good. Somebody's talking."

"Enough so the cops picked up a guy in Port Guinness. Guy named Quince."

"Quince? Mmmmm. Trucking outfit?"

"Something like that. You know him?"

"No, but I think I remember rumors of some tax problems a few years back."

"Well, he seemed to do all right. Big fancy boat. Owns a lot of commercial property. Hung around Chowder's a lot. I knew him just to nod to. Kept his boat at Harvey's yard."

"Instead of at the club? That's interesting."

"We kept our boat at Harvey's too."

"You did it because it was cheap," Brice said good-naturedly. "I bet Quince had other reasons."

"I guess."

"Anyhow, sounds like you and your wife are pretty goddamn tough." A soft, respectful chuckle.

"No. We were scared to death. I'm still scared. Being scared made us strong. And maybe we had a little luck. I don't know. . . ."

"Did the cops tell you you're safe now?"

"Well, they said they thought so, with Quince and those guys arrested in New Jersey."

Landon Brice's expression reminded Kevin of a doctor about to give a patient some bad news. "Hmmmm. That doesn't guarantee anything. They didn't catch the guys who trashed you and your house. Did the cops think the whole thing was connected? The burglary, what happened to you on the boat trip?"

"Cops just told us to be careful. They didn't seem to see any connection."

Brice frowned and shook his head. "Coincidences do happen but . . ."

"Yeah, but."

"Just be careful. You and your wife stumbled into something, and who knows how far it goes, who you're stepping on. You never suspected Quince, or Harvey. Hell, I never even heard anything about them."

"Are you looking into drugs?"

"Could be. I don't like to say too much about what I'm doing. I prefer to ask questions."

"Yeah, I noticed."

Brice chuckled. "Anyhow, watch yourself. Most of us have never been involved with people like this. The pressure's on like never before, and the stakes are higher. The people who stay in the game are, if you'll excuse the expression, the best and the brightest. And the most vicious. I know mob people—physical, enforcer types—who are scared to death of drug people."

"Yeah, include me in that."

"And the people at the top are harder to catch than ever. They've got the best brains and the latest technology. All paid for in cash. They arrange their drop-offs and pay-offs at the last minute and make it all go like clockwork. Very high-tech. They do their business right next door to the supermarket or the shoe store, while some cops are still staking out warehouses at night."

Brice was making Kevin very uncomfortable. "So Quince . . . ?"

"Quince? From what you've told me, he's probably somewhere in the middle. Anyhow, they're dealing coke all over the Island. When my dad had a boat, he kept a jug of Chivas on board. Now, a good host offers his guests a snort."

Landon Brice stopped, shook his head and chuckled softly. "Don't get me wrong, I got nothing but contempt for these people. They're scum. Still, I have a grudging respect for them. Or for their ingenuity. They've forced the cops to rethink their tactics. I've been with them on lots of the usual stakeouts—dark corners, abandoned buildings, Greyhound-terminal lockers, that stuff. But now, with the distribution moving out east as well, the cops have to use their imaginations a lot more. There aren't many abandoned buildings out east, only new ones. And the traffickers use marinas, yachts, the wide-open parking lot of the new shopping malls."

Kevin sipped his root beer, directing the cool liquid over a sore spot in his mouth. He didn't feel safe at all. And Vonnie! Sometimes on her job she drove to out-of-the-way spots near the water. Isolated, winding roads near the shore. Alone. Should he call her?

What was it Brice had said? Or was it something Chili Wilkins had said?

"The winners make big, big bucks," Brice went on in his quiet, authoritative tone. "The losers, they end up like Harvey. Or like the two guys in the story the city desk is working."

"Huh?"

"Couple guys found dead in a car on a side road just off the Expressway this morning."

"Murdered?"

Brice nodded and smiled—grimly, this time. "Unless they decided to chain themselves in the car and then set fire to it."

"Jesus. Who were they?"

"Don't know yet. Cityside is trying to find out. They were pretty well barbecued. The plates were phony, it turns out. Cops were waiting for the car to cool off so they could lift the vehicle ID number. If it's not filed off."

"Damn. Oh, damn."

"Listen," Brice said, getting up to leave. "I know you've been through a lot of shit. If I can help at all, let me know."

Kevin felt slightly guilty for all the times he'd found Landon Brice insufferably pompous.

"Take care, Kevin." Brice grabbed Kevin's hand, shook it warmly, and departed.

Damn, Kevin thought, standing up. Damn. Do I know who my friends are?

On the way back to his desk Kevin passed a young reporter who was wearing a telephone headset and typing furiously. "And you don't know if they were alive or dead when the car was torched. . . . Was there an explosion? Not that you know of. . . . Car was registered to first name Ernesto? Last name . . . spell, please . . . L-U-N-E-S . . . Was he one of the victims? Checking, okay. . . . Some of the chain links were fused by the heat. Oh, gross!"

Kevin felt weak, sick. He was afraid, afraid of what could happen to him and Vonnie.

He got back to his desk and sat down.

"You okay, Kevin? You look kinda white and wobbly." Joe Boles's face was wrinkled in concern.

"I'm okay. I think."

"Feel up to writing?"

God, he had to do the Chili Wilkins story. "Sure, no sweat."

Kevin was thankful the story was an easy one to write; if he had had to *think* he might have lost it. Like a robot, he typed:

"Chili Wilkins, who starred in the Jets's secondary in an era when most defensive backs were pit bulls and later when they were greyhounds, thinks he knows what's wrong with the team's pass coverage."

No, Kevin thought. That's too corny, and not quite accurate. Some of the old defensive backs were fast as well as tough, and some of the new, fast ones could hit.

Screw it. Usually, he made his lead paragraph as grabby as he could, but now he didn't have the stomach to tinker. After typing a few more paragraphs he picked up the phone. Got to tell Vonnie what Landon Brice had said, got to tell her to be careful.

The line was busy. Damn, oh, damn. Vonnie's got to be the only one there, and she's on the phone.

What if someone tried to trick her, telling her to meet them at a house. She wouldn't go. . . . Sure, she would! Real estate people do that all the time. The call she's on right now might be a trick.

Kevin typed a couple more paragraphs, sucked in air to calm himself, hit the "store" button on his computer.

Something Brice had said, or Chili . . .

Kevin dialed again. Busy. He put the phone down, typed some more. Six hundred words was not a lot (Kevin was a fast, facile writer), and he was done before long.

Please, he prayed as he picked up the phone again. Please let her answer this time.

Ringing. Kevin breathed more easily. Okay, Vonnie, pick up. Ringing, ringing, ringing. Where the hell are you, Vonnie? In the john or what? Ringing, ringing, ringing.

"Kevin, you sure you're okay?" Joe Boles said. "You look awful. You never take sick days. Want one now?"

"Yeah, yeah. Thanks. Story's done. Want to check it out?"

Boles called up the story and scrolled through it while Kevin dialed Vonnie's office again. Busy.

"The story's fine. Get out of here."

Kevin almost trotted toward the exit. One last time he stopped, picking up a phone at a corner desk. He dialed. Please, God.

Busy.

Kevin would drive to her office, would stay with Vonnie and protect her. He would get some more time off from work, quit if he had to, and he would take Vonnie away where she would be safe. Where *they* would be safe. Vonnie and he, and Tess.

The last thing he heard as he ran out the door was the busy clickety-click of the keyboards (reporters reducing agony and death to electronic impulses on green screens) and the impersonal hum of the computers.

Dear God, just let me do this right.

16

Yvonne was looking forward to getting back to the office, back to where she would meet people whose worst aggressive behavior would be to try to steal her customer. She wondered whether she would ever stop looking over her shoulder. Even yesterday when she had gone to the supermarket, she had looked at perfectly harmless people and suspected that they were the thugs who had broken into her house or were behind the men who had boarded the boat at Edgecliff.

Perhaps she would be back to normal by the time school started in a couple of weeks. Maybe seeing the kids again would snap her out of it.

The kids. Would they seem more precious and fragile to her now that she had lost one of her own? Would she be more appreciative of the stories about the things they had done during the summer, more tolerant when they misbehaved?

And they'd all have new clothes, pristine notebooks, sharpened pencils. She remembered how it felt to go back to school, with new dresses, new shoes, a new bookbag, and . . .

Suddenly her thoughts were full of DeeDee, who had been there on all those first days of school every September, and who wouldn't be back in front of her own classes for a while.

Yvonne was thankful that DeeDee wasn't blaming Kevin and her for what Quince's men had done. Yvonne had gone to DeeDee's place with DeeDee's mother to clean up and had been nauseated by the sight of so much blood. Mrs. Lockwood had ended up comforting Yvonne. Yvonne could think only how close her friend had come to death.

Yvonne wished that she could believe in a heaven. She thought death would seem less awful if she could look forward to seeing people again whom she had lost. In a heaven, maybe the baby would eternally goo and ga.

She envied those who were certain in their faith, who were sure that death was just a door to another world. Somewhere in the Bible she had read about people who think too much. Could she put all the thoughts away and just blindly believe? How do you get faith? Pray for it?

She wondered if she would get another chance at motherhood. Maybe a little girl to name after DeeDee.

Her head was starting to ache. Too many things that she couldn't do anything about.

She'd put those thoughts away and pick out the clothes she would wear to the office. Tangibles were easier to deal with.

Yvonne chose light clothing, short sleeves, and to heck with the bruises showing. But she would take a sweater, because the office air-conditioning was always churning. Rosalie kept the office below seventy-five because, she said, it was better for the electronic equipment not to get overheated. However, Yvonne knew that Rosalie hated to sweat. Her house was kept as cold as the office, and so were the cars, for that matter.

Rosalie was just leaving when Yvonne arrived, and Yvonne asked her how she felt. It upset Yvonne that Rosalie had been beaten on her visit to her house.

"A little achy, but not too bad," Rosalie answered.

"You look wonderful. I would never know they laid a glove on you," Yvonne said, smiling.

"Makeup," Rosalie said. "Those bastards. How are you doing? And how is Kevin? And Tess?"

"We're all recovering. Kevin creaks a lot, though. I'm afraid he got the worst of it."

"Poor thing."

"You know, I was playing possum and heard one of them talk in a normal voice."

"Good for you. Did you recognize the voice?"

"No. But the police are coming to the house again tomorrow to pick our brains anyhow. Cripes, I am sick of this. What more do they think we can tell them?"

"I thought they had wrapped it up when they arrested Quince."

"I guess they want to be sure that the robbery isn't related to the drug ring. They're inclined to think it's just your plain-vanilla robbery. But Kevin and I don't think so."

"Ah. Why's that?"

"Well, for one thing, they didn't take the VCR."

Rosalie laughed. "That is odd."

"And they left a lot of the little kitchen appliances, too. It was like they were after something specific. Maybe looking for drugs there, too. I don't know. It makes my head ache to start thinking about it."

"You've been through hell," Rosalie said, patting Yvonne on her arm right where there was a big bruise.

Yvonne pulled her arm back. "Ooh. You got a sore spot."

"Oh, dear. I'm sorry. Oh, how clumsy! Listen, are you going to be in the office for a while? I'll be back late this afternoon. I'd like to talk to you then. You haven't changed your mind about going back to teaching, have you?"

"No, no," Yvonne said. A conversation with Rosalie frequently took some sharp turns.

"Too bad. See you later."

Yvonne watched her walk quickly across the sidewalk in front of the office and get into the back of her car, already cooled and waiting at the curb. Carlo, who worked in many capacities for Rosalie, today was driving a stretch limo. Business must be good, Yvonne thought, entertaining briefly thoughts about real estate as a full-time venture.

There were two other salespeople in the office today: Merle Bentsen, a sixtyish man who specialized in commercial rentals; and Betty Cavendish, whose face was in a perpetual smile from numerous face-lifts, whose blond hair was always poufed and sprayed and windproof, and who flirted with every man who walked in the office, regardless of age. Betty rarely sold anything, but she took a lot of floor time and was good at answering phones, otherwise Rosalie would have sent her packing long ago. But real estate people don't get salaries, so Rosalie had an extra secretary, gratis. And Betty actually seemed flattered whenever Rosalie asked her to do something. Yvonne almost never talked at length to either Merle or Betty, but since they were very solicitous about Yvonne's injuries and the robbery, Yvonne felt obliged to talk to them about it for a little while. She also wanted to dispel the rumors, which Melba had told her about, that Kevin and Yvonne were all banged up because they had come to blows in their marital discord. Yvonne wondered where the story had started, and suspected one of the nurses in the emergency room of being the source.

When Yvonne got to her desk, she returned the more pressing phone calls. A psychiatrist was interested in one of the houses she had listed, but he wanted to hold therapy sessions in his basement. Yvonne told the saleswoman from another office that the zoning was okay for that, but that he might have a problem if there were too many cars parked outside all the time. The saleswoman was excited, Yvonne thought. She smelled a sale. Yvonne remembered when a sale would do that to her, but that thrill had gone now. It was only money, after all, for the salesperson; but for the people it was their house, their investment. For some, it was all they had. She couldn't think about customers as sources of money anymore. Maybe that meant that she wasn't a good saleswoman. Money drives the real estate machine. "You have to apportion your day to maximize your income," the teacher of the real estate course had said way back when Yvonne had first started.

No. I can't be that way, Yvonne thought. It wasn't the first time that she found herself going one way, and the crowd, the other.

Yvonne was eager to get to work on the computer. She would be able to buy a new one, the insurance adjuster had said, because she would get full coverage on the one the thieves had taken. After all, there was nothing to depreciate; it had been brand new, still in the box. Actually, she thought the insurance adjuster had been quite liberal in the allowances he had made for their losses. She had expected him to be a lot tougher.

Before she started work on the computer, Yvonne had one more item on her agenda. Melba had called to ask Yvonne to crew for Thursday's race, and Yvonne had said she would be delighted, but her arm was still bothering her and she thought she might be slow on the winches and lose the race for Scotty. Yvonne went next door to Scotty's office and found Scotty and Erik hunched over a computer terminal.

"My God, you're working," Yvonne said in mock horror.

Scotty turned a cheerful face toward Yvonne. "Hello, beautiful. Oh, you poor baby," he said, pointing to the bruised arm. "Come sit on Scotty's lap and let him console you," he said.

Yvonne laughed. "I came to tell you that my arm is bothering me and I don't want to lose the race for you if I'm too slow."

"You wouldn't lose the race for us. We do that for ourselves every week. Besides, Erik will do all the hard work. I want you to navigate."

Yvonne was flattered and said so. "I hope I can come up to your expectations," she said.

"He has the expectations of a dirty old man," Erik said. "But don't worry, I'll protect you."

"You two. . . . Hey, what have you got there? A new computer?" Yvonne was curious about new equipment in an office that seemed so quiet. Since it was the same brand as Rosalie's—and Yvonne's stolen machine—Yvonne wondered if hers had been fenced already.

"We ordered it last week and it just arrived," Scotty said.

Yvonne berated herself silently for her suspicions.

"Big R has been nagging me forever to hook into the twentieth century before it's the twenty-first," Scotty said. "We really can do wonders with it. We were just getting Cunard and the *Queen Elizabeth II* sailings on the screen. Wanna watch?"

"No, thanks. I've got to get to the green screen on the other side of the wall. I've got work to do. I'll be happy to navigate tomorrow. What time do you want me to show, Captain?"

"We can't sail on an empty stomach. We'll have an early dinner or late lunch at Chowder's at four-thirty. The race starts at six. You have to dine with the captain so that he can supervise your diet."

Yvonne laughed. "See you at four-thirty," she said and gave a little salute before she turned to go. She turned back, remembering that the police were coming tomorrow. "Listen, Scotty, I may be late. The cops are coming over to talk to us again."

"You people with criminal tendencies . . ." Scotty said.

"Rosalie told us the cops had it all wrapped up. What do they want with you guys now?" Erik said.

"That's what we thought. But they want to go through the whole thing again, in case the burglary at our house has any connection to the other stuff. I hope they get through it fast. Anyway, I'll meet you at the boat at six even if I have to bounce the cops out of my house bodily. If I get loose earlier, I'll meet you at Chowder's."

"Tell the cops that you have to discuss strategy with the captain," Scotty said.

"I'm sure they'll understand," Erik said.

"I'm beginning to wonder if they understand anything. At least so far as Kevin and I are concerned. They tell us to be careful, they say they are watching over us, and two guys come in and beat us up and clean us out."

"Yeah," said Scotty. "Big R says they really bashed Kevin."

"Yeah, they did. Me too. And your mother, although not quite as bad."

"Rosalie said they had on bright ski masks and jackets," Erik said.

"Yeah, and they mostly whispered," Yvonne said. "But I heard one talk in a normal voice when he thought I was unconscious."

"Good thing you didn't let him know you heard him," Scotty said. "They might have . . . well, they sound like bad guys."

"The worst," she said. "And one of them was very trim and wiry. He moved like a cat, even when he was carrying the big computer box."

"Oh, say, I was sorry to hear about your computer," Scotty said. "Big R said you hadn't even unpacked it. What a shame."

"The insurance will pay for most of it, but I won't have it set up and be working at home until September—if I'm lucky. Soooo I guess I'd better get next door and get to work. At least I did one thing right. I left the discs that I had copied Rosalie's office programs onto here in my desk, so I still have them."

"You're lucky Rosalie let you copy hers. When we told her we were getting our computer, she wouldn't let us use any of her systems," Erik said.

"She's probably got them refined so that they work specifically for real estate," Yvonne said.

"She's got some bookkeeping systems that would be useful," Erik said. He was pouting.

"Well, maybe she'll relent after a while," Yvonne said. "Gotta go."

Yvonne returned to her desk and started to run the programs for updating the listings. There hadn't been many sales during the summer, leaving a bumper crop of listings. That means a buyer's market, Yvonne thought, and when the sellers figure it out, they won't want to list their houses, because in a buyer's market you have to sell cheap. After she checked for the closing date for her listing that had sold, she started to research neighborhoods and price ranges that were selling.

After about an hour of slow going, wading through the electronic files and digging into the paper files that the rest of the staff used, Yvonne remembered that Rosalie had a program for this type of research.

Yvonne tried to remember which disc it was on and what the program was called. She started to search through the directories, trying to find the right file. She remembered that when she watched Rosalie use it, Rosalie had called up the file and then had just followed the instructions that were in it. Rosalie had set up a number of files that way, so that they would be easy for the office staff to use. "I have to set it up so that even Betty can use it," Rosalie had said.

Merle left the office at two and Betty left about a half hour later, leaving Yvonne alone. Yvonne was interrupted by the phones frequently, taking messages, making notations of who borrowed what key, who was showing what house. A couple of times she didn't get to answer a phone before whoever it was gave up. Finally the phones quieted down and Yvonne was able to concentrate on finding the program she wanted.

The office seemed colder than ever and when Yvonne looked outside, she saw that the sky was getting dark. Rain, she thought. It's probably getting colder outside, so in here it's like a refrigerator. She buttoned her sweater but shivered anyway.

She decided to turn down the air conditioner despite Rosalie's orders to the contrary. But the thermostat was in Rosalie's office, and the door was locked. When Yvonne looked through the glass panel that separated Rosalie's office from the rest of the room, she saw that Rosalie's computer terminal was on and hooked up to the phone.

Yvonne knew that the multiple-listing service sent out their updates early in the day, so what was the computer doing? Another crochet lesson, maybe. A bag of yarn was on the desk next to the terminal.

Yvonne could see why Rosalie would lock the door. Now that Scotty had his own computer, he might walk in and meddle with hers. Scotty had a mischievous streak, and he wasn't always considerate of things other people thought were important. He was capable of butting in on a crochet lesson and tripling the number of stitches in a sweater just for the fun of it.

Short of breaking into Rosalie's office, there was nothing Yvonne could do about the temperature. She considered going next door to borrow another sweater, but she really wanted to get on with what she was doing. So she went back to her search.

When she had gone through all of the discs but two, she hit a malfunction. At least, she thought that it was a malfunction. When she called up the directory on a disc labeled "East End," she got a list of supermarkets and malls that all seemed to be located on the eastern end of Long Island. When she tried to call up one of the files, none of the office programs worked. She tried file after file, but she could not get the computer to do anything except show the directory of the disc. Yvonne decided to ask Rosalie about the disc and go on to the last one.

Strange, though, Yvonne thought. This office has never done commercial real estate and never had any properties way out in Suffolk County.

Yvonne decided to have one more go at the East End disc. Perhaps she had copied the original incorrectly. She went to the cabinet where Rosalie kept the office working discs and took the box of discs over to her desk. She went through them one by one to make sure that everything she had copied coincided. But there was no East End disc in the office file.

Well, another question for Rosalie, she thought, and put back the office discs and began searching the last disc for the research program, which, of course, was right at the top of the directory, clearly labeled SERCHUS. Eureka! Yvonne thought, and slipped a disc of sales into the second disc drive.

In seconds the computer was racing through the lists and collecting the information she wanted. Yvonne was delighted and decided to print out her data. She could take that home to study. She hit another glitch in the system, though, when she tried to engage the printer. No dice. Then she remembered that Rosalie was using the modem and wondered whether that would interfere with the printer. She thought that Rosalie had mentioned something about needing more capability. Another question for Rosalie. Well, Big R would be along soon, Yvonne thought, remembering that Rosalie had something to talk to her about. Meanwhile, I can watch to see if that program that's running in Rosalie's office will shut down. Maybe then I'll be able to use the printer.

Yvonne would be able to tell when the program was done, because the light on the phone extension would go off. She picked up the phone and pushed the button next to the light. The phone was whistling and whining.

Yvonne wondered if she could tap into Rosalie's crochet lessons if she plugged her terminal into the phone. Would it show the same thing on this screen that it was showing on Rosalie's? I'm as bad as Scotty. Sticking my nose into someone else's business.

Her curiosity overcame her sense of propriety, and she hooked into the phone with her computer. The data on her disc began to get scrambled and she quickly disconnected.

She scolded herself for not realizing that the office programs wouldn't work with the East End disk. Yvonne realized that she had lost a good part of her research in her experiment and told herself about curiosity and the cat.

She intended to pick up the SERCHUS program and repair her data, but having picked up the East End disc in error and having called up the directory, she thought she'd try that disc with the modem, logic telling her that if the office programs didn't work, perhaps this odd disc would key into Rosalie's crochet lesson. Besides, she thought, the disc is missing from the office file. Maybe Rosalie is using it.

Yvonne congratulated herself on finding her way through the electronic thicket. The East End disc clicked into the modem and began spewing numbers and abbreviations across the screen. Yvonne took them to be the shorthand that crochet lessons are given in. But there were slashes and colons mixed in. An intricate pattern, Yvonne thought. But then it would have to be.

It certainly was a long crochet lesson. But why would a crochet lesson be coming in on a disc labeled "East End"? Yvonne couldn't very well ask Rosalie that question without admitting that she had been nosy.

Yvonne had corrected her research at about the time the light on the phone went out. She had just finished printing her information when Rosalie returned, looking harried and rushed.

"I have to talk to you," Rosalie said, after greeting Yvonne perfunctorily. Rosalie went directly to her office, where she reclosed the door and began to work at the terminal. Yvonne saw Rosalie talking angrily into the phone and then reattach the receiver to the computer modem.

Yvonne packed up her papers and tried to get Rosalie's attention to tell her that she was leaving. When Rosalie finally looked through the glass, her face bore an uncharacteristic worried expression, which was washed over by her habitual cheerful mask as soon as Yvonne caught her eye. Rosalie signaled Yvonne to wait and held up two fingers.

Yvonne waited, but more than two minutes, flipping through the research that she had printed. In the section of houses priced at half a million, Yvonne saw about a half page that looked like the crochet lessons.

Oh, God! I guess those discs aren't completely incompatible after all, she thought. Yvonne flipped to the next page—and hoped she didn't look too guilty—when she realized that Rosalie was coming out of her office.

"Sorry to keep you waiting, Yvonne dear. But some days I can't seem to shake loose from my list of shoulds. I feel I'm neglecting you. I had promised to get you started on your computer and then those yeggs walked off with it. I can give you more instruction here in the office, but of course this is all set up and all I can tell you is how we did it."

"I didn't do too badly today. I'm rather proud of myself," Yvonne said. "Although I have a long way to go to get in your league. I got all my discs to work except for the one marked 'East End.' That one doesn't respond to the same commands as the others. All it does is give the directory."

"Your discs? Where are they?"

"Lucky for me, and maybe for the office, too, the robbers didn't get the ones I programmed. I remember just before I went to Chowder's last Thursday I was thinking that I ought to stop in at the office to pick them up. With all the upheaval with Kevin I had just forgotten to take them home. I guess some things happen for the best," Yvonne said, but she was thinking again about DeeDee and resenting any divine plan that could countenance the terrible assault.

Rosalie smiled. "Oh, yes, lucky. I'd hate to have them fall into the wrong hands."

Yvonne returned the grin. "Does that include Erik and Scotty? Erik was complaining that you wouldn't lend him your software."

Yvonne thought Rosalie looked annoyed.

"Scotty, although I love him dearly, is like a bull in a china shop in all respects. I wouldn't lend him anything but the simplest electronic equipment. Something with one button that says, 'Push here.' As for Erik, he's too nosy. He'd be checking my bank balance before I even taught him how to log on."

Yvonne hoped her guilt didn't show when Rosalie mentioned nosiness.

"By the way," Yvonne said, "the East End disc isn't in the office file. I looked for it when I couldn't get mine to work. I thought maybe I'd made an error when I copied it."

"Ah yes, the East End disc. I was coming to that. It's in my office, but it seems to be malfunctioning. I wanted to ask you about that."

Yvonne was sure Rosalie knew about her electronic eavesdropping.

But Rosalie said, "Remember this morning I said I wanted to talk to you?" Rosalie's mood had shifted. She was talking excitedly, happily now. Without waiting for Yvonne to answer, she said, "We're invited to a little get-together on the East End. I have been so busy, and what with all your adventures, I didn't get around to telling you. Anyway, that rich client that I introduced you to a couple of weeks ago says he wants to work with you. Tonight he's having a cocktail party and he particularly asked me to bring you. It should be a good party. He has a great spot on a little peninsula that juts into the Sound."

"But I'll have to go home and change," Yvonne said.

"Oh no. You look fine. And it is getting late. Just because we'll be drinking champagne doesn't mean we have to dress formal. You will come, won't you. Especially if I apologize for not telling you sooner?"

Rosalie rattled on about how wealthy the guy was and how much he wanted to buy a place in Port Guinness, all the while packing up to leave and putting the office systems in their overnight mode. Yvonne realized that Rosalie had not waited for an answer; she had just assumed that Yvonne would comply.

Oh well, she is good to me, Yvonne thought. Sits with my dog. Lends me money. Listens to my troubles. Although I haven't really bent her ear about Kevin and me. Wonder why. Probably because I haven't seen her as much this summer. I stayed home and sulked too much. But she's been busy, too. She hasn't been in the office when I've been here.

"Carlo is waiting out back with the limo," Rosalie said.

"Uh, I could drive my own car."

"No, no. Carlo won't be drinking. You won't have to worry about driving under the influence. Come on. We'll have a wonderful time." Rosalie seemed ecstatic.

Yvonne gathered up her files and put the discs in her top drawer.

"Is that where you kept the discs to foil the thieves?"

"They've been there since I copied them."

"Did you use the East End disc at all today?"

Yvonne squirmed and was sure her face had reddened. "I tried to," she said. "It doesn't work the way the others do, though."

"No," Rosalie said. "It's not supposed to."

Yvonne wanted to blurt out the truth, but she was too embarrassed and uneasy. She hoped that Rosalie would explain the way the disc worked, would show her the crochet lessons. Then Yvonne wouldn't have to worry about letting anything slip. Yvonne regretted the mischief now. It was getting to be too big a thing.

17

Kevin cheated on four or five traffic lights, honked his horn when any car delayed him more than two seconds, drove more recklessly than he had since he was a teenager. When he was held up he shouted curses to himself. He followed the curses immediately with prayers: Dear God, just let me get there and see Vonnie's car in the parking lot, then find her safe in the office. Do that, and I'll make everything else up later.

At last, he was in the outskirts of the village of Port Guinness, driving by the pizza place where they had been regulars, past the hardware store, past the video-rental place. Finally, he turned a corner, one of the busiest and slowest in Port Guinness, and he could see the real estate office and the parking lot behind it.

And there was Vonnie's car. Thank you, God.

Kevin swung into the lot, steered into the space next to her car, saw a limousine parked at the end of the lot near the building. Probably for Rosalie, Kevin thought.

He got out and started walking toward the building, then saw Yvonne and Rosalie coming out of the office into the parking lot.

Rosalie saw him first and said something to Yvonne, who waved awkwardly.

Kevin waved back. What would he say to her? What the hell, Kevin thought. Try the truth.

"Kevin, what are you . . . ?" Yvonne began.

"What brings you here?" Rosalie said, smiling and poised.

"Hi, Rosalie, how are you? Vonnie . . ."

Yvonne cocked her head, as she often did when she was puzzled, and waited for him to go on. "We were just leaving, Kevin," she said.

"That's okay, I mean . . ." Don't lose it now, he told himself.

"We're taking a trip, Rosalie and I."

"On our way to Suffolk. A rich prospect invited me for a little gathering at his summer place on Smithtown Bay."

"He could be a really big prospect, Kevin. Rosalie says it could really help if he feels comfortable with me, too. In a business sense, I mean. You don't have to—"

"Yeah. Well, great. I guess. Uh, Vonnie, can we talk?"

"I'll wait in the limo," Rosalie said.

"Kevin, can this wait?"

"No. I had this feeling at work. Not just a feeling; I was talking to Landon Brice."

"And?"

"He knows everything that's going on. And he told me we had to be really careful. But I already felt that. I came over, praying you'd be okay. I tried to call."

"Well, the police are coming again tomorrow. We can go over it again with them. All of it." He's really wound up tight, Yvonne thought, feeling some of the same tension herself.

Kevin felt a gentle hand on his arm, turned and looked into Rosalie's face. Her smile was bright and inviting, despite the slight discoloration around her cheek.

"Rosalie, you too. You've got to watch. Look what they did to you the other night. . . ."

"Listen to me, both of you," Rosalie said. "I couldn't help but overhear," Rosalie gently pushed Kevin and Yvonne toward each other, kept her hands on their shoulders. "You two broke my heart when you separated, you want to know the truth. I know, I know, it's none of my business, but I love both of you. Well, we're not going to stop living, no matter what. Kevin, are you through with work for the rest of the day?"

"Yeah. I was so out of it, my editor sent me home."

"Excellent. Then it's settled. For old time's sake, tomorrow's sake, you're coming along."

"I hate to invite myself," Kevin said. In fact, he liked the idea of spending another evening close to Yvonne.

"You're not inviting yourself," Rosalie said. "I'm inviting you.

Have to keep good relations with my close friends in the press. This guy is a terrific football fan. He'll love talking to you."

"Well, am I dressed okay?"

"Are you kidding?" Rosalie said. "He and his rich buddies wear cutoffs and Top-Siders all summer."

"Come on, Kevin," Yvonne said. "It'll help you unwind." For some reason, the idea of having Kevin along was appealing.

"No more arguments," Rosalie said. "Get in the limo. We're going the last leg of the trip on my boat. With any luck, there'll be a few interesting people there. I know there'll be plenty of booze and food."

Kevin was trying to work up to the idea of gulping champagne and devouring stuffed mushrooms and making totally harmless small talk about pro football. At least Vonnie would be close. "I never met a party I didn't like," he said, though this time he would have preferred just to be with Yvonne. On the other hand, he had fond memories of get-togethers with Rosalie and her rich clients.

"Carlo, if you please!" Rosalie said to the chauffeur in her social-organizing voice.

The chauffeur, Carlo, a lean, wiry man who looked as if he could have been a welterweight boxer, smiled and opened the door wide. Yvonne got in the back, followed by Kevin. The chauffeur, business-like behind dark glasses, nodded and smiled.

The limo seats were deep and comfortable. Kevin and Yvonne touched hands for a moment, smiled and settled back.

"This is all right," Kevin said, feeling some of the tension drain out of him.

"So what got you so strung out?" Yvonne asked.

Before he could answer, Rosalie settled into the front seat, turned to them and said, "Excuse me. Let me give you a little privacy, and I'll make a few phone calls." She smiled as a transparent plastic shield slid up into place between the front and rear seats. Then Carlo got in and the limo took off.

"Strung out," Kevin said. "The other night, those guys. There's gotta be a connection. Landon was sure Quince isn't the end of it. Like today . . ." He started to tell her about the two men who had been burned in the car but decided it wouldn't help. "Anyhow, I got worried about you."

"Well, I'm here and I'm okay, and I'm going to be careful. Just don't act too hyper, okay? There might be some people there who are important to Rosalie."

"I promise not to get drunk."

"You've said that before."

"Yeah, well, I guess you have a point. A small one. Maybe I'll get drunk tonight anyhow."

"Well, if you want to loosen up a bit tonight I guess we both deserve it. And we're not driving."

They tried to relax in the quiet, cool isolation.

"I could learn to travel like this," Yvonne said. "How did they treat you at work your first day back?"

"Okay. Couple people gave me funny looks, because of my face. I was vague when they asked questions. Talked to Chili Wilkins about the Jets's pass coverage."

"He's the one in the United Way commercials."

"He got me started worrying. He hears a lot."

"What?"

"When we were talking he told me rooting out drugs is like chopping wild berries—"

"Kevin, look!"

The limo had stopped. Kevin leaned over to see a couple of dozen geese waddling lazily across the road. Duck and geese crossings were so commonplace around Port Guinness that the village fathers had erected diamond yellow crossing signs like those near schools, except that the signs pictured ducks and geese.

"Cute," Kevin said.

"Oh, they are so darling . . ."

After a minute or so, Carlo shook his head impatiently and honked his horn. Several of the last geese jumped for a moment, then proceeded indignantly.

Kevin and Yvonne saw Rosalie scold her chauffeur.

"Good for her," Kevin whispered. "I like people who watch out for animals."

"That's why she's such a wonderful dog-sitter. Next to us, Tess loves her more than anyone."

"I'm really glad we still have Tess with us." Something stirred in Kevin's mind, then was gone.

"You were telling me about your talk with Chili Wilkins," Yvonne

the box of discs too." Yvonne felt a slight, inexplicable shiver go through her. Before she could pin her thoughts down, the limo swung into a service station. It stopped at a row of pumps, and Rosalie slid back the screen.

"We'll just be a minute," Rosalie said.

Just before Rosalie swung the screen into the closed position again, Carlo opened his door to get out. A tiny breeze blew in, past Yvonne's face, just enough breeze to carry a familiar smell. Yes, of course. Musk! And that other smell. Cedar! Of course, cedar! That's what I smelled the other night.

"Maybe I'll go to the john," Kevin said.

Before Yvonne could stop him, Kevin was out of the limo. Yvonne looked out the left side and saw Carlo chatting with the teenager pumping gas. Carlo was graceful. Though Yvonne tried not to make too many comparisons, most men moved more gracefully than Kevin. Still, Carlo was something else altogether. Quick and catlike. And strong: Yvonne could see that easily. Had she imagined recognizing the smell? No, she didn't think so.

God in heaven, Carlo was built like one of the men from the other night. Think, Yvonne told herself. Think. You're the logical one. Pretend you're talking to the police, and you're remembering everything you can. Damn it, I wish Kevin would hurry. I need to filter this through him. He doesn't always let logic get in his way. . . .

Of course. The insurance man had noticed it. The burglars hadn't bothered to take the VCR, but they had taken the computer. More than that: They had taken the box of discs, which weren't all that expensive. There was nothing special about them, except . . .

What had Kevin said? Something about the computers in his office going bonkers and a lot of unexpected stuff coming out. . . .

Yvonne watched Carlo get back into the car.

She managed a faint smile as Carlo's eyes in the mirror met hers. Carlo looked away, then his eyes darted back to the mirror, catching her stare again. Was he measuring her reactions? She had to say something. . . .

"Did you pay already?" She managed not to stammer.

"Rosalie's gonna pay," Carlo said matter-of-factly. "As soon as she's done on the phone."

On the phone? "But . . ." Yvonne started to say, *There's a phone right here in the car.*

Kevin moistened a paper towel and wiped his face. He studied himself in the mirror. Well, he didn't look too bad to go to a party; maybe he would tell people he'd fallen on his boat or something if they asked about his bruises.

Kevin was feeling less enthusiastic about the evening. What he really wanted to do now was go home—home to the house, not his apartment—and have one or two beers. Maybe bring Tessie up on the sofa with him.

Kevin felt his memory stir. It was like the feeling he'd had at the goose crossing. He would have to talk to Vonnie about it.

The hum from the fluorescent light over the sink sounded like a computer.

Computers, computers. The computer in Vonnie's office. Vonnie's own computer, stolen. By people who beat the hell out of us and trashed our house. First they put the dog out of commission. They had to know the dog was there. They came prepared with a tranquilizer. She was knocked out quietly.

I have to run this by Vonnie. Breathe deep and think.

He walked back to the limo. Carlo got out to open the door for him, then stood outside.

"Where's Rosalie?" Kevin said.

"Making a phone call. Something's wrong."

"I know, I feel it."

"Carlo smells like one of the men from the other night. Cedar. That's what the other smell was. He moves the same."

"Can that be?"

"How many men do you think I've smelled, for God's sake?"

"Oh, Jesus. We have to tell Rosalie."

"Here she comes. Don't tell her yet."

Carlo opened the door, closed it when Rosalie was seated. Rosalie slid the screen open. "We'll have a good time," she said. "I'm glad Kevin could make it."

"Me too," Kevin said.

Kevin's and Yvonne's hands met in the middle of the seat.

"Did you tell me how many people will be there?" Yvonne said.

"A few dozen maybe." Rosalie kept smiling.

Kevin tried to smile back at Rosalie, but she saw something in his face, and her expression changed.

"I'm still a little sore from the other night," Kevin said. "Inside of my mouth was cut."

"Ah. I was a lot luckier."

"Well, a drink will make me feel better," Kevin said.

Rosalie slid the screen shut.

Rain had begun to lash the windows. The drops and the rhythm of the windshield wipers created enough noise that Kevin and Yvonne dared to speak to each other quietly.

"Something's wrong," Kevin whispered.

"I know. Tell me your feelings, and don't waste any words."

"Somebody knew we had a dog."

"Carlo."

"Would Carlo . . . ? Would he beat up Rosalie? Wouldn't she know him? You recognize him now. Your computer, Vonnie . . ."

"The burglars wanted my computer, and the discs. Look." Yvonne slid a page of her printout toward Kevin. "The East End disc has a list of shopping malls and plazas," she whispered. "It was running all afternoon. I butted in, and this is what came out."

Kevin looked down at the sheet and frowned. "Numbers and letters. Do you know what they mean?"

"Looks like crochet abbreviations. SC for single crochet, DC for double, CH for chain. But Rosalie is much more advanced than that, and I don't understand all of it. The symbols and numbers."

Kevin studied the colons and slashes. "Dates and times?"

"In a crochet lesson? In a disc about malls on the East End?"

"Not a crochet lesson. What did you tell her about your discs?"

"That I put them in the drawer. I had them in the office all the while. That the men the other night didn't get them."

"You snooped in her computer. You intercepted something."

"Intercepted?"

"You loused up her transmission. That's how drug deliveries are set up. By computer, at the last minute. That's how they move it so fast."

"You're saying Rosalie . . ."

Through the plastic screen, as Rosalie talked business with Carlo,

Kevin saw the familiar tough set of her jaw. Yes, Rosalie was a tough one, all right, and she had bounced back so quickly from getting beaten up. . . .

"Rosalie never got hit as bad as we did," Kevin said.

"No. We went to the hospital. She didn't."

"What about tonight? This rich guy's place on the water?"

"I was only invited after I asked about the East End disc."

"There isn't any party," Kevin said. "She just wants to get us on her boat. She must be the next layer. Quince's boss."

"The first chance we get, we run. Anywhere. Keep smiling. Just keep smiling."

The limo turned off the highway onto a two-lane road toward a boatyard. Rosalie slid the partition open. "Almost there," she said.

Kevin and Yvonne had always boarded Rosalie's boat at the Port Guinness Yacht Club. They didn't know the road they were on now, didn't know the boatyard they were entering.

The limo stopped. Carlo got out and opened the door for Rosalie. "Come right down to the dock," she said, smiling.

Carlo opened the door for Yvonne, who got out and stood on shaking knees. Kevin slid across the seat, got out slowly and saw something in Carlo's expression and stance that revealed a second's worth of carelessness.

In that second, Kevin pushed the door into Carlo, who was knocked back against the side of the limo before falling to the ground.

"Run," Kevin said.

They did, heedless of the gravel that seemed to stab at the bottoms of their feet. They fled toward a jungle of boats, putting themselves farther from the road.

Yvonne stumbled, felt a sick emptiness in her stomach but righted herself before her knees touched the ground.

"Jesus, Vonnie." He was not angry with her, only alarmed. Now he wondered—insanely—if he should tell her he was not mad, before it was too late to tell her anything.

"I love you," he said. His voice sounded crazy in his ears.

"Run," she said, so breathless she thought she might faint. To herself she said: God, just give us another chance at life, and I promise . . .

Shouts, other feet on the gravel behind them.

Just ahead lay a long gray metal building. To its right, as they approached it, lay an area mostly open except for a few boat cradles. They ran toward the building's left, where there was a virtual forest of cradled boats—old, new, plastic, wood, power, sail.

They sprinted into the maze of boats, less clumsily now because the ground surface was more hard sand than gravel.

Shouts again, behind them, slightly farther away.

"Aquí! Aquí!" a pursuer shouted. (Here, here, Kevin remembered.)

"Hide. We have to hide," Yvonne breathed. "Can't run away. Can't surprise them. Not anymore . . ."

"There," Kevin said. He pointed to an ancient wooden sloop that rested atop a tar-stained cradle. Boat and cradle looked forgotten, forlorn. Around the base of the cradle, directly under the hull that showed chalklike stains from barnacles long gone, weeds grew knee-high.

Kevin and Yvonne crawled under the boat, Kevin banging his right knee on something metallic as they knelt. "Oh, damn . . ." His knee hurt.

Yvonne saw that he had bumped into an old half-gallon paint can. She picked it up; someone had left paint in it. A weapon? It was heavy enough to do some damage.

Rubbing his knee as he crawled low, Kevin peered through the weed tops, scanning the boatyard, as much as he could see of it.

"Aquí, aquí." The voices were farther away now, but still between their hiding place and escape.

And where was Rosalie?

The voice again. Still distant.

"I haven't heard her voice," Yvonne whispered.

"No. She could be anywhere. Maybe waiting for us to head back to the road."

The air was getting colder and it smelled of rain. Thunder rolled across the sky like a barrel.

"If it storms, they won't be able to hear us. Maybe we can hide longer."

"But not forever." Kevin didn't finish his thought: that a storm could also drown out the sounds of guns—or screams.

Kevin was scanning the yard through the weeds. Deeper into the maze, about fifty feet away, a gleaming white-and-blue twenty-six-foot O'Day sloop rested in a pristine cradle. The boat had a "For Sale" sign hanging from one side. In late summer, every yard had a couple of spanking-new boats put on the market by first-time owners lured by the romance of the water but turned off by the reality of maintenance.

A shiny aluminum stepladder stood next to the boat. If they could get there, they could climb into the cockpit and pull the ladder up after them and be out of sight.

"There, Vonnie. That's where we want to be."

Yvonne agreed.

The voices were still on the other side of the long gray building. Thunder rolled over the Sound, closer this time.

"Maybe we should try now," Kevin said.

It was almost a question, Yvonne thought, hearing the fear in his voice, and knowing (how many times had this happened before?) that she must help him be braver than he imagined he could be.

"Right now. Quick and quiet," she said. It was not that she was braver, just that she saw the truth.

Kevin stood up and peered as far as he could down the aisles of cradles. Nothing in sight.

"Let's go," Yvonne said.

Kevin saw Yvonne pick up the paint can. "Good," he said, thinking she meant to bring it as a weapon.

Yvonne had another idea, had figured the odds were against their being able to get to the boat, get up the ladder, and pull the ladder up after them without being seen. Unless . . .

She took a deep breath, remembering her days of playing softball, and flung the can as hard as she could in the opposite direction from their route to the boat.

Kevin could hardly believe his eyes as he watched the can hurtle through the air, over the near corner of the long gray building, landing with a clatter out of sight.

It worked. As Kevin and Yvonne moved across the open space to the foot of the ladder, they heard the voices move toward the noise of the can. Kevin steadied the ladder as Yvonne scrambled up. He shook with fright as he climbed, and for a moment thought the ladder would topple. Then he was in the boat and he and Yvonne were hauling the

"I don't see a radio,'' Yvonne said.

Kevin looked through one of the long, shallow windows, seeing only cradles and boats and a flash as lightning danced over the Sound. Thunder crashed overhead, then silence, then tap, tap . . .

"Here it comes," said Yvonne, as raindrops hit, heavy as coins.

Kevin opened the door to the V-berth in the bow of the boat. Just what he expected: the anchor nestled far forward on coils of line, a plastic paddle, winches along the shelves, a life preserver, a couple of full sailbags, a sparkling white ring buoy—all of it spread on bright cushions.

Thunk. Over the sound of the rain, a ladder hitting the side of a boat. Closer now. The voices again. Men's voices.

The paddle could be a weapon, Kevin thought. Then he saw it, partly concealed by a sailbag. It was an orange plastic cylinder about a foot and a half long: a standard Coast Guard–approved distress kit.

"Flares," Kevin said.

Kevin pulled it open and dumped the contents onto the cushions: a pistol and a packet of cartridges. He picked up the pistol, broke it open with trembling hands.

"Oh, Kevin . . ." Yvonne took the packet and bit through the plastic wrap holding the cartridges. They were red, thumb-thick, like shotgun shells.

Kevin took one cartridge from Yvonne, plunged it into the chamber, snapped the pistol shut.

"What's to lose?" he said. The scraping of the ladder was only a few yards away now.

"Go for it," she said. "They're over there, so shoot it out the starboard porthole."

Kevin opened the porthole, pointed the pistol at the purple sky and squeezed the trigger.

He felt Yvonne's face next to his as they watched the tiny rocket hurtle through the rain with a pop-pop-pop, trailing sparks.

Several hundred feet up, the shell burst like a firecracker, a huge hissing orange light leaving behind it a plume of bright smoke as it fell slowly earthward.

Voices from the ground, closer.

"Fire another, Kevin."

He broke open the pistol, chucked the smoking empty shell onto the cabin floor, plunged home another flare cartridge, closed the pistol, put his arm through the porthole and fired again into the rain. This time, the shell did not go straight up, angling off instead toward the road before it burst.

"Again, Kevin. Someone has to see."

"We only have two shells left." He loaded one into the gun.

Then Kevin spotted a propeller peeking out from a narrow storage space. "There's an outboard motor," he said.

"So?"

"If the guy's got a spare motor, he might have a gas can on board."

Kevin scrambled into the galley, banging his head on the V-berth door. "Son of a bitch," he said, rubbing his scalp.

"They're getting closer."

He flung aside the cushion over the starboard bench to get at the storage hold below. He opened the hold, but all he found was a couple of charts and a few yachting magazines.

By that time, Yvonne had got to the storage hold on the port side. She opened the hatch and saw the red can.

"Here, Kevin, but it's almost empty."

Kevin saw a smaller can in the hold and picked it up. Almost full. It was alcohol fuel for a galley stove.

Voices closer outside, and the sound of a stepladder clanging against a nearby boat.

"A fire," Kevin said. "We're going to set a fire if those bastards come on the boat. Come on."

They went into the V-berth, and Kevin latched the door that separated it from the galley. The latch could stand one or two hard shoves from a strong man, but no more than that.

Kevin took one sailbag and set it against the door. He poured some of the alcohol on the bag, then he set the gasoline can on top of the bag. He emptied the small can so that some of the alcohol splashed over the gasoline can.

"What are you doing?"

"Fumes," he said. "We can set off the fumes in the gas can."

Kevin knew the small brass screw on top of the gas can was meant to ventilate vapors that always build up inside a gasoline container, even a nearly empty one. He turned the ventilating screw slightly. A high-pitched whistle filled the V-berth.

"Okay," he said, retightening the screw.

A ladder slammed against the side of the boat.

The V-berth smelled of alcohol and gasoline fumes and fear sweat.

Kevin stuck the last flare cartridge in his pocket. "We go up through the hatch when we hear them in the galley. We don't want to cut it too close."

The boat shook as the pursuers climbed the ladder and landed in the cockpit. Curses and shouts as they pulled out the hatch cover. Loud thumps as the men jumped into the galley. "Here! Here!"

Yvonne opened the hatch, stood up so that her head was exposed to the wind and rain and her hands were resting on the outside of the boat. She hoisted herself up and out and stood up on the deck. She looked toward the ground, directly into the face of Carlo, who was waiting next to the boat with another man. Carlo and his friend (they were the pair from the other night, Yvonne knew) stared at her. A blade gleamed in Carlo's hand. Their clothes were soaked and their skin glistened in the rain.

"Kevin!"

"Here I come!"

He stood up, feeling raindrops on his face. As he was climbing out, he heard the slam against the V-berth door, once, twice. He banged his left leg but still managed to get it up and out. As he hauled himself up, right leg still dangling in the boat, the V-berth door burst open.

The sailbag fell softly on its side, the gas tank clattered to the floor and hands grabbed his right leg. Kevin kicked furiously, freeing his leg for a moment, and before the hands could get a good grip again he pointed the flare pistol below and pulled the trigger.

A light as bright as a welder's torch flashed in the V-berth. Then several things happened nearly at once. There was a loud metallic whump as the whole boat shook. The red gas tank flew up and slammed into the ceiling of the V-berth, just missing Kevin's dangling leg. Kevin managed to get his leg up and out of the boat, an instant ahead of the red-orange flame tongues that hissed out of the opening. Kevin lost his balance, and he expected to fall onto the bow. Instead, a moment after his shoulder came down hard on the boat, he found himself looking at the sand.

"Kevin!"

The thud knocked the wind out of him. The next thing he knew, he was lying on his back, staring up at the flames that flicked higher and higher into the rain. He heard shouts of rage and pain from inside the boat. As if in a dream he thought, someone's on fire. An odd sort of peace came over him; he knew that, even if he could get up, he couldn't run fast enough to get away. No, he couldn't. He hoped Vonnie would understand.

A pair of feet landed in the sand a couple of feet from Kevin's head, and then he was looking up into Vonnie's face. He thought she looked very beautiful in a way he had never seen before and surely never would again: hair and skin wet, catching points of light from the flames, her mouth and eyes set in determination despite the fear. . . .

"Kevin, the flare!"

Oh, yes. "Pocket," he heard himself say. He raised himself up a little, and Vonnie pulled the flare out. Then he felt his fingers being twisted as she pulled the gun out of his grasp.

"Stay away! I mean it, goddamn you!"

As she reloaded the flare gun, she faced Carlo and another man whose tattered shirt had singe marks. Another man knelt several yards away, holding out his bare burned arms to the cooling rain.

"Stay away!"

She backed away from the boat. She was aware of the smell of burning plastic and burned hair. The flames from the boat hissed in the rain.

Kevin started to crawl toward Yvonne, tried to get up, but one knee buckled.

"We're all going for a boat ride," Carlo said.

"No, we are not," Yvonne said. She backed up another step, but the three men were not coming after her. They stood behind Kevin, and Carlo knelt down next to him.

Carlo held up his knife. "End of argument," he said to Yvonne. "You and your shit-for-brains husband can come with us on the boat, or we can leave him here with an extra hole in his throat and just bring you along."

"Where's Rosalie? We were friends. She wouldn't let you—"

"Look, you stupid bitch. Make up your mind."

In the distance a siren. No, more than one. Yvonne read urgency on Carlo's face.

"You decide right now," Carlo said.

Kevin had regained a little strength, and he knew he could push up with the leg that had buckled under him only a moment ago. They were not going on any boat ride, and no one was going to cut his throat. . . .

Carlo reached around Kevin with his free arm, started to bring the knife in for the cut.

Kevin lashed out with one elbow, pushed up with one leg, rolled onto the wet sand, out of the way.

Carlo started to go after Kevin again, but before he could get close with the knife, Yvonne stepped forward.

"No!" she shouted.

All the pain and fear she and Kevin had endured, all the guilt she had felt over the slashing of DeeDee Lockwood crystallized for Yvonne. The feeling was enough to make her point the flare pistol at Carlo and pull the trigger.

Carlo shrieked as the flare buried itself in his shoulder. He went on screaming as he flopped like a fish on the wet sand, grabbing at the flare that sizzled yellow, hissing in the rain as it cooked his flesh.

And Yvonne screamed, because she could not bear Carlo's agony, could not bear the thought of what she had done. She screamed again, her scream caught up now in the sirens from the fire truck and police cars that were racing into the boatyard.

Carlo's companions had run into the thicket of boat cradles, toward the water and the boat where Rosalie must have fled.

Carlo's shrieks subsided to moans as the flare burned itself out. His head lolled to one side and his eyes closed.

Kevin had stood up, and he put his arm around Yvonne.

"Look," Kevin said.

A big powerboat, a sixty-footer at least, was backing away from the pier in a hurry. The sides scraped against pilings, sending the vessel's rubber fenders into the water with splash after splash. Kevin and Yvonne heard the sound of other boats' rigging and trim being ripped away as the big boat swung around to head for open water.

"Rosalie," Yvonne said. "Rosalie."

Now there were other sirens, from the water. Kevin and Yvonne recognized the blue-and-orange trim on the Nassau County Police boats. Several men carrying rifles and shotguns stood on the bows as they blocked the big boat's exit.

Shivering in the rain, Kevin and Yvonne saw two ambulance attendants put Carlo on a stretcher, cover him with a blanket and take him away.

A man in a raincoat stood behind Kevin and Yvonne, placed his gentle hands on their shoulders. Could this be? Yes. "Let me take you inside somewhere," federal agent Bleucher said gently.

Kevin and Yvonne nodded.

"As I said, we didn't think you had hurt her; it made no sense. Kevin, you mentioned two men boarding the boat while you were sleeping, how they rooted around in the galley area."

"And jumped off when a police boat came by to shut up a bunch of drunks," Kevin said.

"Yes. Well, we checked, and sure enough, a marine patrol unit recalled a minor incident with some partygoers. So we asked ourselves, how come those guys didn't look through the entire boat? The answer is, they didn't have to look through the boat. Because Harvey sent them.

"We know who the people working with Harvey were," Bleucher went on. "Ernesto Lunes and Felipe de Leon."

"The roasts on the LIE," Kevin said.

"Roasts?" Yvonne said.

"Yes, burned in a car," Bleucher said. "We think that when they couldn't contact Harvey, they went into hiding. But they couldn't hide from Rosalie. They didn't even know who she was."

Kevin recalled what Chili Wilkins had said: "I don't know who they are. I just know they are."

"What about the guys who roughed us up at the marina?" Kevin said.

"Quince sent them," Bleucher said. "They were there when Harvey was deep-sixed. Harvey told Quince you two didn't know anything about the stuff on the boat. But by that time Harvey had told so many lies—"

"To save his life," Yvonne said.

"To save his life," Bleucher said. "He told so many lies, Quince didn't know if you were in on it or not."

"Neither did you," Kevin said. "But if Quince had already talked to Harvey, how come Quince's men at the Haviland Marina didn't know where the stuff was?"

"Harvey never told where it was," Bleucher said. "He kept saying he didn't know, because if he had told—"

"He would have been admitting he'd put it there," Yvonne said.

"Exactly. So he waffled back and forth, digging himself in that much deeper, until Quince was done with him."

Kevin and Yvonne sipped their coffee and wrapped themselves in the blankets a deputy brought.

"As for Miss Lockwood . . ."

"Poor DeeDee," Yvonne said.

"They thought you had delivered the drugs there. Obviously they didn't find them, so they continued to tail you."

"I'll always feel guilty about dragging her into this," Yvonne said. Kevin shook his head.

Bleucher spoke quietly. "None of this was your fault. A broken sink fitting? If Harvey hadn't put the drugs on your boat, that's all it would have been. Who's to say Harvey didn't weaken the sink fitting himself? Accidentally, I mean, lying on his back to jam the cocaine way back out of sight. His shoulder might have bumped the fitting."

The agent went on in a consoling tone. "You might be dead if you hadn't stopped where you did. Quince's men might have been watching you at Edgecliff that night and been scared off when *they* saw that police boat. They might have been told by Quince that you were working with Harvey. Who knows? Mrs. McNulty—"

"Yvonne."

"Yvonne. You just missed the bunch that hurt your friend. She opened the door to them after you'd gone. She had no reason to be suspicious."

"My life might have been saved just because I get up early," Yvonne said.

"Harvey and his people were in way over their heads, second-stringers," Bleucher said. "Quince and his people—and Rosalie, of course—they were the varsity."

"And we beat the varsity," Kevin said. But his heart was as empty as his voice.

"God may have been on your side."

Kevin and Yvonne studied the agent's face for a sign of cynicism. There wasn't any.

"Of course, there were more earthly reasons. Quince's people were never quite able to get you two alone for any length of time, where they could . . . well . . ."

"They came close enough at the marina," Yvonne said.

"By that time, we figure, they not only wanted their cocaine back. . . ."

"But Rosalie might have told them not to kill us because she needed to find out where my copies of her programs were." Yvonne shivered. "The night I told her I had copied the discs . . . that night when I came home from Chowder's, Tess was growling at something outside."

"You never told me about that, Vonnie," Kevin said.

"I thought it was an animal. I . . . all this other crap hadn't happened yet. Even after she knew where the discs were, she needed to know how much I knew . . . and who else knew."

"Very likely." Bleucher looked very tired as he rubbed his eyes with his fingertips. "I hope I wasn't too rough on you before. I probably was. This kind of work, it can consume you. The business in Colombia, it's been worse than most people know."

They waited for Bleucher to go on.

"This is off the record, please. Not so long ago, I had a colleague. An anti-drug agent for the Colombian government. Total courage, total integrity. A family man. We became good friends, actually. Anyhow, they managed to kidnap him."

"What happened?" Yvonne asked.

"They cut off his hands and feet. Even after that, they weren't done cutting him. . . ." The agent stopped, shook his head.

"You mean he was still . . . ?" Kevin's voice tailed off.

"He wouldn't talk, you see," Bleucher went on. "Wouldn't give them what they wanted. His body was found by a country road with, well, something in his mouth. I try not to dwell. I just throw myself into the job, saving as much as I can for my wife and daughter."

Bleucher's face changed; an emotional curtain had come down.

"I'll drive you home," the agent said. "We can talk some more in the car, if you'd like."

As Kevin and Yvonne stood up to leave, Kevin put an arm across her back and hugged her to him. She didn't resist.

Sitting in the back of the government car while Bleucher drove wasn't as luxurious as riding in a limo, but they preferred it.

The rain fell steadily, but more gently, and there was no more thunder crashing overhead. The sound of the windshield wipers was oddly comforting.

"Are you still going to sell the boat?" Bleucher said.

"We'll see if we still have a buyer when you guys release it," Kevin said.

"It's a good boat," Yvonne said. "I always liked the way it looked in the water. But I guess we'll have to sell it. Probably . . ."

Kevin saw the agent look in the rearview mirror. "We think Harvey's scheme started to unravel even before you took the boat away."

"How so?" Yvonne said.

"Well, that friend of Harvey's, the one they called Tolly?"

"The guy who found that booze and carbon monoxide don't mix."

"Stop trying to be a hard-ass, Kevin."

"You hit it on the head, Kevin. Medical examiner's office is taking a closer look. At first it looked pretty cut and dried. Guy with a reputation for liking his booze works on an engine in close quarters, gets too much exhaust. Ingenious, really."

"Somebody killed him?" Yvonne said.

"The pathologist noticed what looked like a freshly chipped tooth, and that just under the gum line he found a tiny, tiny chip of glass. Do you see?"

"He was force-fed the booze," Kevin said.

"That's our theory. I'm betting the tests on the tissue samples are going to show an abnormally high level of both alcohol *and* carbon monoxide, and that they both entered his system around the same time."

"Jesus," Kevin said. "Meaning he was force-fed the gas too."

"Now you can see how Harvey was in way over his head."

About a hundred feet over, Kevin thought. He kept that sick joke to himself.

"You tell me where to turn off, okay?" Bleucher said. "Are you, uh, both going to the same place?"

"Our cars are in the parking lot at Rosalie's office," Yvonne said. "But we'll probably both stay at Duck Point Lane tonight."

Kevin realized he didn't want to be anywhere in the world but there on this night, even if he slept on the sofa.

"This is just all so sad and terrible and way too much to digest," Yvonne said.

"If they'd got us on that boat, Rosalie and Carlo, what then?" Kevin said.

"I don't want to think about that," Yvonne said.

"I can guess," the agent said, "but I'd rather not. Of course, they had to have you alive until they were sure what you knew about her computer program—"

"Which made it easier to fight them off, because they couldn't kill us right away," Kevin said.

"—but on the boat, and Mrs. McNulty—I mean Yvonne—with your relationship with Rosalie she would have had ideas on how to get the information."

"She was nice to our dog," Kevin said. "That's one of the things that dawned on us. Isn't that crazy? Didn't have the heart to kill our dog."

"I can understand that," Bleucher said. "I have a dog."

Something dawned on Kevin. "Wait a minute," he said. "How did you know we were in trouble, and how did you know where to find us?"

"A combination of good police work and outside help. Once the Port Guinness police got over their embarrassment at having let your house be raided that night—that was a setup, by the way, because Rosalie—"

"We knew that already," Yvonne said.

"It took us awhile," Kevin said.

"And us," the agent said. "Anyhow, once the Port Guinness police started to look at things objectively, with some help from us, the only thing that made sense was that the thugs had never come down Duck Point Lane."

"Because they'd come from Rosalie's," Yvonne said. "Maybe by boat first, to Rosalie's place, and from there to our place."

"Right," the agent said.

"Turn down here," Kevin said.

"I still don't know how you found us exactly," Yvonne said.

"For one thing, we traced some of Quince's phone calls to Rosalie."

Yvonne remembered the computer-telephone hookup in the office. "And you saw a bunch of long calls that made you suspicious. The ones where the computer was running."

"Yes. She was scheduling deliveries."

"The computer calls were supposed to look like crochet lessons," Yvonne said. "She kept a bag of yarn next to the phone."

"Crochet?" Bleucher said. "My wife . . . well, anyhow. Besides checking on the phones, there were other things that made us wonder about her. Some I can't talk about, at least right now. And Kevin, you've got a good friend in your office."

The Hudson was still restless, but by midday, with the George Washington Bridge just ahead of them, Kevin and Yvonne were warm enough to take off their sweatshirts.

"The sun feels good on my arms," Yvonne said. "I'm a little surprised there aren't many people out."

"This is the time of year people start thinking more of football. At least those people who give a damn about football."

"Just the same. By the way, I hope your friend Marty Diehl finds another boat."

"Yeah, well, if he wants one bad enough, he will."

"I'm sure."

A grim joke, but not too grim, occurred to Kevin. "You know, maybe he can pick up that one on Long Island for a bargain. I mean the one we set fire to in the boatyard."

Yvonne chuckled a little. Sometimes (not often) Kevin hit a bull's-eye with his humor. Well, that one was in the inner ring anyhow. She would take a laugh wherever she found it.

"Funny how boat people get about boats, isn't it?" Kevin said.

"Meaning?"

"Well, like this Pearson is *our* boat, and meant to be our boat. I mean, we've filled up this boat with memories and . . . and . . . all that sentimental shit."

"And you use words for a living?"

"Still," he said, "we ought to give the boat a name, our name for it, not the previous owner's.

"You're right. *Lark IV* doesn't seem to suit it."

Kevin laughed. "How about *Narc IV?*"

"Not funny."

"I've got it. Really. How about *Happy Ours?*"

Yvonne started to protest.

"Without the *h* on 'ours.' "

"Mmmm, not bad," Yvonne said.

Kevin was making resolutions silently. He would drink less. He would try harder. There would be no more betting on football, at least not with money. A cup of coffee at most.

"I'm going to work at us, Vonnie. I mean, I'm gonna hold on to what's important and—"

"Right now, the most important thing you have a hold of is the tiller. Just keep your eye on the river."

"Yes, dearest."

Good, Yvonne thought. He had taken her remark just as she had intended it. "Sentimental Irish windbag," she whispered, loud enough for him to hear. Lucky he was used to that quirk in her, that need to sound tough, she thought.

The George Washington Bridge thrummed with traffic high above him. Looking up, Kevin thought of the last time they had gone under the span, going the other way.

Shooting the flare into Carlo that day in the boatyard had affected Vonnie. She had been relieved to find out that Carlo would recover, though he would always have a nasty scar.

"What the hell," Kevin said, "a scar will make him look real macho to the other convicts." But Kevin had liked his joke not much more than Vonnie had.

They were near Edgecliff now, about to pass within sight of DeeDee's balcony. She would use it again, one day.

They had agreed that, if they needed to refuel, they would not do it at Edgecliff. Not matter what.

"We have to remember this, Kevin. All of it. If we're ever in a position to make a difference, to, to . . ."

She stopped, out of words but with her composure intact, and welcomed his arm across her shoulders.

"I think I'm done with violence," he said. "For life. In movies, books, whatever. Except for football."

For a little while, they flowed along with the river and the silence. Then Yvonne had an inspiration.

"You know," she said, "we should have Landon Brice and his wife over for dinner."

"You think so?"

"You know we'll find things to talk about."

"Yeah, it's just that he's so shy and withdrawn."

She elbowed him gently. "We really should."

"Okay."

Kevin remembered the last time he had seen Landon Brice. After the mess in the boatyard and Rosalie's arrest, he had asked for time off from work yet again. But he had had to stop in the office to see Landon Brice.

Brice was one of a very few reporters to have his own office. His was a tiny corner cubicle jammed with gray metal file cabinets on which rested stacks of notebooks and old newspapers.

Kevin saw that Brice was on the phone (he wore a headset that was hooked up to a tape recorder). Kevin turned to walk away but stopped when Brice looked up and motioned for him to come in.

Brice nodded, smiled, pointed to a chair. "*Oui, oui, je comprends,*" Brice said into the phone and conversed for several more minutes in what sounded to Kevin like perfect French.

"*Au revoir,*" he said finally.

He took off the headset and turned to face Kevin. "A mob source from Montreal," Brice said. "Calls me every few months just to shoot the *merde*. That's French for—"

"I know. *Merci*, Landon."

"*Encore?*"

"Thanks. You know, for maybe saving our lives."

"Ah, that. Well, it sounds like you saved your own lives. How did you guys know enough to run?"

Kevin told him how they'd compared notes in the limo and things had fallen into place.

"Yeah," Brice said, "Rosalie was running the whole East End operation."

"And Yvonne recognized Carlo from the way he walked. And from the cedar smell."

Brice chuckled. "Some of the traffickers pack coke in cedar chips. They think it fools the dogs."

"Does it?"

Brice chuckled again and shrugged. "How would I know?"

"Anyhow," Kevin said, "it might not have done us any good, shooting the flares like that, if the cops hadn't been on their way already."

Brice smiled in an "aw shucks" way. "I happened to see you on the phone, just before you left the office. Dialing, then slamming the receiver down, like you were all upset. I knew what a tough time you'd had. So I was worried about you, and I decided to call your home to tell your wife."

"And she wasn't home," Kevin said.

"No. So I checked the city desk Rolodex and got your wife's work number. But I dialed a couple of times and couldn't get through. So I began to think that's where you'd been calling and you couldn't get through either."

"So then you called the cops."

"Not right away. Then my scalp started itching, like it does when I have a hunch. I didn't buy that theory that the robbery was unrelated, and I decided I had to call the cops."

"So you steered them to Yvonne's office."

"They were already pretty sure you were clean. I mean, when you got the crap beat out of you in your house, what else could they think?"

"That we were drug dealers who'd been beaten up by other drug dealers. You know, a double-cross . . . ."

At that, Brice threw back his head and guffawed. "Naw, Kevin. Not you. Not your wife. What's your big vice? A six-pack?"

"Or two. And betting on football."

"Anyhow," Brice went on, "I told the cops to find you, find your wife. Fast."

Kevin realized that Brice, sitting back now in his chair with his feet on the desk, had reverted to his customary I-know-more-than-you-do manner. A shield, Kevin thought.

"Besides," Brice said, "what I told 'em dovetailed with what they were piecing together on their own."

"So things were starting to point to Rosalie?"

"Yeah."

"So why the hell didn't the cops move faster and save us a lot of grief?"

"Couldn't. Not enough to go on, for one thing. If they'd moved in too fast on Rosalie, they wouldn't have had a case at all. See, Quince started to talk when the cops connected him to the break-in at your house."

"How'd they do that?"

"They found pink and canary jackets on Quince's boat. They knew the robbers hadn't passed the stakeout on Duck Point Lane. So they figured the robbers came by boat. And only Quince knew about Rosalie, and he was coming around slowly."

"So the cops weren't just using us as bait?"

"Not at all. See, that thing at your house, that was smart thinking by Rosalie, but you know what her mistake was?"

"What?"

"Not having those guys hit *her* as hard as they hit you and your wife."

"Well, Vonnie and I finally figured it out. Then there was the dog tranquilizer . . ."

London chuckled. "Dumb of her."

"Well, I'm glad she was soft on our dog."

Brice told him how puzzled the police were at first that only Kevin and Yvonne, not Rosalie, had gone to the emergency room after the house was trashed. "Not only that, the cops couldn't find any doctor who had treated her."

"How would they know where to look?"

"They have their ways." Brice's eyes sparkled, a signal that he was debating with himself how much to tell his naive listener.

Kevin found the familiar Cheshire-cat grin momentarily irritating. "Cast a flickering torch into the vast caves of my ignorance," he said.

Brice laughed. "Plastic surgeons! A handsome, wealthy woman with a face that's messed up is gonna see a plastic surgeon. Only, the cops couldn't find any plastic surgeon who'd treated Rosalie. So they were on to Rosalie, and after I talked to them they raced over to your wife's office—"

"And saw both our cars in the lot."

"So they decided to check the marinas and boatyards along the North Shore, partly because of what happened to Harvey. They were working on the water as well as on land."

"There's a lot of marinas, though."

"But the cops knew about what time you and your wife had left her office. They asked Rosalie's son and the other guy in his office, and then they double-checked on the limo, just in case Scotty was in on the deal."

"The limo . . . ?"

"The phone in the limo."

"Bugged?"

"You see? That narrowed it down. They did their best, put a lot of manpower into it, figuring they'd let you down once already. They got lucky. That's how it goes sometimes."

"Well, thanks anyhow."

"Hey, all in a day's work. . . . And one more thing . . ."

Kevin could tell that Brice was savoring the moment. "Okay, Landon. Hit me with it."

"Your motel room up in Tansytown?"

"Yeah?"

"I've got a real close source in the DEA. I hear your room was bugged."

"Bugged . . ." Of course, Kevin thought. No wonder the cops were so thoughtful: fixing us up with a room, bringing us food. And beer, bringing us beer, for God's sake. Hey! What if Vonnie and I hadn't been technically separated, what if we . . . ? "Any more surprises, Landon?"

"Well, the cops did look through your house just before you got back from the boat trip."

"Why, those dirty . . . I never gave them permission. . . . Goddamn!"

Landon chuckled softly. "Hey, Kevin, the cops offered to check in on your dog. I'm sure one of the officers thought he might have heard something in the house. Just doing their jobs."

Kevin had wanted to say more to Landon Brice that day, to suggest that maybe they could have a beer or two or three. But Brice's phone had rung, and the reporter had put on his headset and waved good-bye.

"We will have Landon over," Kevin said. "Do me good to talk to someone like him. It's not his fault he's a genius."

"From what you told me, I think he's a little shy."

Kevin kept his skepticism about that to himself.

"Besides," Yvonne said, "we have to build a new social life."

Kevin heard her voice catch, did not ask her why she went forward to sit on the bow.

When Bleucher had given Yvonne a message from Rosalie, Yvonne had felt repelled.

She remembered playing possum the night of the burglary and hearing one of the thugs say in a normal voice. "They're both out." But the "both" meant the thug was referring to Kevin and Yvonne and talking *to* Rosalie. "Boss," one thug had called her.

One of the intruders had mentioned that Yvonne and Kevin would be moving: another clue that pointed to someone who knew them.

It was all so clear now. There was no more denying, and the sense of betrayal was almost immobilizing.

Then Bleucher had brought a message from Judas herself. The feds were setting her up with a new identity. She was going to testify against Quince and the others, and there were even bigger fish.

"She wanted me to tell you that she would never have hurt you or Kevin or Miss Lockwood," Bleucher said. "She puts the blame for all the violence on Quince. We think she might have got into the business by inheritance."

"By inheritance?" Yvonne had asked.

"We think Rosalie's father might have been a gofer for the mob years ago, and that she herself started running errands for them."

"You say you just think that?"

"We've done a lot of background research on Rosalie," Bleucher said. "Her tracks are pretty well covered. Even some of the stuff she told her son wasn't true."

"My mother told me she'd heard Scotty's father wasn't Mr. Durer," Yvonne said. "There was some rich shady guy who showed up now and then."

"We traced that," Bleucher said. "We couldn't find anything. In fact, beyond a certain point in the past, Rosalie doesn't exist."

Doesn't exist, Yvonne thought. "Where are Scotty and Melba?"

"They had to leave Port Guinness for their own safety. Also to make Rosalie more useful to us. If someone kidnapped Scotty or Melba—"

"That would shut Rosalie up as a witness," Yvonne said.

"Scotty and Melba didn't have the faintest idea where most of the money was coming from," Bleucher said. "They were innocents."

"Extravagant ones at that," Yvonne said. "I wonder what they'll do now."

"We'll take care of them for a while. And that brings me to a job we have for you, Mrs. McNulty. Yvonne, I mean. Rosalie wants us to let you see to the sale of the family assets. Hers, Scotty's, and Melba's. The commission is very good."

Bleucher went on: "The government will take most of the money, but there'll be many personal items we won't care anything about. Those things will be yours for the taking. We'll be glad to have someone see to the details.

"You'll need to keep good records. Rosalie says Program Add-Up on Disc D will work fine. You have a copy of that, Rosalie says."

Yvonne asked, "What I want to know is, is she trying to bribe me with this bit about selling her assets?"

"That may have crossed her mind. She is a devious person. But we got the okay and you can do it if you want. One of our legal people will contact you and he or she will get the signatures you need."

"I don't want anything of hers," Yvonne said. "I'll sell everything and give the money to some organization that takes care of children."

"Rosalie told us that you'd say something like that," Bleucher said.

"She's good at reading people," Yvonne said, lowering her chin so that her tearing eyes would not be so obvious.

"We'll have to watch her or she'll be setting up new enterprises," Bleucher said.

Yvonne came back into the cockpit. Kevin recognized the look on her face; it was the one she got when she had put something behind her and was ready to move on.

"We'll have a little more money," she said. "And you won't be paying rent on an apartment."

"You thinking of some projects?"

She laughed. "Your guard is always up. As a matter of fact, the living room could stand painting. So could the boat."

"Hey, painting the boat! That idea I like. Seems right, somehow. Maybe we can hire someone to paint the living room and do the boat ourselves."

"I didn't think painting the living room would be such a big deal, work-wise."

Kevin caught on: Before they separated, Yvonne had liked to share projects with him. "Okay. A deal. Next time I get two days off in a row, we'll do it. How about a nice purple?"

"Gag, puke. How about a nice eggshell white?"

"You win again. But of course it'll have to wait until after football season."

"No dice. Football season is never over." Yvonne smiled and punched his arm playfully. She would work him into the painting gradually. Once the living room was done, they would think about a color for the corner room. That room was to be the nursery before. Who knows? Maybe they would try again. But not yet.

"We do have some work ahead of us, don't we?" she said.

"Yeah, we do. We both do."

"Well, I'll do my best."

"You always do. So will I."

It was time for lunch. "Turkey or tuna?" she asked.

"Tuna sounds good."

She handed him half a sandwich, then took out one of the cans of beer she had surreptitiously stowed. "Here," she said. "A small celebration."

"All, *RIGHT!*" Kevin had been drinking a lot less and enjoying it a lot more. Right now seemed like a good time for a beer.

"Maybe pizza tonight?"

"That sounds good too."

They rounded the Battery. This time there were no Staten Island ferries or barges in their way. Yvonne took note of the wooden pilings in front of the ferry slips. The pilings were short, meaning the tide was high. That bothered her, but she didn't know why just yet.

"There's no one I'd rather have a beer with, Vonnie."

"Well, that's a good sign."

"You know what I mean."

"No." But she did.

"It means I love you, for God's sake."

"Well, that's as it should be. Because I love you too."

They motored in silence for a while—an easy silence this time, with sightseeing and beer-sipping.

As they neared Hell Gate, Yvonne thought the snake-like ripples were coming at them instead of going with them.

"Uh, Kevin, you did check the tide chart?"

"Of course I did."

Now she knew what had bothered her about the pilings at the ferry